HELLO TROUBLE

KELSIE HOSS

Editing by Tricia Harden of Emerald Eyes Editing.

Proofreading by Jordan Truex.

Accuracy reading by Brian, Alissa and Amy.

Cover design by Najla Qamber of Najla Qamber Designs.

Have questions? Email kelsie@kelsiehoss.com.

Readers can visit kelsiehoss.com/pages/sensitive-content to learn about potentially triggering content.

 Formatted with Vellum

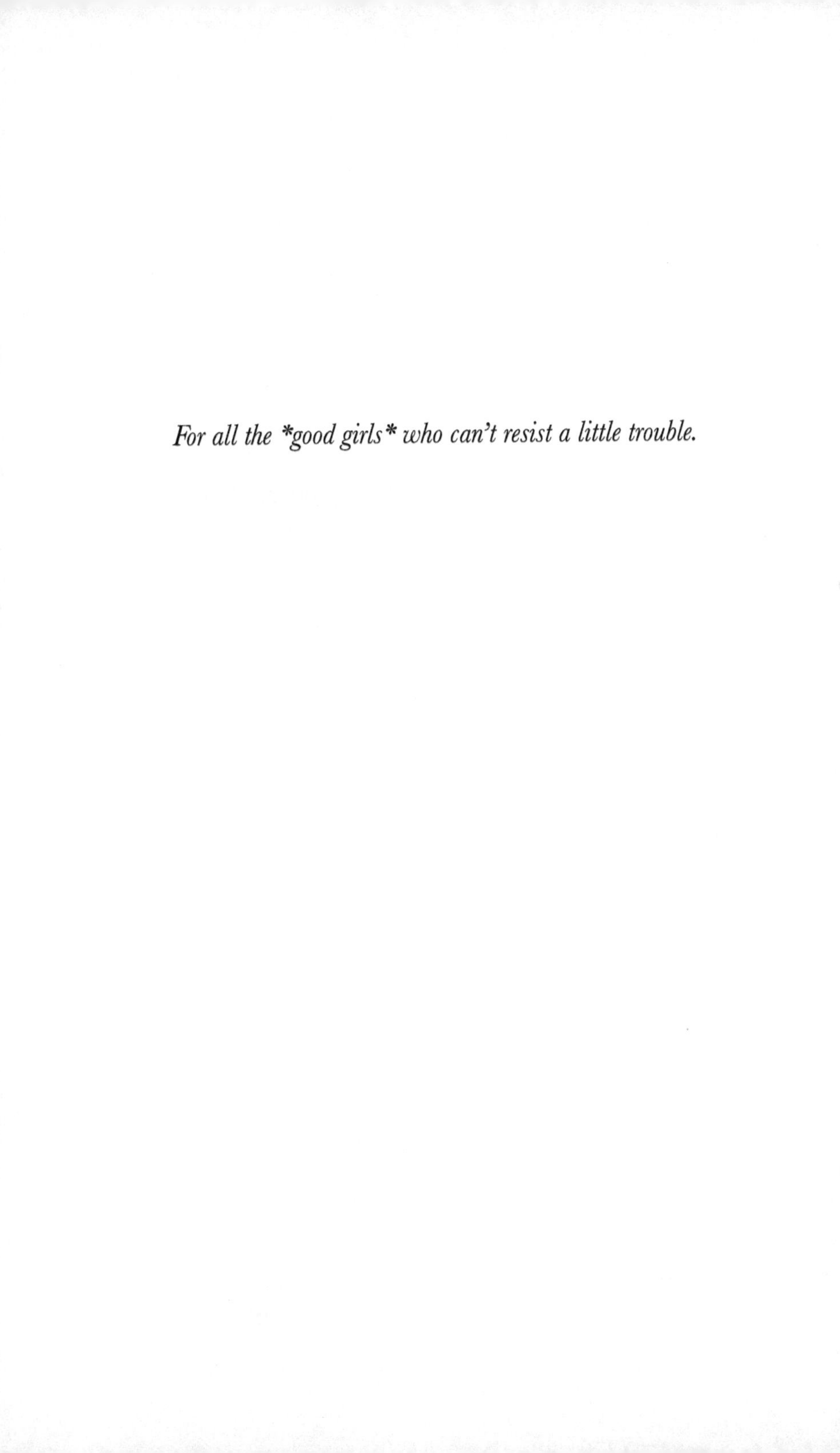

*For all the *good girls* who can't resist a little trouble.*

CONTENTS

1

———

HAYES

A SMALL PIECE of pink paper stuck out from under the windshield wiper of the car I was about to tow, and it said *READ ME* in cutesy cursive letters.

So, of course I pulled it open.

PLEASE DON'T TOW ME YET. I just had to get a snackie. I'll be right back. Promise!

I raised my eyebrows at the note. What the fuck?

A snackie?

I was definitely not in the mood for this nonsense because one, it was cold enough to freeze the balls off a brass monkey, and two, I had half a dozen things to catch up on at my auto repair shop. Waiting for a woman I could never be with to get a "snackie"? Not in my schedule.

I glanced up toward the diner across the street, searching through the windows for her familiar mane of curly red hair. I instantly spotted her, curls spilling from a pink beanie.

She was chatting with the cashier, making him laugh.

My jaw clenched, and I crossed the street, taking long strides to get there faster. But just as I reached for the door covered in town flyers, she came out and smacked into me, slopping hot chocolate all down my front.

"Oh no!" She frowned down at the brown liquid steaming on my coat. "I'm so sorry! Are you burned?"

My jaw clenched. "Just annoyed. I don't like to be kept waiting."

She looked up at me with apologetic pale green eyes, framed by dark lashes. "But I got you a hot cocoa for your trouble... although I spilled it." She gestured at my coat. "You can have mine, though!" She offered the cup that was still intact. "Extra whipped cream."

I shook my head, turning to walk back toward her car across the street. "I don't drink that shit."

"Excuse me?" She trailed after me. "You don't drink hot chocolate?" It was like I told her I hated puppies or something.

"No." I crossed Main Street, which was empty, to the tow truck, checking the winch again to make sure it was set up right.

She caught up to me and said, "You're joking, right? Everyone loves hot cocoa. Especially when it's this cold out."

I arched an eyebrow at her. "Does it look like I'm joking?"

Even though I was focusing on the chains, I could hear the frown in her voice as she said, "But I even asked for marshmallows."

"More useless shit to go on top of a useless drink," I muttered as I finished hooking it up. I knew I was being an ass, but it was a way for me to keep my distance from her. She was my sister-in-law's best friend, which made her completely off-limits. Even if her full pink lips distracted me as much as her curvy body.

She folded her arms across her chest, making her slick coat swish. "Christmas has been over for a few months now. You don't have to be a Grinch anymore."

Ignoring that comment, I said, "Get in the truck while I lift this up."

"Grinch," she muttered, walking toward the front of the tow truck. I pushed the button to start the lift. But then she called over. "A little help? I can't carry my cinnamon roll and my cocoa up the steps."

I smirked at her. "Sounds like a personal problem."

"Hayes!" she chastised. "My best friend is married to your brother. Doesn't that earn me a *little* special treatment?"

"You don't want to know what would earn you that." I sent her a wicked grin where she waited by the passenger side door.

"I'm feeling less and less sorry for spilling hot chocolate on you," she retorted.

I watched out the corner of my eye while she set her cocoa on the sidewalk, then struggled to open the truck door in her mittens and climbed in.

Yes, mittens.

Why a grown adult was wearing those things, I didn't know.

After two trips up and down the steps in her mittens, she had her cocoa and "snackie" in the truck.

Satisfied the car was hooked up correctly, I went to the driver's side and got in, shutting the heavy door behind me.

Della greeted me with a major side-eye. "You're a real piece of work, Hayes Madigan. Not liking cocoa..." She shook her head with an air of disappointment.

Why did her annoyance amuse me so? I shouldn't be feeling anything for her other than that of an acquaintance. Of two people who lived in the same small town. Of the mechanic about to take care of her car. "What's the deal with your ride anyway?" I asked as I fired up the truck. The diesel engine rumbled to life, making our seats vibrate.

With a heavy sigh, Della said, "The heater's on, but it's not blowing any air."

I stared at her, my hand still on the gear shift. She called a tow truck... because it's not blowing hot air?

"What?" she asked over a bite of cinnamon roll. She had a fleck of frosting on her pink upper lip that I ignored.

"You can drive a car without a heater!" I protested. "You could have brought it by the shop without taking me away from other projects."

She shrugged, completely unbothered. "*Technically*, I *could* have driven it to your shop... but my insurance pays for a tow to get it fixed *and* I get a ride in a warm truck with *fabulous* company." She winked at me.

I let out another groan and put the truck in gear. "Okay, Moonshine. Let me get you home... *and out of my truck*," I added under my breath.

"Heard that," she sang back, completely unaffected. "But you know, most people don't utilize all the benefits their car insurance companies offer. In fact, I'm doing the world a service with this tow ride."

I turned down the street toward her house and sighed. "I'll take the bait. How are you doing the world a service?" I was actually interested to hear her take. It was sure to be wild.

"Because, you towed me on Main Street. Everyone in the diner's going to be talking about it. When they ask me what happened, it'll be easy to start a conversation about the services our company offers to its clients. Boom, more clients, more business for you, too. It's a win-win."

I studied her in my periphery. There was a fine line between genius and crazy, and it was sitting right next to me sipping hot chocolate in mittens. "You should get paid to make Super Bowl ads," I teased. "Marketing genius like that."

She proudly brushed invisible lint off her shoulder. "Just another day's work."

"I was being sarcastic!" I groaned. "Call an Uber next time, Moonshine." I parked in front of her house, eyeing the pink siding and white trim. It looked like a damn dollhouse.

She took a bite of her cinnamon roll and said, "And deprive myself of a few minutes with you? Not a chance." She gave me a peeving grin as she opened the door. "Have a great day! Although I don't know how you will without hot cocoa."

She got out and walked toward her driveway, and I shook my head as I towed her car away, fighting the small smile tugging at my lips.

2

———

DELLA

THE TOW TRUCK'S engine idled until I was safely inside my home. Once the door closed, I heard it rumble as Hayes drove away.

Interesting. For all his rough edges, it was pretty chivalrous to make sure I was inside safely before leaving. Or maybe that was a coincidence. I imagined him getting out his phone and giving Woody's a one-star review online for serving hot cocoa and giggled to myself.

It was totally something he would do. And probably with that salacious smirk on his face. It was too bad he wasn't into relationships because damn, did he look good in that dangerous *I could rip your heart into a million pieces and have you screaming my name while I did it* kind of way.

Shaking my head, I set my drink and snack down on the side table, shucked my gloves and coat, and went to the kitchen to get ready for dinner with my parents tonight.

We ate together and watched *The Great British Bake Off* every Wednesday. But today, I had news for them, and I knew they wouldn't like it.

But it was time to tell them what was going on with me—the truth and not the happy façade I'd been putting on for longer than I cared to admit.

With the sense of dread growing in the pit of my stomach, I got out the lasagna ingredients and got to cooking. Experimenting in the kitchen was one of my favorite things to do, and I couldn't wait to hear what my parents thought of this new recipe, made by rolling the noodles up with ricotta cheese and spinach then covering it with a creamy alfredo sauce mixed with shredded chicken. A little sprinkle of mozzarella on top would make it look pretty coming out of the oven later.

I just wished I could figure out how to make a sourdough loaf to go with it, but so far, all my attempts turned out like frisbees.

A knock sounded on my front door, and before I could respond, it swung open, letting a gust of cold air and my parents inside.

"Hurry in!" I called from the kitchen. "It's freezing!" This springtime cold front was unusual for these parts of Texas, and I was ready for it to go away.

Mom and Dad rushed inside, my mom tugging a hand-knitted cap from her mop of blond curls. Dad stood behind her, holding on to her shoulder for balance as he kicked off his boots.

The sweet little gesture had my heart twisting with a pinch of jealousy. My parents had the kind of partnership I'd always admired and hoped to have for myself one day. But with my fortieth birthday coming up and no love interest in sight, the odds were looking slimmer and slimmer all the time.

With their outer gear off and hanging on my vintage coat tree by the entrance, Dad shut the door. It squeaked a little on the way, and he said, "Where's your WD-40? I'll take care of that for you."

I barely said "garage" before he was on his way to handling it, his dusty white socks slipping over my hardwood floors.

Mom came to join me in the kitchen, rubbing her hands together. "I can't remember the last time we got a chill this bad in March."

"Come sit on the couch," I said, steering her back to the living room. "I'll start the fire for us."

Mom blew on her fingertips while I pushed the button for the gas fireplace and grabbed a throw blanket for her. Dad walked back behind us, and I could hear the whoosh of the WD-40 can being sprayed and the latch of the door coming open.

Soon, there were no squeaks at all. "Got it," Dad said.

I smiled over at him. "Thank you. I keep meaning to do that but never get around to it."

"That's why I'm here, sweetie." He smiled at me and then asked, "Need help with dinner?"

"I just need to prep a salad. Everything else is in the oven," I said.

Soon, Dad and I were at the table, slicing lettuce and tomatoes and chatting about work. He was a great listener, and he didn't just ask questions for the sake of conversation. He actually cared about my answers.

Which was making this really awkward.

I'd never kept a secret from my parents before, and it was eating me up inside.

Dad used a pair of forks to toss the salad as he said, "I heard you got towed today. You know you could have called me."

"It's okay. Hayes gave me a ride in the tow truck."

Dad grunted his disapproval. "Wish there was more than one mechanic in town."

Mom and I both gave him curious looks. "What do you mean?" Mom asked. "He always does a good job for us."

With a reluctant nod, Dad conceded, "He does a fine job, but he's such a womanizer. He's been by the co-op to see the receptionist. And the branch manager. And the janitor! I don't want people to think I'm condoning that kind of behavior."

My eyebrows raised. "Tell us how you really feel, Chuck."

Dad rolled his eyes at me. "It just gets me riled up is

all. There's a way to treat a woman, and 'disposable' isn't it."

Some small part of me felt defensive for Hayes, but I didn't have a chance to stand up for him before Mom chimed in from her perch on the couch.

"We've all got our faults," she said. Which was her way of changing the subject. Dad replied, "I'll get the silverware and drinks for everyone."

While he did that, I went to the oven and pulled out the lasagna. The cheese was just beginning to crisp on top, and the scent of thyme and oregano had my mouth watering. I carried it to my table in potholders and then set it out for us to eat.

There wasn't much talking as we served ourselves and took the first few bites. But then Mom said, "Your car must really be worrying you... You're usually talking our ear off at dinnertime."

I shook my head, setting down my fork. "It's not my car. It's... something else."

That had my parents' attention. They both looked at me—Mom with her pale-green eyes. Dad with his light blue. And I took a deep breath. It was time to tell them...

"I'm moving away from Cottonwood Falls." The words tumbled from my mouth in a rush, wrecking the mood like a bowling ball into the kingpin.

Mom's fork clattered to the table, and a dip formed between Dad's eyebrows.

"What?" Mom asked first while Dad kept watching

like he was trying to understand some alien language. "Your job is here. Your friends. I don't understand."

"I was offered a job in Dallas," I said. Despite practicing my explanation a million times, the words still sounded wooden coming out of my mouth.

"What job?" Dad demanded, brow still knit.

So I explained that Griffen Industries needed an in-house insurance expert, and Gage Griffen (the founder and a friend from Cottonwood Falls) thought of me.

"But why?" Mom asked. "Your life is here."

My cheeks flamed, and I had to remind myself to breathe. "It's hard to explain."

"Is it about the money?" my dad pressed.

I shook my head. It wasn't about money—although the bump in pay would be nice. There were other goals I hoped to reach in my life. Ones that weren't happening here.

My breath shook, and so did my hands, so I wrung them in my lap. "I'm almost forty, and I don't have any relationship prospects in sight. Everyone in this town is paired up, not interested, or an ex. And I *want* what you both have with all my heart. I want a husband, a family. I want a happily ever after. It's just not finding me here."

Tears pricked at my eyes. Of embarrassment. Of loss. It was hard to feel like there wasn't something wrong with me, being passed over for love all these years.

If twenty-year-old me could see my current self—

still single with no prospects in sight—she'd be devastated. And to tell the truth, current me was devastated too. I was running out of time to have a family of my own.

Mom and Dad exchanged a silent conversation, and then Dad said, "When do you start?"

"In three months."

I had three months to pack up my entire life, say goodbye to my friends, and start all over.

Dallas, here I come.

3

___

HAYES

THE OFFICE PHONE rang on my desk, but I ignored it. No business calls past six—unless it came through the emergency line. I put my feet up on my desk and started my nightly routine of scrolling through the long list of women in my phone.

What did I want tonight after the kind of day I'd had?

Kinky to distract me from the monotony?

Vanilla to comfort me from a stressful workload?

Loud to drown out all my thoughts?

Efficient to get the job done before I got too tired?

Every option was there in the list of names and numbers.

But then a new message came through on my phone, interrupting my search.

Unknown Number: Sorry I'm running late! Be there in five! – Della

My eyebrows drew together.

Hayes: How'd you get my personal number?
Della: Liv gave it to me.

"Fuck," I muttered, making a mental note to have a chat with my sister-in-law. Della may have been Liv's best friend, but that didn't mean she needed special access to me too.

In a small town, you learned to set up boundaries. Otherwise you'd have random farmers calling you at four a.m. because they couldn't stand waiting until the shop opened at eight. Anyone who I wasn't related to or fucking got my business line. Or the emergency line. Not mine.

Hayes: Shop's closed.

I tapped away from the thread, but her response was immediate.

Della: I'm almost there. See you soon!

Frowning, I thumbed out a response.

Hayes: Do not come. I won't open the door for you.

Della: This is about to get real awkward...

I was about to say *bring it on,* but then I heard a knock on the office door.

Fine, she could knock all she wanted. Didn't mean I'd let her in.

Della: I know you can hear me.

I smirked at my screen.

Hayes: Hayes can't come to the phone right now. Leave a message after the tone.

The knocking stalled for a moment.

Della: You can't pretend to be an answering machine by text message. It doesn't make sense.
Hayes: BEEP

I was chuckling to myself at my own damn joke when the knocking stopped again. I leaned back in my chair, basking at the sound of blissful silence—no one needing me, no calls coming in, no one banging on tires or cursing at a stubborn bolt.

As the owner of Madigan Auto, I had to be "on" all day. Dealing with customers, handling delayed orders for parts, making sure my employees were satisfied... it took a lot out of me. And I learned early on if you didn't set boundaries with your customers, you'd run yourself ragged working all hours of the day and night.

Della was gone and could get her car in the morning. I knew her parents or my sister-in-law would help her out if she really was in dire straits. No need to stress, I reminded myself.

And then a new text came through on my phone.

Jessica: Baby, I'm outside. We can hook up on the tire stack again. ;)

That had me standing up and rushing to the front door. I unlocked it and opened it up, looking for Jessica, but then a mess of curves and curly red hair brushed past me, carrying a big red cooler inside.

"The fuck?" I muttered, following the determined woman into the lobby.

She set her cooler down on the coffee table, giving me a happy smile. "Don't be mad. I come bearing gifts."

My eyebrows drew together, and I went back to the door, poking my head outside and looking for Jess.

"She's not here," Della sang wickedly.

I stormed back to her, incredulous. "What the fuck is going on here?"

Della smirked as she opened up the cooler. Inside were several thermoses, along with Ziplock bags of different food items and a can of whipped cream. "I knew you and Jess had a thing. She owed me one." She shrugged before squirting some whipped cream in her mouth and licked her lips.

My mind went dirty places, but I folded my arms across my chest, the corner of my name tag rubbing against my forearm. *Della is off-limits.* "I'm holding your keys hostage all damn weekend."

"That's fine. I have a spare." She took a paper cup from the cooler and started opening one of the thermoses.

Now I full-on gaped at her as she seemed to be making herself right at home. "Then what's all this about? Why are you here?"

"Well, I keep thinking about how you hate hot cocoa and how miserable your life must be without it." While talking, she poured a drink into the cup, then used the can of whipped cream to add an obscene pile atop the brown liquid. "So I wondered if you just had a more bougie palate than everyone else. To test my hypothesis, I brought a few different flavors and toppings for you to try out. This one's dark chocolate." She passed me the cup with shining, expectant eyes.

I stared at her. She was like a puppy following you around the kitchen, not realizing its food was in the dog bowl in the corner. "I think I'll pass."

"If you try it, I'll get out of your hair," she tempted me, wiggling the cup.

"I don't do sugar unless it's in alcohol or off a woman's body." I folded my arms across my chest, eyeing her up and down. "Maybe we could try a body shot?" I arched a brow.

Della's cheeks flushed red in a way that made me want to touch her skin and see if it had heated. But I shook the thought just like she shook her head at me. "Stop trying to rattle me," she said. "I'm not leaving until you try this."

"So if I drink this, you'll get out of here?" Why did I feel like this was a trap?

"This... and the four other flavors I brought." She nodded resolutely.

I groaned, knowing her well enough to know she wouldn't be giving up anytime soon. That's why she and my sister-in-law were such great friends.

"Oh, come on. Don't be such a sourpuss. I'm trying to help you."

I dragged my hand over my face, about to explain that she could help me by leaving, but I had a feeling that would fall on deaf ears. "Fine, I'll try it, and then you'll leave."

"Great." She handed me the cup and watched eagerly as I took a cautious sip.

The bitterness of the dark chocolate actually improved the flavor a lot, but there was no way I'd give her the satisfaction of saying so. "Next," I said.

She frowned. "Really? I thought that would do it. Okay. Next one..." She opened another thermos, and I took a covert taste of the first one while her back was turned. Dark chocolate was really growing on me.

But I set the cup down when she had another one ready. This time, she handed me a drink topped with foamy milk and a grid of caramel sauce.

"This one is salted caramel," she said. "*So* good."

I took the cup and sipped it, maintaining a poker face. It definitely was a level up from regular cocoa, but dark chocolate was still in the lead.

She rubbed her hands together, a light shining in her pale eyes. "Tell me you love it."

"Want me to lie to you?" I murmured.

"Ugh." She turned and had to dig through the cooler. My eyes trailed to her backside, the jeans gaping at her waist and revealing a thin strip of black lace.

That had my eyebrows rising with appreciation. Curiosity. The dark fabric was such a contrast to her pale skin...

But then she turned back to me with another cup. This one had a mint leaf atop a swirl of whipped cream. "Mint hot chocolate," she explained.

I absently wondered if it would taste like Thin Mints as I drew it to my lips. That was my favorite Girl Scout cookie. The only one worthwhile, really, if you asked me.

My lip ring butted against the cup as I sipped the best fucking hot chocolate I'd ever tasted. But I was careful not to drink for too long before handing it back with a bored expression. "Do I really have to suffer through another one?" Damn, I should have gone to acting school. I was *that* good.

Undeterred, Della said, "That's okay. I *know* you'll like this one." She bent over again, and I took a moment to appreciate her curves without her looking. Without my sister-in-law reminding me that her best friend was strictly off-limits.

I bit down on my lip ring to keep myself from reaching out for her round waist before Della turned back around. My eyes trailed the constellation of freckles across her cheeks as she said, "Irish cream." Her eyebrows waggled like I was in for a treat. As if I hadn't just gotten one.

I took the drink from her, a frothy light brown color, and drew it to my lips. The whiskey was strong, just like I liked, but the hot chocolate didn't really add anything. "Better with coffee," I muttered.

"It's decided then." She folded her arms across her chest, and it took all I had not to stare.

"What's decided?" I asked.

"You're from another planet. Are you sure your house isn't secretly a spaceship?" she deadpanned.

"Come home with me. I'll probe you on my ship." I was only half teasing.

But she laughed dismissively, turning to gather up her hot chocolate supplies.

I tried not to be bothered by the brush-off, even though nothing could ever happen between us. I had a phone full of women, after all. Women who wanted to come over and do more than shove sugary drinks down my throat.

So why the fuck was I bothered?

Knowing I needed a distraction from the strange reaction to this woman, I said, "Leave the whipped cream."

She turned back to me, red eyebrows drawing together. "Why?"

I smirked. "Shall I show you?"

Della's breath caught, and she fumbled with the lid of the cooler, but only for a second before getting it shut and latched. "Hayes Madigan, you tease." She shook her head at me like I was exasperating to her.

She had no fucking idea I wasn't teasing.

That my self-restraint had worn thin after all these years.

She picked up the cooler and left, taking the whipped cream with her.

Pity.

4

DELLA

SATURDAY AFTERNOON, I drove my car—with its now-functioning heater—through the country to my best friend's house just outside of Cottonwood Falls for a get-together. The cold front had thankfully left the area, leaving us with pale-blue skies, soft-yellow sunlight, and the beginning tells of springtime passing out my window.

Just as I crested a hill on the dirt road, a gorgeous white farmhouse came into view. I smiled at the sight of it standing out amongst miles of rolling meadows. The picturesque home was the personification of Liv's happily ever after with her childhood friend. Hard to believe they'd gone from neighbors growing up to husband and wife with three children between them.

They'd had a whole tumultuous love story and made *multiple* humans while I remained single.

It was like I was sitting in this car, watching life blur by out the windows but never really getting anywhere.

A heavy ache settled in my heart as I slowed and pulled into their gravel drive. I hoped this impending move to Dallas would give me a chance at the same happiness they'd found together. Even if it meant leaving the town I loved.

Once my car was parked behind Liv's truck, I turned it off and took a look around at all the other vehicles outside. Both Liv and Fletcher came from big families. Her with three siblings, and him with four. So there were plenty of people here—most of them married with children of their own.

I took a few deep breaths to brace myself for the cookout today.

This would be one of the last times we all got together before I moved away. And even though I wanted what they had... I'd miss my friends beyond comprehension.

The roar of an engine broke the silence. I twisted in my seat to see an old black-and-gray Ford rumbling down the driveway, Hayes Madigan at the wheel.

And since he clearly hadn't noticed me yet, I let myself stare.

Tattoos covered every spare inch of skin, curling up his neck and only pausing at his face, all hard lines and edges with a silver ring curling around his bottom lip. Shaggy, dark blond hair dusted over blue-green eyes— the kind of gaze that caught you like a mouse in a trap.

So with every inch of him screaming *danger*, why was I still staring?

Maybe because he fascinated me.

The human version of a massive red button that said DO NOT TOUCH.

His truck stopped next to me, and the abrupt pause of the engine's roar had me jumping.

I scrambled for my phone, pretending to be busy texting until I heard his truck door open and shut. Dad would have needed an entire can of WD-40 to fix those hinges.

After what I hoped was enough time, I opened my door and got out of my car, grabbing the pan of yeast-risen rolls I brought for a side. The sun hit my face, nice and warm, but a brisk breeze followed it up, making goosebumps rise on the back of my neck.

Shivering, I shut the door and turned to walk around my car, slamming into a wall of muscles and tattoos. I nearly spilled the pan of rolls, but he caught it, covering my hands with his own.

"Not again," I groaned, having flashbacks of hot cocoa and his grumpy face.

"Anyone ever tell you it's rude to stare?" he asked, his voice low.

His hands still covered mine, holding me in place. There were hints of his job on his skin, oil stains and calluses marked each hour in the shop. I looked into his eyes and found him staring right back at me.

Unabashed. His jaw muscles flexed, and I realized he was still waiting for my answer.

I finally remembered to breathe. Better to play his game and tease him than let him discover how his simple touch affected me far more than it should. "Where did you attend charm school?" I retorted. "So I can leave them a one-star review online. Or possibly send you back for a do-over."

But my comment didn't deter him one bit, and my body wouldn't listen. My skin hummed underneath his, vibrated with electricity. A slow smirk tipped his lips as he said, "They wouldn't take me back." He took the pan from me and started walking toward the house.

I took a few seconds to gather myself, then walked beside him to the backyard. It was sunny back here and just warm enough to be comfortable in my jacket if I didn't stand too still.

Liv and Fletcher's little girls came toddling up to us. "Uncle Hayes! Aunt Della!" they cried. Maya followed behind her sisters with her cousins, Emily and Jackson. It was like a whole parade of children running up to us.

Hayes held the pan in one hand and easily scooped the four-year-old, Leah, into one of his arms. He held her close, tattoos contrasting with the white of her sweater. And then kissed her cheek. Leah giggled happily at the scratch of his stubble. And when he set her down, she came over to me, arms in the air.

I picked her up, relishing the soft feel of her cheek against mine. "Hey, sweet girl."

Out of the corner of my eye, I watched Hayes greet all his nieces and nephews who looked up to him like the hero in their favorite movie. And that grumpy guy I saw in the body shop? Completely gone. This tatted guy had eyes shining with happiness. Tender hands that tickled and hugged and carried. And damn, my ovaries needed to remember that he reserved this special brand of warmth for select people in his life. I was not one of them.

"Della!" Liv came over, glowing with her pregnancy. I let Leah down so I could give Liv a big hug. I definitely needed it.

"Let's go inside," she said, leaving her arm around my shoulder. "All the ladies are in there. What's new?"

It was a simple question, but it automatically had my gut sinking. "Oh, um..." I still hadn't told her about the new job. And word would surely get out soon, especially since they all knew the people I'd be working for.

We went into the house, and I saw our best girlfriends sitting around the island. This was where we hung out while the guys spent their time outside around the grill trying to find the perfect char of meat.

Henrietta, Maggie, and Larkin all waved and said hello. I smiled back at them thinking with the five of us here, we felt complete somehow.

Hen was married to Liv's brother, Tyler. She had gorgeous dark skin and natural curly hair and a smile that could brighten even Hayes's dark mood. Maggie, the brunette with pretty brown eyes, was married to

Liv's other brother, Rhett. Larkin was the most recent to marry into the Madigan family, living her own happily ever after with Knox after a nasty divorce.

And here I was, sliding into a barstool at the island, the old maid. People had married, divorced, and remarried in the time it took me to change the wallpaper in my living room.

I took my time with decisions, big and small. I made fewer mistakes that way. But maybe taking so long with my decisions was a mistake all its own.

Hen poured wine into a glass for me and passed it my way. I took a long sip, relishing the warmth that filled my mouth and drained down my throat. "Why has it been so long since we've had a girls' night?" I asked them.

Liv pointed at her belly. "All-day sickness."

Maggie said, "The salon has been crazy busy."

And Hen answered, "Tyler and I have barely been in town the last month."

I nodded, trying to ignore the pang of jealousy that went through me.

But then Larkin said, "What have you been up to lately?"

This was the perfect chance to tell my friends about my move, but I couldn't... So I simply said, "I found out Hayes hates hot chocolate."

They all looked at me, incredulous, and Liv said, "Seriously?"

I nodded. "I brought him some for towing my car

the other day, and he acted like it was liquid manure in his cup." I left out the part where I spilled it all over him. Minor details.

Liv tilted her head in confusion, making dark hair fall over her shoulder. "But he ordered mint chocolate hot cocoa for the party tonight... Had it shipped here yesterday."

A smug smile formed on my lips. "I freaking knew it."

Hayes Madigan wasn't as tough as he'd seemed. Maybe I'd gotten under his skin as well.

5

HAYES

"LEFT, RIGHT, LEFT, SCOOT," my teenaged niece, Maya, ordered, showing my brothers, dad, and me the moves to the "Boot Scootin' Boogie." She had been learning it in dance class and insisted the whole family learn it, too, for the Cottonwood Falls Spring Festival. Her class would be performing and their families were encouraged to join in.

I swore this girl would run the world one day. Just under a month ago, she and my other niece Emily were giving a presentation on why I should finally settle down and pick a girl to marry. They had bullet points and everything. Never mind that the list included impractical options for a partner, like their teacher, my brother's sixty-year-old nurse, and my sister-in-law's best friend—Della Dwyer.

Immediately at the suggestion, Liv had said, "Absolutely not," reaffirming my reasons to stay away from Della.

It should have been easy to steer clear, with *billions* of people on the planet. But something about her was magnetic. Or maybe I was just as stupid as a bug drawn to a light.

"Hayes!" Maya groused. "That's not how you scoot!"

While my brothers snickered at me, I arched an eyebrow. "I can scoot on outta here."

Maya was undeterred by my smart-assery. "Like this." She squared up in front of me, lifting one knee so she did a half-skip to the side. "Now you try."

I did it as she asked, exaggerating the movement.

Her little lips pursed. "Good. But without the atti-tude next time."

That had everyone cracking up.

I gave my brothers a look and said under my breath, "Sorry, I do my best dancing with a partner." Then I winked.

Knox shoved my shoulder. "Stupid."

But Maya soldiered on. "From the top!"

She yelled out the moves, no doubt in a perfect imitation of her music teacher, and we all followed along. My brother Knox was a great dancer and prob-ably knew the moves already. Our oldest brother, Fletcher, followed the steps like a robot. And Dad surprised me with how well he kept up. My other brothers, Ford and Bryce, couldn't make it today since they lived out of town. Lucky bastards.

When we made it through the song a couple times with minimal errors, Maya squealed. "I have to show Livvy!" That's what she called her stepmama. "Stay right there."

The blood drained from my face—the last thing I needed was an audience. Especially knowing Della was among them. Oblivious to my panic, Knox elbowed Fletcher and said, "Maya could start a cult."

Fletcher made prayer hands and closed his dark brown eyes. "*Please*, God, let her use her powers for something productive."

I shook my head. "So far we have a PowerPoint on why I should get hitched and a choreographed dance. I'm not convinced."

My dad and brothers cracked up at my joke. But then the door swung open, and we glanced over to see Liv coming outside with Maya... followed by all the other women.

I bit down on my lip ring to keep myself from saying something stupid. Especially since I'd soon be performing for them. Usually, I wasn't shy. But something about Della's eyes on me felt different.

I could feel her stare just like I could earlier.

And it bothered me that I even noticed.

Why the hell did I notice?

Women staring at me was part of my everyday life. When you lived in a small town and had as many tattoos as I did, had a reputation like I did, you drew attention.

But Della's attention felt different.

Probably because she got under my skin—especially lately. Why was she so intent on making me like hot chocolate? I used to be fine with plain black coffee, but now that shit was like a drug. And unreasonably hard to find. I ordered over fifty bucks worth just to get free shipping.

But Maya's performance went on, regardless of my spinning thoughts. The song started playing over speakers attached to the back of the house, and she shouted out the moves.

The women hooted and hollered their support, and... Della's eyes were still on me.

If she was watching...I might as well put on a show.

I ran through each step, easily following the beat. Between spins, I sent her a wink that had her pale cheeks flushing with color, her eyes darting away. Some part of me was satisfied that I could fluster her like she distracted me. Even if nothing could come of it, at least I wasn't on an island of my own destruction.

When the song ended, everyone was cheering. Hell, maybe I was even smiling a little bit, despite being voluntold into dancing.

Maya walked up to me, holding out her hand for me to shake. "Good job, Uncle Hayes."

I shook her hand. "Good job, squirt. I better vote for you for governor one day."

She grinned easily. "I'd prefer a vote for president."

"Done," I said. "Lord help the other countries with you at the helm."

Giggling, she went off to her dad and stepmom, who praised her teaching skills. As I watched after her, Knox patted my back and said, "Pull those moves at the bar and you'll have the ladies all over you."

I scoffed at him. "I don't need moves for that to happen."

Someone snort-laughed nearby, and I found Della flushing bright red under all her freckles.

"Yes?" I asked.

Knox's eyes darted between us.

"Nothing," Della said, humor crinkling the corners of her eyes. "Nothing at all."

"Enlighten us," I drawled.

She shrugged, despite the teasing smile playing on her lips. "I'm just thinking you may need those moves when you lose your hair."

Instinctively, my fingers went to my scalp, and Knox cracked up laughing. A sly smile formed on Della's lips, and I flipped off both of them before going to get some grub.

Why was she so good at getting under my skin?

FOR THE REST of the evening, we sat around the firepit outside—eating, drinking, and shooting the shit

—while little kids ran around like seagulls, picking food off peoples' plates and playing games with each other.

But eventually the kids got tired and people started heading home. Liv, Fletcher, Della and I were the last ones around the fire when Liv glanced through the glass back door to the house and let out a sigh. "Looks like the movie's over. Better tell Maya to get some sleep."

Della stood up and gave Liv a hug. "I'm going to head home. It was great seeing you."

That was my cue to leave, too.

While Liv and Fletcher went inside, Della and I walked around the side of the house to the driveway where our vehicles were waiting for us.

We were almost to our cars when she said, "Hayes?"

It was a tentative question, the way she said my name. Color me intrigued, because I leaned up against my truck. "What's up?"

Her eyes darted in every direction but never landed on mine. "Never mind... It's embarrassing."

"More embarrassing than the Boot Scootin' Boogie?" I cracked a wry smile.

She chuckled. "No, nothing's more embarrassing than that."

My hand went to my chest, wounded.

"Kidding," she replied. But something was off about her tone. It was falsely light. Something was going on. And I might be a grump, but I'm not a dick. "What is it?" I pressed.

She bit her bottom lip, and my gaze lingered there a moment longer than it should have. "I just wanted to know... How do you do it?" she asked, her words halting and shy. So unlike her.

"Do what?" I asked.

"How do you stay single? How do you... enjoy it?"

I tilted my head, examining her. What a strange question, considering our interactions had never gone very deep, even in years of knowing each other. "What makes you ask?"

She glanced down quickly. "Reasons."

I raised my eyebrows, waiting for more.

Extra color started at her neck and wound its way up her cheeks. "Forget I said anything." She turned back toward her car.

But the thought of her driving away from me when I didn't know what was behind her question had me saying, "Follow me."

Now it was her turn to be surprised. She spun back toward me. "What?"

"Get in your car and follow me. It's easier if I show you."

I got in my truck, half expecting to see her head-lights go another direction, but when I made the turn, she was right there with me.

6

DELLA

I WEARILY EYED the house in front of me before
Hayes's long stride crossed my headlight beams and he
stopped, waiting with his arms folded over his chest.

I got out of my car and gave him a suspicious look.
"I'm not sleeping with you, Hayes Madigan," I said.

He smirked, still lit up by my headlights. "No one
said anything about sleeping."

I gaped at him, but he just chuckled. "Get your
mind out of the gutter, Princess. Follow me."

My heart was beating faster than normal as I
walked behind his long, lean form to his front door. He
pulled it open without unlocking it—no one in this
small town ever locked their vehicles, much less their
houses. And then he led me inside.

I'd never been inside Hayes's home before—even
knowing him most of my life. He was several years
below me in school, and when we saw each other, it was

only in work settings or at family gatherings. Even so, I drank in my surroundings, curious to see what his home would tell me about the enigma of Hayes Madigan.

He was always a bit of a mystery to me. I suspected there was something behind his cavalier demeanor, but I didn't know what.

Realizing I was a few steps ahead of him, I glanced back to see him tugging off his hoodie. His T-shirt lifted up with it, and my lips parted at the view.

Tattoos covered nearly every spare inch of skin I could see, rippling over the muscles of his stomach. When he took off his hoodie and met my eyes again, I knew.

He'd seen me staring. Again.

But he didn't comment on it this time. Instead, there was a pleased look in his eyes as he gestured toward the living room. "Look around. What do you see?"

"A living room?" I asked as I eyed the sparse space with dark leather couches, a glass coffee table, and the giant TV that was a staple in any bachelor's home. Then I frowned. "One that needs a lot more color."

He smirked. "Look again. Hard furniture. Nothing a girl would like to hang out on. No frilly throw pillows. No plushy rug. Nothing that says, 'Welcome home, make yourself comfortable while I make us breakfast.'"

My eyebrows pulled together. But before I could speak, he said, "Follow me."

Dazedly, I fell into step behind him, where he led me down the hallway past his kitchen. "This house has two bedrooms," he explained. "This one is mine"—he tapped a finger on a wooden door to his left—"and the other..." He opened a door on his right, and I stared inside.

The entire room was stacked floor to ceiling with boxes. The only vacant space was an aisle down the middle of the room to access the boxes.

I looked a little closer at the labels, noticing one of them said BRAKE PADS. Another, OIL FILTERS. I raised my eyebrows. "Did you run out of room at the shop?"

He leaned against the doorframe, all lean muscles and carefree confidence. "Hell no. I have plenty of room."

"So you decided to bring your collection home because you love your job that much?" I needled. I folded my arms across my chest, and I watched his gaze lazily trail down my body. It was like all my staring had given him an invitation—one he happily accepted, judging by the heat in his eyes. When they met mine again, a shiver went down my spine. I almost didn't comprehend his words when he spoke again.

"This room sends a message, Moonshine."

"That you really love your job?" I countered. Why was my voice so breathy when I was trying to be pithy and snarky, unaffected by his sex appeal and the intoxicating scent of his cologne?

He shook his head, holding my gaze until I had to look away. "It says the only space for a woman in my home is in my bed, screaming my name."

His words came out a low rasp that told me just how much he enjoyed his time there. And despite the pounding in my heart, despite the breathlessness of my chest, I said, "What are you trying to say?"

His lips twisted wryly to the side. "*That's* how I stay single. I won't have it any other way."

"But that's not what I asked," I said.

"Isn't it?"

I shook my head. "I asked how you stayed single and happy."

"They mean the same thing." He gestured that we should leave the room, so I stepped farther down the hallway and he turned out the light before shutting the door. The snap of the latch against the strike plate was just the cleanser I needed as I walked to his living room, feeling Hayes's eyes on me as I went.

A question was stirring at the edge of my tongue, but before it came out, Hayes asked, "Want a beer?"

I raised an eyebrow, surprised at the question. "Thought the only place for a woman was in your bed?"

He ran a hand through dirty-blond hair. "You don't count."

"And why is that?" I asked, trying not to show how much that bothered me. It was just a reminder of all those times men's gazes slid over me at the bar like I didn't really exist. Or how, when I was in college, guys only befriended me to get my skinnier friends' phone numbers.

My interest in Hayes frustrated me, because he clearly wasn't interested in me.

"Actually, I will take a beer," I said with a sigh.

He went to the fridge, bottles clinking as he pulled them out. Using the hem of his shirt, he twisted off the lids, showing another slice of his stomach, which I tried hard not to stare at.

I didn't meet his gaze again until he passed me a bottle. I pulled it to my lips, letting the tangy liquid distract me from this sinking feeling.

Hayes was known to be a womanizer. What did it say about me that I was the one woman he wasn't interested in?

He gestured at the couch across from him, and I defeatedly went and sat on the cold black leather. Damn, he was right. It was fine for a little bit but wouldn't be comfortable enough to sit on through a whole movie or anything. The first thing I would change about this place would be adding some throw pillows and blankets to make it more comfortable.

His voice was low, eyes trained on his beer bottle when he finally spoke. "I don't shit where I eat, Della. That's why you don't count."

"What does that even mean?" I asked. I picked at the corner of the label on my own bottle, pulling back the paper.

He took a swig of his drink, and it was hard not to stare at his lips forming a seal around the bottle, the bob of his Adam's apple, the swipe of his tongue over his shining mouth. "I don't want my... relationships to make things worse for my family." He held up his fingers to count off a list. "My nieces' teachers, employees, and family friends." He gestured at me. "That would be you... All off-limits."

I put my hand over my chest, pretending to simper. "Did you just call me your friend? Aw, Hayes. So sweet!" Okay and maybe I was secretly relieved that it wasn't just about my looks.

He waved his hands while swallowing his drink. "I said *family* friends. Not *my* friends."

I pulled his move and winked at him. "Don't worry, your secret's safe with me." I set my beer on his coffee table while he looked curiously at me.

"You still haven't told me, *friend*, why do you care so much about finding someone?" Now his eyes were fully on me, unabashedly staring while waiting for my answer.

My stomach twisted uncomfortably. "You wouldn't get it. Not when you've set up your whole life to keep women at arm's length." I was genuinely curious, so I had to ask, "You came from a big family, Hayes. Almost all your brothers are happily married. Don't you see the allure?"

His gaze darkened for a fraction of a second, but then he was back to his cavalier façade. And I realized it was a mask... with something hiding behind it. "I see the allure of a relationship in one place, and that's—"

I rolled my eyes at him. "The bedroom. Yeah, yeah, I get it. You don't want someone around, cramping your... style." I made a face at his couch.

Hayes pretended to be wounded. "You think I'm that shallow?"

I gave him a look. Wasn't it obvious he cared about surface-level things only?

"What would you rather have, Princess? Freedom to do whatever you want whenever you want... Or some dude who farts when he sleeps, leaves his clothes on the bathroom floor, and forgets your anniversary as often as he remembers it?"

"Gee, you're romantic," I drawled, even as my heart was squeezing with worry. Was that really all there was out there for me?

"I'm a realist. And I don't see the point in being any other way. Most women dream of a man who will sweep her off her feet. But the only thing waiting for them is some guy who will lift up his feet for her to sweep under them."

My eyebrows pinched together. "Is that how you think of your brothers? Just losers for their wives to look after?"

"Of course not!" he argued. "But they're the exception, not the rule."

His cynicism was seriously getting me down. Especially considering I was about to move to get a chance at love. "You're forgetting something," I reminded us both.

"And what is that?" he countered, elbows resting on his knees.

"You don't love someone just because of their good qualities. To love someone, and to really be loved, you have to see all their flaws and choose them anyway."

Hayes was quiet for the first time that evening.

After a moment, I set my bottle on the table and said goodbye.

Because Hayes Madigan?

He would never understand.

WHEN I WOKE up the next morning and walked into my living room, Della was on my mind. The disappointment in her face when I reminded her how most relationships went. It was like waiting until Christmas morning to tell a kid Santa didn't exist when they came running down the stairs to look for presents and found nothing underneath the tree.

A small part of me felt guilty. But wasn't it better to know the truth and adjust to reality than waste your life waiting on a dream unlikely to come true?

It reminded me of my mom at home, dying. And everyone praying for a miracle when they all knew damn well she wouldn't survive.

With a grunt, I went to the kitchen, made coffee, and then decided to spend my Sunday at the garage working on my 1969 Harley Davidson. I'd spent the last six months slowly restoring her. When she came to me, the paint was chipped, the leather cracked, and the insides just as much of a mess. Now, she glimmered in all her candy pearl sea-green paint, and the dark leather practically gleamed under the shop lights.

The final part I needed was set to arrive tomorrow morning, and I wanted to make sure everything was ready for the install.

It was early enough in the day that the light still had a pinkish-blue tinge to it as I drove to the garage. Over the lobby windows, the sign shone against the pale morning. MADIGAN AUTO.

My lips twitched at the sign, at seeing my name there. Even though I'd bought the garage over five years ago now, the sight of my name on the building never got old. Most people thought I would never amount to anything, and this sign was a giant middle finger proving them wrong. Proving my small group of supporters right.

With a sense of pride filling my chest, I got out of my truck and walked to the building. It took just a moment to unlock the door, go back to the garage, and roll out my pretty bike.

For the better part of the day, I tinkered with the motorcycle, making sure everything was ready for tomorrow. As soon as the part was installed, she should be ready to go. I hoped.

When there was nothing left to do, I cleaned up the garage and went into the office to do some paperwork. The monthly payment for the business was due, and I wrote the check, thinking of my dad, who made it all possible.

When I had an opportunity to purchase the business, he cosigned the loan. He could have lost everything. Still could if things went south.

It kept me working harder than ever.

I snapped a picture of the check and texted it to him.

Hayes: Thanks Dad.

Within a few minutes, he texted me back.

Dad: Proud of you. See you at lunch tomorrow?
Hayes: It's on me.

With any luck, I'd be riding my motorcycle there.

THE NEXT MORNING, I couldn't help but drop all my projects to install the new part and see if she would run. If all the work I'd put in was going to pay off. I could feel everyone in the garage watching me to see the outcome.

So I gripped the new textured handlebars under my bare palms, shoved the bike forward so the kickstand would go back in place. Then I twisted the ignition key and used my full weight to kickstart the bike.

The engine turned once and died. But my heart was fucking soaring. That sound was better than any song.

Giving it my all, I kicked it again to the same result.

I could feel everyone holding their breath for me.

On the third try, the engine struggled to catch, turning over once, twice, and I twisted the throttle to give it more gas.

It roared to life, growling like the sweetest music in the world.

Whooping roared through the shop, my guys cheering for me as I kicked it into gear and slowly pulled out of the garage. A grin split my face. This was the best feeling ever. Fixing something broken, bringing it back to life.

A cool spring breeze ripped around me as I drove through the less trafficked areas, lifting my hair, rippling my shirt around my body, making me feel *alive*.

"Yeah!" I shouted, pumping my fist. "Hell yeah!"

If I was an emotional guy, I might have cried tears of joy. Instead, I steered her up and down the side streets in town, getting a feel for the way she handled before taking her out on the major highways and streets.

At first, I took it easy, but then I pushed her, seeing how far this rebuilt engine would go. She felt alive underneath me, responding to my touch and every shift of my body, like a woman would.

I lifted my wrist to check my smartwatch and saw it

was about time to meet my dad and brother for lunch at Woody's Diner.

Perfect timing—I could show them my girl.

Excited at the thought, I revved the engine and sped back into town toward the chrome-topped diner where my dad ate lunch every day. It was his social hour—and a chance to see the waitress who he insisted was only a friend.

When I pulled into the cracked blacktop parking lot, my ears hurt from the cool wind blowing by for the last hour or so and my eyes were watering, but I was grinning ear to ear. I adjusted my shirt and walked through the doors, noticing most of the diners checking out my motorcycle through the window.

A feeling of pride seeped through me as I walked straight to the booth where my dad always sat—the one closest to the coffee pot. Probably so he could talk to Aggie without interrupting her work too much. A move I'd used myself (although on other waitresses).

Dad scooted over so I could sit by him, and Fletch nodded at me across the table. "Got the bike up and running?" Fletcher asked.

I grinned like a kid on Christmas morning. "Finally. She runs like a dream, too."

"That new voltage regulator did the trick?" Dad asked.

I nodded, annoyed I had to wait so long while it was on backorder. "Finally got in this morning."

Fletcher said, "My daughters aren't allowed to ride on it outside of the driveway."

"Fine," I grunted. "But you never said anything about your pregnant wife. She'll love it so much she'll get pregnant twice." I winked.

Fletcher went white, and my dad shoved me. "Hayes, don't make me get a spray bottle out for you again."

I smirked at him. "Wet T-shirt contest?"

Fletcher was composed enough to roll his eyes at me while Dad only gave an exasperated shake of his head. But then Dad's gaze snapped to a woman approaching the table. She was Hispanic, curvy, with black hair broken up with streaks of gray. Her smile crinkled her eyes as she approached. "Some of my favorite guys!" I swore her eyes lingered a little longer on my dad, and he grinned back at her.

"Can't beat the service here," he said.

She pretended to flip her hair back, even though it was up in a ponytail. "You're just happy I ignore the two-refill limit for you, Gray."

Dad happily lifted his full coffee cup. If this sugar fest continued, I might gag. "I'll take a coffee—black," I told her. "And a burger with fries."

Dad gave me a look.

"Please," I said, putting on my most charming grin.

"Of course, baby," she said, jotting it down in a notebook. I glanced out the window to check on my motorcycle. I bet the green paint caught the light just perfect this time of day.

But then I noticed someone touching the leather seat. Someone with bright red curls and far too colorful of clothes.

"The fuck?" I muttered, annoyance making my pulse speed up. "Excuse me," I said before getting out of the booth to go outside and yell at Della. Didn't her parents ever tell her to look with her eyes and not her hands?

When I pushed past the customers paying for their meal at the register and got to the parking lot, Della was already walking back across the street to the insurance office where she worked.

As I jogged toward my bike, I called out at her, "Don't you know better than to lay hands on a vintage Harley?"

She turned in the middle of the dead Main Street, completely unbothered, and waved at me. "Just left you a note," she called, then she turned and walked the rest of the way to the front door. And maybe I spent a little too long looking at her ass in that fluttery skirt, but wasn't that my whole point? Look, don't touch?

I reached my bike just as the mirrored glass door closed behind her and saw a hot-pink sticky note on the seat with something written in the same curly handwriting from the other day.

24X more people die riding motorcycles than cars. WEAR A HELMET. – Della

My eyebrows rose at the note. Seriously? Now that I had her number, I pulled my phone out of my pocket and fired off a text.

Hayes: Looks like someone cares about me. How sweet.

I looked at the building where she worked, even though I couldn't see her inside. And soon a text came back.

Della: Don't flatter yourself. Just trying to avoid the extra paperwork when your family files a claim.

I smirked at her message, then pocketed my phone and went back inside.

8

______

DELLA

HAYES RODE that damn motorcycle to the diner—without a helmet—every day that week. Of course, I couldn't ignore it when my office window overlooked Main Street and the diner. Especially since his motorcycle was so loud, it was like an alarm alerting me to his presence.

So every day, I walked a sticky note across the street with a fact about motorcycle accidents—each tidbit gnarlier than the one before it.

It was fun to rib him—to see the annoyed look on his face when he picked up the note and shoved it in his pocket. But even though Hayes and I teased each other, I'd hate to see him hurt. He was as much family as anyone else in Cottonwood Falls.

Although, my concern seemed to do no good. Until Friday.

I stared out the window in disbelief as he drove up to the diner and parked. Saying a quick "Be right back" to my boss, I scurried across the street to eyeball the thing sitting atop the black leather seat of his motorcycle.

I grinned at the red and black helmet.

That's when I noticed a yellow sticky note on the side, but it didn't have a message on the front. I plucked it from the helmet, turning it over to read Hayes's messy scrawl.

Happy now?

I grinned, knowing he was watching me. I'd won. Basking in my glory, I looked back at the helmet and saw what the sticky note had been covering—a sticker of a middle finger.

I rolled my eyes and pulled my phone out of my dress pocket. (Those were seriously the best. Who even wore dresses without pockets anymore?)

Della: Rude.

Hayes: Exactly what I call getting adhesive on a brand-new leather seat.

If I kept rolling my eyes at this rate, they'd unscrew from the sockets. So I sent back another text instead.

Della: You're welcome for protecting your head.

Hayes: *smirk emoji* I'm already good at making sure that's covered.

My cheeks flamed bright red.

Hayes: Want to see?
Della: Keep it in your pants.

I turned and walked away from his motorcycle, knowing he was probably laughing inside the restaurant. I was tempted to raise a middle finger as I walked away, but between all the other innocent people in the diner and my boss inside the office, I restrained myself.

Barely.

Hayes Madigan knew how to press all my buttons. Maybe it was time I pushed some of his too.

I WAS BACK at the office, working through a stack of paperwork when my phone started vibrating like crazy.

Group Chat
Della, Henrietta, Larkin, Liv, Maggie
Liv: EMERGENCY MEETING AT DELLA'S HOUSE.
TONIGHT @ 6. Ya bitches better be there.

Private text message
Liv: You're MOVING?

I SWALLOWED HARD, seeing the flurry of text messages coming through my phone. Liv had found out I was leaving—before I had a chance to tell her. Now, not only did I feel like a shit friend for moving. I was a shit friend for keeping it from her.

Della: How did you find out?
Liv: I saw your mom at the grocery store. She thought I knew already. LIKE I SHOULD HAVE. wtf Del?

I set my phone on my desk and rubbed my temples. I was guilty. Liv was pissed. And now I had to explain. This wasn't what I had in mind.

Della: I was going to tell you all on Saturday, but I couldn't bring myself to say it out loud... I'm really sorry you had to find out this way. Forgive me?
Liv: We can talk all about it tonight.

Letting out a heavy sigh, I locked my phone and tried to focus on the rest of the paperwork I had to do this afternoon. This was already the part of my job I enjoyed the least, but now it was like torture, knowing I only had a couple hours before all my friends would be at my house demanding answers it hurt to give.

I even put on a podcast recapping the latest *The Great British Bake Off*—a.k.a. *GBBO*—fan predictions, but that did nothing to distract me from my worry.

Eventually, I finished up my papers and crossed the lobby to my boss's office.

I knocked on the doorframe, and the older woman with light brown hair and giant Coke-bottle glasses looked up at me. She pushed the frames up her nose and smiled. "All done for the week?"

I nodded. "Any plans for the weekend?"

She tilted her head to the side, but her hair stayed in place thanks to gallons of Aqua Net. "Other than coming up with a scheme to keep you here?"

My lips curved into a sad smile. "Having a boss like you already makes the decision hard enough." Edna had taken a chance on me fresh out of college. I'd grown here as a professional. As a woman. "It's going to be hard not seeing your face every day."

"Oh hush." She waved her hand at me, wearing a satisfied smile that deepened her wrinkles. "Have a good weekend, Dell."

"I will," I said, mentally adding, *I hope.*

There would be four extra women at my house soon who all needed answers. And since I didn't have much at my house, I stopped at the store to grab a meat and cheese tray and some wine. Multiple bottles of wine. Plus some of that sparkling water Liv liked to drink while pregnant.

When I got to my place a few blocks away, I uncorked a bottle first, pouring myself a glass and taking a long sip of the liquid courage.

Gah, maybe *this* was why I was single. I could handle conflict with people like Hayes all day every day. But my friends, my family? I ran from hard conversations like they were zombies and I was barefoot in a nightgown trying not to die.

But this conversation couldn't be avoided. Not now that I could see headlights shining through my front window, cars parking in my driveway and along the street.

My friends were here, and I had some explaining to do.

Liv walked inside first, carrying a giant notepad and a tripod. I didn't have a chance to ask her what that was about before Henrietta, Larkin, and Maggie followed her inside.

"Anyone care for wine?" I asked. "I have some charcuterie on the table too."

I helped pour drinks, watching while Liv set up the tripod with the notepad. She clicked the lid of a big black marker in her fingers, waiting for us all to be ready. She meant business.

"Enough with the snacks," Liv said, tightening the ponytail at the back of her head. "Everyone sit down. We have a problem to solve."

"What do you mean?" Larkin asked, her gaze tracking between Liv and me.

Liv gave me a pointed look. "Tell them."

Everyone went to sit down in my living room while

I stood awkwardly in the dining area. All eyes were on me, and despite *hating* all the attention, I raised my chin up high. "I got a new job in Dallas at Griffen Industries. I'm moving in two and a half months."

There was a mix of gasps, worried smiles, and frowns. Henrietta said, "That's not so bad. Dallas is just two hours away."

"Thank you," I mouthed to her. She'd moved to Texas from California, so at least she had a different perspective. Not like Liv and I, who had spent most of our lives in Cottonwood Falls.

"Not so bad?" Liv countered. "It's terrible!"

Henrietta said, "It's a good job, right?"

I nodded, thankful for her prompting. Wringing my hands around the stem of my wine glass, I said, "It's a significant bump in pay. I'll even be leading a team for the first time."

Liv frowned. "That's all fine and good, but..." She uncapped the marker and wrote a headline on the paper. REASONS DELLA SHOULD STAY

Maggie held a cube of cheese in her hand and said, "No more random drop-ins if she leaves."

I gave her a betrayed look, and she gave me an embarrassed smile.

"Sorry, I'll miss you!" Maggie said.

Larkin nodded. "It's been fun having a girlfriend in town to talk to."

Liv said, "All your nieces and nephews love you."

My heart ached as Liv wrote each reason on the board, and finally, I'd had enough of the ambush. I went and stood by Liv, taking the marker. "Look, it's not like I want to leave!"

Now everyone looked confused, but Liv voiced it. "You don't?"

I shook my head and started pacing anxiously. "Of course not! I love it here. I have you all. My parents. My job is great. And my house." I gestured around me. I had decorated it exactly how I liked, using peel-and-stick floral wallpaper and window clings that caught the light and cast little rainbows on the floor. Even my hanging plants had character, with pots that looked like disco balls. It was a bona fide Della Dreamhouse. Finding its match in the city would be nearly impossible, even with my new and improved salary.

Liv's hands extended out at her sides. "Then why the hell are you moving?"

"Because I'm lonely!" I nearly shouted, embarrassed but hoping they would understand. "All of you have found your person. And each day I'm reminded that I don't have one." Humiliated tears pricked at my eyes, and I quickly pressed at the corners to keep them at bay.

Matching looks of sympathy found their faces, which I hated almost as much. I didn't want them to be sorry for me. I already felt sorry enough for myself. Everyone said you should feel "complete" on your own.

But I'd lived almost forty years alone, and I wanted more.

"Look," I explained, "the dating pool in Cottonwood Falls is very small. And the definition of insanity is doing the same thing over and over again and expecting a different result. Well, I've tried staying here. I've tried waiting for love to find me. Now, I have to change something to find my person too."

Liv flipped over a new sheet of paper. "But that doesn't mean you have to move to find him. We just need to catch with a wider net, right?"

I eyed her doubtfully while my other friends nodded in agreement.

Liv said, "Let's make a list of all the eligible bachelors. We have two and a half months to make something stick."

I rolled my eyes. "You've got to be kidding me." This wasn't some high school revenge movie. It was my life.

But Liv came up to me, taking both my hands in hers. "I know you said you haven't found your person yet... but you're *my person*, Della. I can't let you leave without at least trying."

My throat felt tight with emotion, and I blinked back tears. I wanted to stay here too—even if the plan to make it happen was a moonshot. "Okay, we'll try."

A cheer erupted around the room. And for the next half hour, my friends listed every single, non-terrible guy within a sixty-mile radius. Once we accounted for no major age gaps, there were only four on the list. And that was the problem. I didn't want non-terrible. I didn't want bottom of the barrel.

I wanted real, heart-stopping, all-consuming, life-long *love*.

Liv frowned at the paper. "Only four guys? I could have sworn there were more."

"Oh!" Larkin said. "Give me the marker." She got up from the couch and took the marker from Liv. In steady strokes, she wrote HAYES MADIGAN.

Maggie whooped, and Hen giggled. Liv only frowned. "We have two and a half months," Liv said. "It'll take a lot longer than that for him to be ready for a woman like Della." She crossed his name off the list.

Hen replied, "It's a solid start."

Larkin nodded. "You only need one, right?"

I tried to act positive for their sake, but looking at the names on the list, I wasn't so sure. As much as I hated to admit it, maybe Hayes was right. Maybe I was stupid to hope for a happily ever after.

BENNETT SMITH
    Ethan Miller
    Joshua Jones
    Matteo Garcia
    ~~Hayes Madigan~~

. . .

ALL THE GUYS listed had lived here for over five years, and nothing had happened yet. But even so, a small glimmer of hope battled for a hold on my heart. I didn't want to end up grumpy and cynical like Hayes. I wanted more.

Maybe we *could* find a way to make this work.

And if not... Dallas was waiting.

9

———

HAYES

SO I MIGHT HAVE LIED to Della about no place in my house being for women. Because in the bottom of my closet, I kept a basket I fondly referred to as my treasure chest. Any item left behind got tossed into the basket, where it waited for its owner to claim it. Some items had been in there over five years—half a dozen lipstick containers, hair scrunchies, a pair of Buckle jeans, Silly Putty, slippers. It all went in the treasure chest.

When I was old and gray and sagging, I'd sit in my rocking chair telling the younger generation about my adventures.

But I was about to add a strange item to the treasure chest—a pink, frilly throw pillow. The chick I was with last night must have brought it for a comfy place to lay her head (although I had no idea how it could be comfortable with all the sequins) and forgotten it entirely.

I dropped the pillow in the basket and then finished getting ready for work. The shop was about half a mile from my house, and I got on my Harley for the ride. My helmet waited on the back seat, and I pulled it over my head, thinking of the infuriating woman with the luscious hips who led to the purchase. Her face when she discovered the sticker would be imprinted in my memory forever. If only that moment could make it in the treasure chest too.

With a shake of my head, I gunned the engine and drove the short path to the garage. It was cool in the morning, but I knew by the afternoon, I'd be thankful for the massive fan in the shop pushing air around.

The morning went by quickly, even though I was in the office handling paperwork. Owning your business sounded like fun until you learned how much fucking not-work you had to do. A lot of the hours I used to spend under the hood were traded for meetings with accountants, calls with suppliers, request forms that needed to be filled out. The list was never-ending. Add on communicating with customers who want the repair done fast and cheap? Yeah, the headaches are real.

So I was thankful when Liv came into the office with Leah and Mira. Seeing my nieces always brightened my day. Leah ran around the desk as fast as her four-year-old legs would carry her and hopped into my lap. "Do you have a sucker and a Gatorade for me, Uncle Hayes?" She blinked big puppy-dog eyes up at me.

I grinned at her. "Of course I do. If it's okay with your mama."

Liv nodded, shifting the youngest on her hip. "Sure thing."

I kicked off the ground, making my wheeling chair spin toward the mini fridge in the corner of my office. Leah squealed with laughter as we spun, and the sound made me smile. Chuckling, I bent down to the fridge and opened it. "Looks like we have blue or yellow. Mama said red dye was no good for you."

Leah's little hand darted out, grabbing a blue bottle. Then I spun us back to the desk again. She giggled on the way and then picked a sucker out from the drawer.

Mira was grunting and squirming in Liv's arms, her soft blond hair curling up in sweet little tufts. "Looks like she wants in on the fun," Liv said.

"Come on," I said, reaching my hands out for the little girl. She and Leah sat on my lap for a little bit, giving Liv a chance to use the bathroom, while we played and spun around my office floor.

Maybe being an owner wasn't so bad if it meant I could make time for things like this.

I heard the shutter sound and looked up to see Liv had snapped a photo with her phone. "Send it to me?" I asked. "I need something to put on my desk."

"Will do," she said. As she looked down at her phone, Leah and Mira crawled off my lap and started playing with an empty box in the corner of my office. Never mind that I kept a basket of toys especially for them.

"Hey," Liv said, "I have a question for you. Can you get me Ethan's number?"

I raised my eyebrows at her. "My mechanic Ethan? Why?"

She nodded. "I was thinking he and Della might be good together, you know?"

My eyebrows drew together thinking of Della, who spouted her belief in love, with *Ethan*. Fuck that. "Shut the door," I said to Liv.

She pushed the door shut and then leaned in, whispering, "What? Is it juicy?" Her brown eyes were way too lit up for some gossip.

"Cool your jets. It's nothing bad—Ethan's a nice guy and a hell of a worker, but he's also a functional alcoholic. Della wouldn't be interested." Someone who talked about love and romance like she did wouldn't be satisfied with someone who couldn't be counted on after six o'clock because he'd be three sheets to the wind. Not a chance.

"Ohhh..." She glanced toward the door. We couldn't see them, but all the guys were working on the other side. "Ethan, really?"

I nodded slowly. "On to the next harebrained idea, I guess." Although some part of me was far too satisfied that Della wouldn't be dating a guy from my garage.

But then Liv said, "What about Joshua? You were in the same grade in school, right?"

I shook my head. "He's got a family in Oklahoma he pretends doesn't exist."

Liv's jaw dropped open. "You're kidding, right?"

"Wish I was." Skipping out once kids got involved was as low as you could go. "Looks like your days of playing matchmaker are over." Why did that bring me so much satisfaction?

"Not quite. We still have some options."

Well shit. "Like who?"

"Don't worry, you're not on the list," Liv said like that was supposed to make me feel better. And it should have.

Why the fuck didn't I feel better?

Mira screeched at her older sister, and Liv and I both flinched. "Leah, let your sister have a turn in the box please."

Leah huffed out, "*Fine.*" But it sounded more like "*Dine*" because she couldn't say her Fs yet.

Liv and I both held back a chuckle, and I turned my face away so the little ones wouldn't see me grinning. Once we both got our composure, Liv said, "I better get these two to the car so we can pick up Maya. See you around."

I waved to Liv and then gave my nieces each a hug

before getting back to work. But it was hard to focus knowing Liv was actively trying to set up Della and obviously had shit taste in men for her best friend.

It was none of my damn business.

So why did I care so much?

10

DELLA

WITH ALL THE hubbub of the list, nothing changed over the week. I went to work. I had dinner with my parents. And on Friday night, I washed the sticky bread dough off my hands and then picked up my phone to see who the new text was from. I was going another round with my sourdough. The last loaf I attempted was a flop, but I hoped this one would turn out better.

Liv: Bad news or good news first?

I took the phone to my couch and sat down.

Della: Bad news? (Need something to look forward to!)
Liv: Ethan and Joshua need to be crossed off the list.

I frowned.

Liv: Ethan has a drinking problem. Joshua's a deadbeat dad.
Della: That's half the list!
Liv: Which is where my good news comes in... Matteo is
picking you up for dinner in an hour.

My jaw dropped—both at the late notice and the name. Matteo was one of the better-looking guys on the list we made. He worked as a realtor in Cotton-wood Falls and was always dressed and groomed nicely for client meetings. Meanwhile, my pajama set was already speckled with flour, and my hair was twisted into a tight bun atop my head.

Della: I ALREADY TOOK OFF MY DAY CLOTHES.
Liv: Put 'em back on, babe!
Della: My hair is in a bun. My curls will NEVER BEHAVE.
Liv: Straighten it! No excuses. I'm keeping you in town
even if I have to whore you out to every single guy in a fifty-
mile radius.

I rolled my eyes at my friend. When she set her mind to something, she almost always got her way.

Liv: What are you waiting around for? GO GET READY!
Della: How did you know?
Liv: I've known you forever. Just go and have a good time.
See what comes out of it. And then call me and tell me
EVERYTHING.

I let out a sigh. Of course Liv was right. I needed to stop making excuses and start getting ready. But there was also a small voice in the back of my head saying that if Matteo really wanted to date me, he would have at least asked me out by now.

Either way, he'd be here soon, according to Liv. So I covered up my sourdough to rise and then went to my bedroom to get ready. I decided to keep my hair up in a bun and dressed in leggings and a flowy floral top.

I was putting on a fresh layer of lip gloss when the doorbell rang and sang a cutesy song I fell in love with at the hardware store. With a small smile, I capped the lip gloss, grabbed my phone and purse, and went to the door.

Matteo stood on my porch in a pair of dark wash jeans, a light-blue button-down with the sleeves rolled. His olive skin and dark eyes were so yummy to me, especially since all my skin ever did was burn.

"Hey, Della," he said warmly.

"Hi there." In that moment, it hit me that I wasn't good at dating. My last serious relationship had been a few years ago and not a lot had come my way since then. "Would you like to come in, get some water or something?" I asked.

"Sure," he said with an easy smile that crinkled his eyes at the corners.

My heart fluttered nervously. Was he just being nice, or was I doing the right thing? While I went to get a glass from the cabinet, Matteo paced my living room. "I love this wallpaper," he said.

"Thanks," I replied over my shoulder as I filled the glass designed with etched flowers. "My dad helped me put it up."

"Is it permanent?" he asked.

"Peel and stick. In case I changed my mind," I said.

"Smart." He took the glass from me and drank a few sips. "Have you done lots of other work on the place?"

I nodded. "Want to see?"

"Definitely." He grinned. "It's always nice to get a feel for a place if you'll be coming by more regularly."

That had a smile on my lips. He thought he'd be coming by more often—that must mean I'd done something right. Or he's presumptuous, but I preferred to look on the brighter side of life. So I gave him the grand tour of my pride and joy. All three bedrooms and two bathrooms. It was colorful and quirky and entirely *me*.

"It's obvious you've taken a lot of pride in it," he commented as we went outside to his car waiting in the driveway.

"It's been a labor of love." I told him about painting it pink the prior summer with my dad and some of my friends. It had been a fun project, and we made a whole event of it with free-flowing lemonade and a watermelon feast.

I got into the passenger seat of his SUV. It was

impeccably cared for, clean on the inside, and it smelled like his cologne. I could get used to riding around in this.

"I thought we could go to Woody's," he suggested. "They have a chicken fried steak special tonight."

"Sure," I said, secretly thrilled. It had to be promising that he was taking me to the most frequented place in town. He wasn't embarrassed to be seen with me or worried about rumors that were sure to follow a public outing together.

When we got to Woody's, the date seemed to go really well. We talked about his background—he told me about going to college for sales and how many deals he'd been able to close as a realtor since moving back to Cottonwood Falls. It sounded like he'd had an incredible run working in real estate.

I was thinking he could be a really viable option for a partner, one that had been right under my nose, until he said, "A house like yours is going to take a specific kind of buyer, but I think we can get it sold faster if you're willing to take down some of the wallpaper and touch up the paint behind it."

I blinked. "What?"

"I know you love the house, but buyers like to see a home as more of a blank slate so they can make it their own."

My head was spinning. "Sorry, I'm confused... I don't want to sell my house. I'll rent it when the time comes."

His eyebrows drew together. "But Liv said I should take you out to dinner since you were moving soon and she didn't want me to miss my chance with you..." Then realization hit his features. "Oh... Della, I'm sorry. I like you, but I don't really see you like that. You showed me around your house, and I thought—"

I held up a hand. "That's okay, Matteo. Sorry for the miscommunication."

He gestured down at the meal, clearly flustered. "I'll cover this."

"Oh no," I said. "I'll get it... for your professional advice." My cheeks were freaking on fire. "In fact, you should go. I've already taken up so much of your time."

"I don't mind driving you home," he said.

"That won't be necessary," I replied. "I think I'll stay for a milkshake," I added, just to get him out the door sooner. I had to keep at least a shred of my dignity.

"Okay..." He stood up and stayed by the table for a moment, opening and closing his mouth like he was about to say something, but I chirped, "Bye, Matteo!"

He gave me an awkward wave and left the restaurant.

And I got out my phone to text Liv.

Della: Matteo thought he was selling my house.

Liv: *shocked emoji* What??

Della: I am so embarrassed. *monkey covering eyes emoji*

I'll be wearing a paper bag over my head until my last day of work.

Liv: Don't give up! Bennett's still on the list!

Della: I think I've had enough embarrassment for a decade. Now to find a paper bag...

Liv sent me a text with a link to order paper bags in bulk.

Della: You're such a dear.

Liv: Sorry, Dell. I really thought I was clear with him.

Della: Swing and a miss. Ttyl.

I tucked my phone back in my purse and got up for the long walk home. Too bad I couldn't call the tow truck for a ride home due to broken pride.

11

HAYES

IT WAS a perfect night to take the Harley out for a ride. Spring was finally starting to give us some warmer days, and the sunset burned the horizon like the painter in the sky forgot to use pastels today.

I drove around dirt roads outside of town until the sun set and then took the bike slow down the side streets in Cottonwood Falls, listening to nothing but the hum of the motor and the rush of wind over my helmet.

A few people were sitting on their front porches doused in soft golden overhead lights, but not many. The sidewalks were empty until I saw a tuft of familiar red hair shining like a beacon in the dark and the swing of hips under flowy floral material.

What the fuck was Della doing walking around town after dark? And over a mile away from her house?

I slowed down next to her and flipped back the

shield on my helmet. Then I killed the engine so she could hear me. "Couldn't remember the tow truck's number?" I called over to her.

She stopped and turned to me, an exhausted expression on her features. "God, I wish that was it."

I raised my eyebrows. "Care to explain?"

"No."

Wow, Moonshine was really not in a good mood. Something must have happened tonight, and a strange urge to incapacitate anything or anyone that upset her overwhelmed me. Taking a deep breath, I said, "Then care for a ride?"

Now she raised her eyebrows at me. "You're kidding, right?"

I pulled off my helmet. "You can wear the helmet, and we won't go over twenty. Most you can get is a lady boner from riding on such a sexy bike."

She snorted, then covered her mouth. "Did you just tell me I'll get a 'lady boner' from riding your motorcycle?"

I dipped my head in answer.

Her lips twitched. "Unfortunately, that's not covered by insurance."

"I won't charge," I retorted. "Now get your ass on the bike. I know you're not walking all the way home in those shoes."

She glanced in the direction of her life-size version of a dollhouse and then back to me. "Promise you won't go over twenty?"

"Cross my heart."

"And you'll stop at every stop sign?"

"And hope to die," I replied.

She let out a sigh. "Guess there's a first time for everything."

I passed her the helmet, but soon she realized she couldn't pull it over her head with that bun sticking up. So she groaned and undid the knot, letting her curls flare wildly around her face. The way she looked went straight to my cock, so I tore my eyes away.

"Don't say a word," she huffed, pulling the helmet over her head. The ends of her hair stuck out under the red and black helmet, and I had to smile at her with the middle finger sticker on the side of her head.

"I didn't say anything," I replied, trying and failing to fight my smile. "Now get on."

She placed her palm on my shoulder, the spot heating instantly under her touch. The bike shifted as she threw her leg over and then placed her feet on the foot pegs behind mine.

"Can I hold on to you?" she asked.

"Depends on where," I teased over my shoulder. "The lower the better."

She rolled her eyes and put her hands around my solid middle. Something about her soft hands and forearms sent my blood thrumming. That was until she pressed her full chest to my back. And damn, if anyone was getting a boner, it wasn't her, and it wasn't because of the bike.

I took a breath and did my old trick of listing off the parts of an engine to keep my mind from picturing her riding me on this bike.

Pistons...

Valve spring...

Spark plugs...

And it took a little of the edge off as I kicked the bike into gear and took off down the street.

She shrieked just loud enough for me to hear and gripped me tighter, and it took all I had not to push the bike to the max and get Della holding on to me with all her strength.

But I kept my promise, going under twenty until Della's house came into view. I navigated the bike to park behind her car, uncomfortable at the squeeze in my chest at our ride being over.

Regardless of my feelings, I waited as she stepped off, balancing herself on the gravel. Then I got off the bike, putting the kickstand in place. I turned just in time to see her step back and tugged the helmet straight off her head.

Her hair expanded in a giant poof, and I held back a laugh, despite my eyes shining with a smile.

"You suck," Della huffed, smoothing her hair. She bent over and used gravity to pull her hair into a knot atop her head.

I watched in fascination as her shirt slid up, showing a sliver of her pale lower back. Her leggings were just sheer enough to see the outline of her thong underneath. I bit down on my lip, hard.

Camshaft...

Timing belt...

Oil filter...

She stood up straight, cheeks pink with blood flow. "Thank you for the ride. It wasn't as bad as I expected."

"That's what every guy wants to hear," I returned with a smirk.

She shook her head at me with a smile. "Can I get you a drink, as a thank you?" she suggested, nodding toward her house.

And even though I really wanted a drink and to see where things could lead, I had standards of my own.

Standards that included not fucking your sister-in-law's love-obsessed best friend and pissing off everyone in the family when it didn't end well.

"I better not," I finally said, taking the helmet back from her. "But call me next time you need a not-so-bad ride." I couldn't help the wink I added at the end.

Her laugh did strange things to my chest, like it always did. "Will do. Goodnight, Hayes Madigan."

"Goodnight, Moonshine."

I waited until she was safely inside her house to rev my engine and head the motorcycle back toward home. I was getting a major hard-on, and the bike's vibration wasn't helping at all.

Usually when I got to feeling like this, I'd go

through my phone, find someone to come over and meet the need humming through my veins. But that felt wrong, knowing I'd be thinking of Della's breasts pressed to my back the entire time.

So I walked my happy ass to my room and took care of myself, dangerously thinking it would be better with Della instead.

12

DELLA

I CLENCHED my desk as another memory of last night's dream flashed through my mind.

Hayes Madigan, bending me over his motorcycle, gently knocking my legs apart with the toe of his boot. Running his hand over the exposed skin of my ass.

I blinked, hard, like that could erase the memory.

Never mind the fact that my heart was pounding, my breath ragged, and an ache pulsed between my thighs.

So I forced myself to remember *reality*.

In reality, I knew it would never work. He was a serial womanizer, didn't believe in love or romance, and was grumpy more often than not. I should not be thinking about that torrid dream, especially while I was on the clock.

I was just reacting strongly to riding on the back of his motorcycle. My mind must be trying to process the adrenaline rush. Or possibly distract me from that date gone wrong with Matteo. Or better yet, make me forget altogether that when I invited Hayes into my house, he emphatically said no.

I tried not to let the rejection sting. But knowing he had a continuous parade of women in and out of his house didn't help my confidence.

Another heavy sigh.

I wasn't getting any work done with my mind spinning like this.

I got up from my desk and went to my boss's office. She had Dolly Parton playing softly from her speakers and was bobbing her head side to side.

My lips pressed into a smile. I'd miss this in Dallas.

So I didn't scare her, I knocked softly on the door. And when she looked up at me through her thick glasses, I said, "Hey, Edna, I'm running to get lunch from the diner. Want anything?"

She looked up from her computer, still typing on the keypad. "How about a Cobb salad?"

"Of course," I said. That's what she always ordered at the beginning of the week. Toward the end, there were more fried foods involved. "Anything to drink?"

She held up a giant jug of water that had times listed down the side with motivational quotes. "Got it covered."

"Sure thing," I replied, then gave her a wave and walked outside.

Spring was in full swing—sunny and warm. The

trees were budding, and I couldn't wait for all the flowering dogwoods along Main Street to start blooming. They added the most beautiful pop of color to our little town.

The fresh air and sunshine were already helping ease the tension in my shoulders. Going to the diner had been a great idea. If I weren't busy looking both ways and crossing the street, I'd pat myself on the back.

Inside the diner, the sound of sizzling grease and people talking filled the air like the smell of French fries. I couldn't wait to take my sweet time eating lunch and get a fresh take on the day. If you asked me, it was never too late in the day or week or year to turn over a new leaf and make it better.

But my hopes were soon dashed when I realized there wasn't a single place available for me to sit. Woody's was *slammed*. I frowned, thinking I'd have to take my order to go.

"This seat's open," a warm voice said nearby.

I turned to follow the sound and saw Bennett Smith sitting on one side of a table. He was a big boy, so a booth wouldn't have worked for him. As I thanked him and sat across from him, I felt a heat creeping up my neck, knowing his name was the last one listed on my board at home.

Despite technically being my last resort, he was a genuinely good guy. He had short curly hair sticking out from under a worn and weathered Smith Welding hat that shaded soft blue eyes and a warm smile framed by perpetually rosy cheeks.

But I'd always seen him as a friend, and he'd never indicated a romantic interest in me either.

"It's been a while. How have things been lately?" I asked him, trying not to stress too much about my list.

"Better now." He smiled, and I felt a warmth flutter in my stomach. I was so out of practice with flirting, but this felt like a nice way to dip my toes in the water. "How about you?" he followed up.

I shrugged, picking a menu from the holder on the table. "I've been a little distracted today. Came here to clear my head."

He nodded, taking a sip from the sweating glass of iced tea in front of him. "You know what I do to clear my head?"

I motioned that I didn't.

"It's kind of strange, but..." He leaned closer, whispering. "I gargle ice water."

Surprised, I giggled a bit. "What?"

He nodded, sitting up straight again. "It resets the vagus nerve. Learned that on a podcast driving to one of my jobs. You should try it."

As if she was listening to our conversation, Agatha came by our trouble and asked me what I'd like to order. She looked busy with the lunch rush, so I quickly told her what I'd like and asked for a glass of ice water.

As she walked away, Bennett winked at me.

I smiled to myself, shaking my head. "Do you listen to podcasts a lot?"

"Just when I get tired of hearing the same song over and over," he tossed back. "You?"

I nodded, then leaned forward. "It's a little embarrassing though."

Amused, he said, "Tell me."

"I listen to people rehash reality TV."

That had him chuckling warmly. "*Real Housewives?* That's my mom's favorite show."

"*Bake Off*," I replied.

He laughed again, and I could feel people watching our exchange, but it didn't bother me one bit. This was exactly what I needed—a nice conversation to distract me from thoughts of Hayes Madigan. Maybe I had underestimated Bennett all this time.

Agatha passed by, easily sliding a cup of ice water in front of me. The cubes rattled against the plastic for a second after it came to a stop.

"Try it," Bennett said.

My cheeks warmed. "There's no attractive way to gargle. Maybe I should take it to the bathroom."

"Oh please," he said. "Gargling's sexy as hell."

A laugh easily fell past my lips. "Okay, let's put this theory to the test." I picked up a glass of water and tossed back a mouthful. Then I tilted my head back and started to... gargle.

If my mom knew I was doing this, she'd faint, and

when she came to, she'd give me a lecture on how a lady behaves.

But Mom wasn't here.

After a few seconds, I tipped my head back up and swallowed. Bennett eyed me expectantly. "How do you feel?"

I studied my body for a moment. "Better," I finally said. Although I didn't know if that was because of the water or the company.

And that's when I heard the all too familiar roar of a motorcycle outside, and any sense of ease I had was instantly gone.

13

————

HAYES

I SET my helmet down on the seat of my motorcycle and looked through the diner window to see if my dad, Knox, and Fletcher were already seated. The place was fuckin' packed, which made me want to turn around and go home instead.

But then I saw a bright flash of red hair through one of the windows—and she was sitting across from... Bennett Smith. Smiling.

Something in me raged at the sight of him getting one of her smiles. At the plain-ass smile he sent back to her. He should have fucking heart eyes coming out of his face.

Something irrational and reckless and most of all, fucking dumb.

I didn't date, especially not people intertwined with my family. This was none of my business. So why was I having a hard time believing myself?

I grit my teeth together and walked around the side of the diner to go in and sit with my dad and brothers.

I found them at Dad's usual booth, Knox and Fletch sitting on one side, leaving space for me by Dad. The only problem was that from this angle, I had a great view of Della and Bennett.

The amount of self-control it took to say hi to Dad, Knox, and Fletcher before I glanced her way deserved an award. My gaze was met by pretty soft-green eyes. She quickly glanced down, and I smirked.

She was looking at me while she was talking to him.

Suddenly, the ache in my chest eased, if only a little bit.

"Hayes," Fletcher said like it wasn't the first time he tried to get my attention.

"Yeah?" I turned my attention to him, gently biting down on my lip ring.

"Maya's class is doing a line dancing performance at the spring festival, and she asked me to 'confirm your participation'," Fletcher said.

"No." I reached over and plucked a menu from the rack, even though I always ordered the same thing. Maybe just so I had something to look at other than the redhead across the diner.

But Knox grabbed the menu and eyed me with that no-nonsense cop look. "He wasn't asking. We're all doing it."

I raised my eyebrows. "Why?"

Knox shook his head at me. "Because our niece wants us to?"

"And?" I asked.

Fletcher eyed me. "*You* try telling her no."

"Fair point." I sighed. "When and where?"

Dad snickered next to me, and I said, "Why are you laughing? You're dancing too."

"Oh no," Dad said. "That's for you young guns. I'm a little old for that."

"True," Knox said, a smirk lighting his blue eyes. "He needs to get his doctor's approval for physical activity."

We all swiveled our gazes to look at Fletch, the family doctor. He was grinning as he pulled a pen from his pocket and wrote on a napkin. *Grayson Madigan is hereby cleared for line dancing activities.*

We were all laughing as Dad shook his head at us and ripped the napkin in half. "Oh, grow up," he muttered, an amused look in his eyes.

I had to wipe my watering eyes, but when I looked over, I saw Bennett and Della walking toward the register. And the future flashed before my eyes. Bennett and Della in this restaurant every week. Seeing them together as a couple. Him, putting his hand on her waist, comfortable with her in a way I'd never be.

"What did that napkin do to you?" Dad muttered, nudging my side.

I realized I had a death grip on my napkin and

loosened up. "Guess I'm saving it from you," I popped off.

He rolled his eyes at me and then joined back in on the conversation with Knox and Fletcher about some new machine Fletcher was getting at Madigan Medical. But all the while, I could hear Della and Bennett talking over the restaurant's chatter.

Della said, "I better get this back to Edna before the lettuce gets soggy. Thanks again for paying. You really didn't have to do that."

"I wanted to," Bennett said. "In fact, I'd like to do it again sometime. Maybe Friday night?"

I gripped my knees under the table, straining for her answer.

"Oh, wow... I'd like that." There was a smile in her voice that I could picture.

"Great. Does seven work? There's a great steak place we can go to in Roderdale."

"I know the place. I actually have a client over there I need to see. I can meet you there."

"Sounds great. See you then, Dell."

Dell?

She sounded pleased as she said, "See you then."

The door opened and closed before I could hear my brothers talking again.

"Hayes," Fletcher said. "Are you coming down with something? You're acting really strange."

I blinked, like that would somehow clear the conversation echoing in my mind. Bennett and Della were going on a date. And he was exactly the kind of guy that she would settle down with.

It shouldn't bother me. It should be like hearing there's going to be rain on Tuesday. Or hell, I could even be relieved someone else will be giving her rides around town from now on.

But instead, it felt like rain was falling on me now, thick and all-consuming. The kind that splattered all over the window and even the highest speed of your wipers couldn't keep up.

He didn't deserve her.

He was plainer than vanilla, and she was a fucking color explosion.

"Maybe I am coming down with something...." I muttered. Because I'd never felt this way before. I had to be getting sick. Something had to be wrong with me. After all, my gut did hurt.

Dad said, "Do you need me to give you a ride home?"

I slowly shook my head. "I'm good. Maybe some food would help."

Spoiler alert: It didn't help.

After lunch, I went back to the garage, where that foreign feeling continued blooming in my chest like some invisible masochist was adding fuel to the fire. I was pissed—pissed that vanilla Bennett thought he deserved her. Furious that Della was wasting her time with someone beneath her.

The blaze almost consumed me when I walked through my door to my empty house.

Enough was enough.

I paced my living room and texted Jess to come over and distract me.

Less than half an hour later, Jess came inside without knocking, wearing a khaki trench coat. I could already guess what was underneath. I was sitting on my couch, drinking a beer while *Sons of Anarchy* played on the TV, but muted it at her entrance. "Hey there," I said, eyeing her up and down.

Soon, my body would feel *right*. Turned on and distracted.

She was tall—nearly six feet—and had curves for days visible even under the trench. I reached for the button on my pants, undoing it and watching as she stopped short of me and pulled the coat open to show her sheer black lingerie.

"What do you think?" she asked, slipping out of the coat so it fell in a puddle behind her.

I studied her, wondering why my cock felt limp. I reached into my pants and ordered, "Turn around. Let me see you."

She did as I demanded, letting me see the thong where it disappeared between her ass cheeks. The sway of soft blond hair over her bra clasp. It would snap apart easily under my fingertips.

She even bent over and wiggled her ass to give me a better show, and... nothing.

No twist of my hand over my shaft or mental image of her riding me could get my cock to stand.

What the fuck was *wrong* with me?

When she turned back to me, she must have seen it in my face. "What's wrong?" she asked, full lips pouting. "You don't usually need help to get you in the mood."

I shook my head, letting out a frustrated sigh as I stood and buttoned my pants back up. "I'm sorry, Jess. I shouldn't have called you over."

She stepped forward, putting the back of her hand against my forehead. "Are you okay?"

With a wry chuckle, I pulled her fingers aside. "I'm not sick... But I'm not okay." I held her hand for a moment, looking at her fingers.

After a moment of watching me, she said softly, "The fun's over, isn't it?"

I nodded slowly. It sure was.

14

___

DELLA

I PULLED my Dutch oven out of the stove, feeling heat radiating up from the pot and warming my face. A giddy flutter went through my chest, hoping the perfect sourdough loaf was waiting underneath the lid.

After setting the pot on top of the stove and then shutting the oven door, I carefully lifted the lid.

My jaw dropped open, and I squealed. "It looks like real bread!" I cried, even though no one was around to hear me.

It had taken me a full month to get my sourdough starter going, several failed loaves, and then twelve hours of working with this batch specifically.

And don't get me wrong—it wasn't the prettiest loaf in the world. There was a rip down the center like I hadn't scored the bread deep enough, it wasn't quite as round as I'd like, and the designs I'd carefully cut into the raw surface had more or less disappeared in the oven. But it looked—and smelled—like bread.

I couldn't wait to serve it to my parents with potato soup for supper tonight.

Gripping the corners of the brittle parchment paper, I lifted the loaf out of the pot so it could cool on the counter and then tended to my soup in the Crock Pot. I liked to sprinkle a layer of shredded cheese on top about half an hour before serving it for a nice melty effect.

Soon enough, Mom and Dad were at the door. Dad came in first with a stack of flattened boxes under his arm. Mom was behind him, carrying a box full of old newspapers.

"What's this?" I asked, closing the door behind them.

Dad leaned his boxes up against a wall by the entrance. "Thought you might want to get started packing." He took the newspapers from Mom and set them by the boxes.

Mom brushed invisible dust off her hands. "You know how awful it is to try and move at the last second? You have so much more stuff than you think you do. This way you can start packing up some of your trinkets and decorations."

"You're right," I said slowly. The thought should have occurred to me sooner, but for some reason, the boxes sitting in the corner had a heavy feeling settling in my chest. It reminded me that I really was leaving

Cottonwood Falls, the place I thought I would call home forever.

I tried to remind myself that all hope wasn't lost—I had a date with Bennett on Friday. But I was leaving town in two months. It would have to be the world's most whirlwind romance to change my plans.

"Thanks," I finally said to my parents, putting on a happy smile. "Come check out my sourdough!"

They followed me to the counter, and Dad commented, "It smells incredible in here."

Mom agreed, and they both fawned over my bread like it was my own baby. "Can't wait to taste it," Mom said, brushing thick blond and gray curls behind her ear.

I smiled and replied, "Why don't we get started? You're not supposed to cut it while it's hot, but you know me. I'm impatient."

Dad smirked, making crinkles form around his eyes. "You're about as patient as a bulldozer."

I rolled my eyes at him while Mom chuckled. And it hit me again how grateful I was to have them around. That even though I was nearing forty, they still loved and supported me no matter my flaws.

As we ate the soup, I tried to savor every bite, every moment. And I hoped that this date with Bennett would lead to something big—something that let me stay in Cottonwood Falls.

ON FRIDAY AFTER WORK, I walked to my car in the parking lot on the back side of the building, got in, and pushed the button to turn it on.

The lights flashed on the dash, and the fan started blowing air, but the engine didn't turn over.

My eyebrows drew together. That was strange.

I pushed the button again, but the same thing happened.

A glance at the dash showed the check engine light.

"Great," I muttered, heart sinking. I was supposed to meet with a client before going out with Bennett, but now it looked like I needed a rescue instead.

I picked up my phone and dialed Hayes's personal number, hoping I didn't get the Hyde version of him today.

After a few rings, his voice came over the phone. "Yes, Moonshine?"

I rolled my eyes at the nickname. "Why do you call me that?" He'd been calling me Moonshine for years now, and I'd always chalked it up to one of his quirks.

"To remind myself I should stay away," he replied earnestly, making my stomach flip. "That I'd regret having too much of you come the morning."

He thought he should stay away from me all this time? Why?

Did I really want to know the answer right before I was supposed to go out with another man? I shouldn't be thinking of Hayes when I was with Bennett. Not his tattoos. Not his muscled arms. Not the ring curling around his lip. Definitely not the illogical way he made my heart beat faster.

"Hello?" he said.

I cleared my throat, trying to focus again. "Remember how you offered me a rescue?" I hedged, making my voice sweet.

"Jog my memory."

Looked like I'd need to put this in terms he'd understand. "When your death trap motorcycle gave me a lady boner?"

"Ah, I remember now," he said. I could hear the smirk in his tone.

"Good," I said, shifting my cell to my other ear. "Well, my car won't start, and I need to be in Roderdale at seven at the latest. I already had to cancel one client meeting. Can you help?"

"I was just about to head home, but... I am a man of my word."

I shook my head at his bravado. "My hero."

"Where are you? I'll come get you in the tow truck."

"Still at the office. Thank you so much."

"And why don't you get us a 'snackie'?" he teased. "Since I'm missing dinner for this."

"It's the least I can do," I said sincerely. I asked him what he liked from the diner and then crossed the street to Woody's, hoping Hayes could find a solution to my car quickly. With any luck, the issue would be something simple, like needing a new battery, and not too terribly expensive.

I had his food in hand, along with a side of mozzarella sticks for me, and was paying the bill when I saw the tow truck coming down Main Street. Most women would have been impressed by an Aston Martin, but man, did my heart flutter at the sight of that rusty old truck.

Once I finished paying, I walked across the street and around the building where I worked to see Hayes leaning under the hood of my car. He had on a pair of faded jeans that hugged his lean frame, and his shirt hung loose, giving me a view of his muscled, tatted sides.

Tattoos had never been my thing—something about them usually screamed *bad decision*. But on Hayes? My eyes traced each one, wondering what they meant, if they had any meaning at all.

Something about Hayes carried a mystery I was dying to discover. Why did he have such a cynical view of relationships?

I tried to rack my mind to remember if a high school girlfriend had broken his heart but came up short.

As far as I knew, Hayes had always been this way.

I only realized I'd been staring, lost in thought, when he stood up from under the hood and looked my way.

There was a frown on his face that shed all my embarrassment. "What's wrong?" I asked.

"It's going to take a little more work than I hoped."

"Do you think it could be done by six thirty?" I asked.

"I'll try my best," he said grimly. "Climb in the truck."

15

____

HAYES

"I CAN'T BELIEVE this had to happen tonight," she mumbled, standing in the tall garage door opening, looking all dejected at her car.

"That's how cars usually work—they break down at the worst possible time." Although I wasn't mad at the timing. I walked up behind her, grabbing the takeout bags from her grip and setting them on a table by the workbench.

The shop was entirely empty when we pulled up, all my guys having gone home.

"You can sit there and wait," I said, gesturing at a rolling stool nearby. The plastic seat gleamed under the overhead fluorescent lights, a stark contrast to the dirt and grease covering every other surface. It had just come in earlier today, so it was clean enough for her to sit on while I worked.

"Okay." Della gave a resigned sigh and sat on the

stool. The way her thighs pressed together had me biting my lip.

But I forced myself to look away and lifted the hood again. "So what are you in a rush for?" I casually asked, keeping my gaze trained on the engine.

"I was going to meet a client, and then I have a..." Her sentence trailed off, and I looked over my shoulder at her. The sunset was glinting in through the garage door, giving her hair that golden flame effect. The sun caught her pale green eyes as she looked up toward the ceiling like she didn't know how to explain. Or maybe she didn't want to tell me her plans.

Interesting.

"You have a..." I prompted.

Her cheeks gained some color. "I have a date, okay? I just didn't want to tell you because I don't want your cynicism to ruin it for me."

That surprised me. That she cared enough about my words to let them affect her—she always seemed like a duck letting my words slide off her back.

Strangely pleased, I looked back at her engine, fiddling with different caps to check the fluids even though I'd topped those off the last time she came in. "No cynicism here." I stood up, wiping my hands on a microfiber rag. "I like dates."

"Really?" she said skeptically. "*You* like dates?" She folded her arms across her chest, and I swore God was shining on me today because she was in a V-neck dress.

I walked closer to her, seeing her breath pick up in

response as I leaned across her to put the rag on the counter. "I'll let you in on a secret." I held on to the counter, using it to angle me so my mouth was right near her ear.

She lifted her chin, not shying away.

This close, I could smell the delicate scent of her perfume as I whispered, "I like a date, but I *love* what comes after."

I pulled back just in time to see her eyes flutter closed. "Hayes Madigan, you horndog." But her voice was breathy. Not entirely exasperated like her words suggested.

Flirting with Della was one thing. My body's reaction to hers was another altogether. The way it affected me had me stepping back to clear my thoughts.

Taking a deep breath, I opened the driver side door to the car and hooked up the scanner that would give a readout from the car's computer. After a few minutes, I glanced at the screen, frowning.

"What is it?" Della asked.

"It's an electrical issue." I glanced at her before disconnecting the scanner and wrapping up the cords.

Della's eyebrows rose hopefully. "That's an easy fix, right?"

"Not too bad. A few hours, give or take."

Her features sagged, and I almost felt guilty. But then she told me she needed to text Bennett and cancel, and I felt a lot less bad for her.

"Hey, if you can stick around, I can fix it tonight.

You know, since I offered you a rescue." I forced myself to watch her reaction. How did she feel about spending an evening with me while I worked on her car?

Her eyes widened. "Really, you'd stay late for me?" She seemed genuinely touched.

"Yeah, 'slong as we can eat some food first."

Twisting her lips to the side, she said, "I guess my other dinner plans are shot. Can we eat inside, though? It feels unsanitary to eat out here around all the..." She gestured her arms around.

And I had to chuckle. It wasn't rare for us to scarf down a snack between jobs. Something about Della's finer sensibilities was refreshing and incredibly attractive.

"Let's go to the waiting room, Princess," I teased.

With a roll of her eyes, she picked up the takeout bags, placing the strap through her middle finger. I let her walk ahead, if only so I could see the swish of her dress over her hips. But I quickly realized how bad of an idea that was when all I could picture was lifting that dress up. Digging my fingers into her soft flesh. Pulling her onto my—

She was reaching for the door, but I got ahead of her just enough to pull it open. In response, she gave me an appreciative smile. "So there is a gentleman in there somewhere," she teased.

The compliment pleased me far more than it should. "Dad taught me *some* manners."

She sat down at one of the tables in the waiting

area and began untying the bag. "Your fries are probably soggy by now."

I shrugged, strangely unbothered. "What did you get?"

She opened one of the takeout containers. "Mozzarella sticks. With ranch."

"You and Liv," I said. "I swear she has ranch with everything."

"It's the superior dressing," Della agreed, a sense of finality to her tone. It had me chuckling.

"You take your sauces seriously," I said.

"Is there any other way to take them?"

A wicked thought crossed my mind and made a smirk form on my lips.

"Hayes Madigan," she chided.

I shook my head at her. "Why do you always call me by my full name?" I finally asked.

She lifted a corner of her lips. "Because you're an enigma. It's like calling Evel Knievel just 'Evel.' Doesn't make as much sense."

I lifted my burger from the box. "I can't tell if that's a compliment or not."

She shrugged. "Maybe it's both."

A short silence hung between us while we chewed our food. I wanted to get to know her better, to hear more of her thoughts and perspectives. But an uncomfortable feeling took over my chest—like I was trying to write with my left hand for the first time and the words were coming out all jumbled and juvenile. I didn't know how to do this and definitely didn't know how to do it the right way, without crossing any lines.

But damned if I wasn't going to try. "How did you get interested in the insurance business?"

She gave me a look like the question sounded just as awkward as I felt. But then she swirled a deep-fried stick of cheese through a puddle of ranch. "How does anyone get interested in work? I was out of college, and there was a job open." Her shoulders lifted, making her red curls move. "At first, it was a job to pay the bills, and I really liked working with Edna. The people we served were nice—for the most part. And I was good at it. *Am* good at it. I don't know what else I would do if I had a choice to change careers." She smiled slightly to herself. "What about you? Did you always want to do this?" She gestured around at the waiting room.

"Eat dinner with a pretty girl?" I held eye contact with her. "That was all I ever wanted to do."

A look of surprise crossed her face for a moment, but she quickly wiped it away. "You know what I meant."

Hmm. So she wasn't shying away from the compliment. But I realized she was waiting for my answer, so I wiped a crumb from my mouth and said, "I was always shit at school. It wasn't that I was stupid—I was bored. I couldn't see how any of it mattered. And then we had a shop class my senior year. Most kids took it as a fuck around class, but for me, it was the first time I felt like something I was learning could actually be used in the real world. I got my first—and only—A. Mr. Smith taught the class part time while running this garage, and he offered me a job. Kind of took me under his wing. From there, it was pretty obvious what I should do."

Her lips parted. "I didn't know that about you."

I lifted a shoulder. "Turns out there's more to me than a pretty face."

She chuckled, and my chest lifted. Della always laughed so easily, but it felt special when I was the one behind it. "Wait..." she said slowly. "If your only A was in shop class, does that mean you didn't get one in gym? Everyone got an A in that class!"

Fighting a smile, I shook my head. "She docked me a letter grade for lewd behavior."

"Ah, hitting on your classmates," Della said, amused.

"No, the teacher."

Her laugh could only be described as a cackle as she put her hands together, clapping. "Oh gosh, that's great..." Her phone started ringing, and she picked it up, still smiling. "Hello?"

I looked down at my food, listening to her end of the conversation—sorry, not sorry.

"Oh, that's so sweet of you... I'm at Madigan Auto. Hayes is getting me all fixed up... Yes! I'd love that... See you in fifteen?... Okay, bye."

She was smiling so damn big when she looked at me and said, "Bennett is bringing dinner to me. Guess it all worked out after all—I get the date and my car fixed!" Her shoulders shimmied with her excitement, never mind the fact that I was trying to hide every uncalled-for feeling racing through my chest.

I definitely wasn't hungry anymore. "I'm gonna work on your car. You can wait for him in here," I said.

"Oh." She looked at my half-eaten food. "Are you sure?"

"Yep. Later." I got up and walked out, wondering what the fuck was wrong with me and feeling stupid for trying to do something new. Sex, one-night stands, friends with benefits. That I could do.

Whatever I wanted with Della was a fucking terrible idea.

16

———

DELLA

I WAS STILL WONDERING what had changed with Hayes to make him leave so abruptly when I saw headlights pan over the waiting area through the big front windows.

Hayes and I had been getting along—connecting even. And then he got all grumpy again, leaving to work on my car. I could hear the sound of an air compressor through the waiting room walls and windows. See him bent over my car, a light hanging from the hood.

And part of me missed the conversation we were having. Getting to see behind his protective wall of humor and tattoos. But I couldn't worry about that now. Despite all odds, Bennett and I were going on our date tonight. And a small flutter of hope formed in my chest.

It was a good sign that he'd brought dinner to me—

that he was willing to put effort in when things hadn't gone perfectly to plan.

So I stood up, grabbing the takeout boxes and dumping them in the trash. Then I walked to the front door to step outside and meet Bennett in the parking lot. But it was locked—of course it was locked. The business was closed. So I went back through the garage. I saw Bennett talking with Hayes at the farthest bay, a bouquet of carnations in his hands.

Hayes's shoulders were tense, probably from a long day of work made even longer by my mechanical issues. But Bennett had an easygoing way about him, like he either didn't notice or wasn't bothered by Hayes's stance.

I walked over to them, and when Bennett saw me, his lips parted into a wide grin. "For you," he said, handing me the flowers. They were the kind that came from the grocery store, but I loved them all the same. It was the fact that he'd thought about me, put in extra effort before showing up. It made me feel seen and appreciated.

I sniffed the fresh scent and then smiled up at him. "Thank you, that was so nice of you!"

"Of course," Bennett said.

The screech of an air ratchet made me jump, and we turned to see Hayes bent over my car again, ignoring us altogether.

Compared to his warm attention earlier, this treatment was icy enough to make me shiver. Why did it bother me so much? It wasn't like Hayes owed me anything, or I him.

"So, um, what do you say we get out of here?" Bennett suggested awkwardly.

I nodded. "I'd love that." I was going to stick around a second and thank Hayes, tell him he really didn't need to stay late for me. But then Bennett reached out for my hand, and I took it. His hands were so large compared to mine—he reminded me of a big teddy bear.

"Thanks for everything," I called to Hayes.

He barely lifted his hand in acknowledgement before Bennett and I were in his truck, the smell of meat, mushrooms, and onions filling the cab.

"I wasn't sure what you like, so I got you a little bit of everything. I can park somewhere on Main Street while we eat," he offered.

"I have a better idea," I replied. "Let's go to my place. That way we can sit at the table and enjoy."

It was already clean, since I liked to keep things relatively tidy (except for my closet. That thing was a mess of epic proportions.) So when we walked inside, I wasn't embarrassed or anything. In fact, it was kind of fun to see him so at odds with the girly interior.

He carried the food while I made a show of taking the flowers he got me and putting them in a colorful vase I thrifted.

With the flowers between us on the table, we opened the takeout boxes, eating the slightly cooled food with plastic silverware. For a little while, we were quiet, and I almost missed the banter Hayes and I shared. It seemed like conversation flowed so much easier with Hayes. But then I remembered Hayes was a womanizer and certainly not interested in anything real with me. Unlike Bennett.

So I planted myself firmly in reality and took the first step. "How was work today?"

Bennett wiped his mouth with a paper napkin and said, "It was a real headache. I was on a welding job at the feedlot and the wind picked up."

"Oh no." I winced. "Liv told me the dusty days were the worst out there. Hard to believe they keep water trucks on hand, not just for fires but to spray down the dust."

Bennett said, "Thank God for that. How was work for you?"

"It was fine," I said. "Edna's stressed about end-of-month reports. Like she is every month. So that adds a little pressure."

He chuckled. "You'd think she'd be used to it by now. Pretty sure I remember seeing her when my parents dragged me into her office from time to time when I was a kid."

I smiled because I had the same memories from when I was younger. "I'm pretty sure she'll never retire. She loves it too much."

He nodded and put another bite of Salisbury steak in his mouth. And for a moment, it struck me. I could see us doing this twenty years from now. Eating dinner at the table. Talking casually about work.

And my heart sank at the idea.

Is that all there is?

"Is the food okay?" Bennett asked, studying me.

I must have made a face, so I tried harder to school my expression. "The food is wonderful. So... tell me something about you that I don't know," I suggested, hoping to learn something that would improve the night—to go a little deeper.

He scrubbed his hand over his face, deep in thought. "Hmm..." Then his eyes lit up. "My right foot is a whole size bigger than my left foot. Have to buy two sets of shoes to get one pair that fits the right way."

Facepalm. So much for going deeper.

"Is that so?" I managed through the disappointment rising up and threatening to swallow me whole. This surface-level conversation was an echo of every other relationship I'd had in Cottonwood Falls... and a painful reminder of why I'd accepted a job in Dallas.

He nodded. "Buying two pairs gets a little expensive." He took another bite.

I took a breath. Maybe I just needed to ask a better question. "How did you get into welding?"

"I'm terrible with cars, and Dad wouldn't pay for a four-year degree. So I asked the tech college which job made the most money. Welding it was."

"I see." I chuckled. "Sounds like it's paying off?"

"Oh, definitely. Guess I've always been practical that way." He shrugged his broad shoulders.

Practical.

Isn't that what I'd always wanted? A steady man I could count on like my family could always count on my dad?

I tried to shove down my confused feelings and just be in the moment. Conversation went about the same way until we finished eating. And then Bennett helped me clear away the trash. Some guys would have taken advantage of dining at my place and pushed for more, but he gave me a kiss on the cheek and said, "It was great getting to know you a little better tonight, Della. Liv was right about you."

My eyebrows rose. "She was?" Liv hadn't told me she'd spoken to Bennett.

"Oh yeah, she told me last week I should take you out. I'm glad I did... I'll call you sometime?"

I nodded, holding a smile in place.

But once the door was closed, my smile quickly fell.

Here I'd thought Bennett had finally noticed me of his own accord. But he had to be nudged toward me. Even though I knew Liv was determined to find me a man, I didn't want one who had to be prodded in my direction.

Was it too much to hope that someone would notice me, chase me, *love* me?

I heard the roar of an engine in the distance and sighed.

Maybe it had been silly to hope.

17

———

HAYES

WHY HAD I agreed to check cattle with Dad this early on a Saturday morning? Maybe I hadn't known I'd be in such a pissy mood when I'd agreed, but damn. Between my balls crunching on the saddle, the horse farting underneath me, and my mind constantly replaying Della driving away with fucking *Bennett*, I was beginning to regret my choice.

But Dad rode along easily on Blister, his roan quarter horse. A slight smile tilted his lips as he gazed out over the herd of mama cows and their calves. This pasture was full of hills and ruts. It could be driven, which Dad did most days, but you could see more when you got on horseback. He did that more often while the calves were young. Losing one could cost the ranch hundreds, if not thousands, of dollars.

"Looking forward to the spring festival?" Dad asked. "It's just a couple weeks away."

"Fuck no," I huffed. "Maybe I'll break a leg and get out of dancing."

Dad gave me a look. "I thought you liked dancing."

"I do when it's my own idea," I admitted. "So about that broken leg..."

Dad shook his head at me. "Keep talking that way and you'll jinx yourself."

I rolled my eyes. Dad was superstitious like that. Always giving things a deeper meaning, like God was listening in ready to contradict us.

After a beat, Dad said, "Liv had an ultrasound. Baby's doing well."

"That's good." I managed to smile for a second before it fell.

Our horses walked us into a valley, steep hills dotted with yucca plants on both sides of us. The sun was still low enough in the sky that we were cast in shadows, making it about fifteen degrees colder. I shivered, glad I'd kept my hoodie on.

"Emily won student of the week," Dad added. "They're having an assembly next Friday where they'll tell everyone how nice she is."

"I never won any of those."

Dad smirked. "Wonder why... Oh, and Maya's on the dean's honor roll."

"Stupid—the high school doesn't have a dean."

Dad gave me side-eye. "Did a rattlesnake crawl up your pants?"

I raised my eyebrows. "No?"

"Then why are you so full of piss and vinegar today?"

I had half a mind to ride my horse away from Dad and back to the house. But even though he had more gray hair and wrinkles than he used to, he could still out-maneuver me on a horse. So I was stuck here under his inquisitive stare. "Can you let it go?"

"I let it go the other day at the diner when you were acting off. This is me bringing it back up."

Now I gave him the side-eye. Sometimes I wish he wasn't so damn involved. "Can't you be a deadbeat like Aggie's ex?"

He responded with an exasperated look. "I'm sorry my love and care for my sons is an inconvenience to you."

We reached the end of the valley where a pair of cattle were grazing. They were off to the side, apart from the others, which wasn't a good sign. "Let's get a closer look," Dad said, the interrogation paused for the moment.

I adjusted the reins to fall into step behind his horse while he studied the animals. Growing up, we all did our part on the ranch, so I knew what he was looking for. Either a runny nose, trouble breathing, an injury, or scours.

At the sight of the calf, he frowned and twisted in his saddle to look at me. "I'm gonna rope the calf. Can you watch the mama so she doesn't maul me?"

"Trusting me an awful lot, considering I'm full of piss and vinegar," I said lightly.

Dad gave me yet another exasperated look, then started unclipping his lasso from his saddle. I guided my horse up, pushing back the mama cow. "Back up, babe," I said to her in a low, steady voice. As soon as she'd taken a few steps back, I heard the thwick of a rope, then the snap of it pulling tight. The beller of a calf.

The heifer snorted, trying to run toward the calf, but I cut her off, playing defense on horseback. My adrenaline was kicking up, and finally my mind felt clear, focused on something instead of stewing on an impossible problem.

Thank fuck.

Dad made quick work of medicating the calf, and when he was back on his horse, he called, "All good."

I steered my horse, trotting away from the heifer. She was already running back to her calf, nosing over its body to check out the little guy.

"Everything okay?" I asked Dad.

"Had the scours and needed some electrolytes. I'll check back in on him again this evening."

I nodded, continuing to keep pace alongside him. He turned toward another draw, silent for a moment. But my luck didn't last too long, because Dad said, "Don't make me tie you up too."

I chuckled softly, then gave in, because Dad wasn't giving up. "If I tell you, you can't tell anyone."

The old man held up his pinky. "Want to swear on it?"

I rolled my eyes at him. "Fucker."

Dad chuckled. "It's just you and me out here. What's going on?"

I shook my head slowly, not even sure how to say it. "I've been thinking things lately…"

"That is new," Dad teased. "I can see why you'd be concerned."

"Dad!" I huffed out, holding back a laugh. "I'm being serious."

"Go ahead." He smiled over at me before looking ahead again. It was like he knew I needed space to talk because I was having trouble finding the right words to describe what was going on. "How did you know when it was time to settle down? Weren't you wild back in the day?"

Dad smiled, making the lines around his eyes grow deeper, catching shadows. "You're asking the wrong question."

I raised my eyebrows. "I am?"

He nodded, rocking in tandem with the horse. "You should be asking 'When did you stop fighting the fear of settling down?'"

"What do you mean?" I swore he talked in riddles sometimes.

He shifted the leather reins to his other hand and let out a breath. "When I met your mom, something in me knew she was the one. But there was another part of me that thought 'You're too young, it isn't the time...' all that bullshit. I was thinking of what I'd have to give up to be with her, not what I'd gain by having her in my life."

My throat felt tight. Hearing him talk about Mom that way, when I hardly remembered her, was hard.

"Is there a woman?" he asked, straightforward.

"I don't know. She's always been around, but it's like I'm having a harder and harder time remembering I should stay away. I've never felt like this about her before."

"What changed?" Dad asked.

It was a fair question. And I had to sort it over in my mind to find the right words. We crested another draw, suddenly giving us a view of the horizon. We could see dozens of pairs from here, illuminated by the golden morning sunlight.

"It's like coming over this hill," I said. "The cattle were here the whole time, but I couldn't see them until we got to the top."

Dad nodded slowly. "You know, just because you noticed her doesn't mean you have to do anything."

I couldn't hide my surprise. "What do you mean?" Dad was so happy when all my brothers paired up, got married, had kids. Some part of me always felt like I was disappointing him by not following that same path.

He layered one hand atop another on the saddle horn while he spoke. "Even though I wish I could have come to my senses sooner and been with your mom, I wasn't ready for her yet. I needed to grow into the man she deserved. If I would have jumped into that relationship before I was ready, it would have done us both a disservice."

An uncomfortable, squirming feeling had me asking my next question. "What if she had moved on before you were ready?"

"Then I would have gotten ready real damn fast." Dad chuckled. "The thing about wonderful women is that other people can also see how wonderful they are."

18

―――――

DELLA

I TUCKED my vacuum cleaner back in the closet where I'd stashed the easel holding the list of datable guys in Cottonwood Falls. Before closing the door, I looked over the names written in Liv's messy handwriting.

Bennett's name was the only one left. And I was determined to give him another chance.

First dates were always awkward—maybe we both needed to ease into getting to know each other and the feelings would follow. That's why I agreed to go out with him again later this evening.

But seeing his name on that list didn't give me any sparks. Not like the idea of sneaking this extra throw pillow into Hayes's house.

I picked up the frilly pillow I'd nabbed at a garage sale a few years back, turning it over in my hands. I liked to keep extras in my guest bedroom so I could change them out every so often, but there were plenty of pillows to go around.

Liv had texted me earlier and said that Fletcher was playing poker at Hayes's garage tonight, which meant Hayes would be occupied. I had just enough time to go to his house, complete my mission, and come back here for Bennett to pick me up.

Since I love a good theme, I went to my bedroom, putting on black leggings, a black sweatshirt, and tucked my hair up into a black stocking cap. I even put on my favorite perfume, Black Orchid, because it fit the theme.

Feeling thoroughly spy-ified, I walked outside, got in my car, and drove toward Hayes's place on the outskirts of town.

Even though he was supposedly occupied, a good spy knew not to park too close just in case. So I stopped my car a couple blocks away, turned off the lights, and made the rest of the path on foot. The night air wasn't too warm or cool. And it was quiet in Cottonwood Falls, so I could hear little pebbles scraping across asphalt as I walked—nay—crept toward his house.

It was exactly the kind of prank Liv and I would have pulled in high school. The thought made me smile, remembering that time we tried to TP a friend's car and the wind blew it all away. So when we saw him at school the next day, he only asked why we were giggling so much.

After a few minutes of walking, I reached Hayes's place. The floodlight was on, casting a silvery glow to his driveway and the truck that sat neglected since his motorcycle was up and running.

The motorcycle was gone, so I breathed a relieved sigh and turned the knob to his front door. Unlocked, as usual.

This was too easy. I didn't even need to crawl through a window or anything. (Not that I particularly wanted to.)

I stepped into his house and used the flashlight function on my phone to peer around. The floral table runner I'd left here a few days ago was noticeably gone from his chrome-and-glass-top table. As was the other throw pillow I'd left on his couch.

Smirking, I placed this new pillow, silver-sequined to match my disco ball planner, on his couch.

I could just picture the annoyed look on his face when he found it, wondering which of his conquests was feeling too at home and how he'd missed it before.

But then I heard the roar of an engine and saw a single headlight beam flash through the front window blinds.

"Shit!" I whispered, fumbling with my phone to turn off my light. "Shit! Shit!"

Sure, this was a harmless prank, and I wasn't actually stealing anything, but Hayes was grumpy under the best of conditions. Imagine him finding out I was sneaking around his bachelor pad without his permission.

The engine on the vehicle slowed to a dull roar, idling in the driveway. My heart was racing, all thoughts of being a spy completely gone. And just as I heard the doorknob jiggling, I dropped to the floor, tucking myself up against his dark leather couch. Maybe my black outfit would hide me until I could sneak back out and vow never to return again.

The door swung open, and boots landed on the floor, taking step after confident step toward the fridge.

My mind flashed back to being a kid and playing dead in preparation for my lead role in some princess movie while waiting for true love's first kiss. I'd thought I was so convincing back then. Now I knew I'd never truly had a chance. Why the hell was I breathing so loud?

I tried to take shallow little sips of air, but that didn't help. I swore I was losing oxygen.

And in my delirious state, I realized Hayes had left his front door open. Didn't he know heating and cooling a house wasn't cheap? How much money had he wasted in these few moments?

He shut the fridge, and I heard the familiar clink of glass bottles in a six-pack. He must have been on a beer run.

I let out a sigh of relief. He would be in and out before he even noticed me.

But that sigh was a mistake, because he froze.

My heart stopped with him.

Shit. Shit. Shit.

"What the fuck is that doing there?" he muttered to himself. Then I heard the clink of bottles.

More footsteps.

HE WAS WALKING AROUND THE COUCH.

I squeezed my eyes shut like that would somehow make me invisible. And then I peeped through one eye, spying him through a fringe of eyelashes.

He had the shiny pillow in his hands and was looking at it like... well, like it had snuck into his house.

Shaking his head, he turned to leave the living room. And then his eyes fell on me.

He yelled out in shock, jumping backwards, which made me scream too.

"Della?" he yelled. "What the fuck are you doing down there?"

"I—I..." Let me tell you, there is no good way to maintain your dignity while dressed in all black and lying on a bachelor pad floor. But I did my best as I stood up, anxiously running my hands over my pants to dry my sweaty palms.

His eyes traveled from me to the pillow in his hands and back again. "You?"

This was it. My moment. The one where I decided which type of villain I would be.

I could be the calm, confident one who used her moment in the spotlight for a killer, quotable mono-logue. Or the one who stammered and backed away slowly, then ran outside and never showed her face again.

I needed to go to the gym more for the latter to be an option.

So I lifted my chin and said, "I thought your place could—"

He held up his hand, wagging his finger, and walked back to his bedroom.

Really? He cut off my villainous monologue? Didn't he know how this spy thing worked?

I followed him back to his room, half expecting to see some kind of freaky sex den with ropes hanging from the ceiling and leather cords spilling from the closet.

But it was... normal.

A king-sized bed. Matching nightstands on either side.

There was even a book on one bedside table. I squinted, trying to make out the title, but I couldn't before Hayes stood up from the closet, holding a giant laundry basket in his hands.

"What's that?" I asked.

"The treasure chest. But now it's full of your shit." He held up a frilly pink pillow. "I'm assuming this is yours."

My cheeks were so hot they could have lit a candle.

He pulled out a floral table runner. "And this?"

"Matched perfectly with your chrome table," I pouted.

He stacked it on top of the pillow.

Then he pulled out a potted aloe vera, the ferns drooping sadly. "Yours as well?"

I gasped. "You didn't even water it?"

"Fuck no!" He picked up the pile and passed it to me. "Plants say 'I can take care of things.' Like a *child*. Or a piece of furniture that needs put together. Or your dog that just got neutered and looks all sad at you in those stupid cones." Even though I was holding the pillow and table runner in my hands, he didn't back away. Instead, he leaned in. This close, I could see the ink curling up his neck. The glint of the light off his lip ring. Could smell his cologne mixed with the earthy scent of his garage.

And damn if it wasn't just as intoxicating as too many trips to the box of wine in my fridge.

My eyes traced his lips as he said, "Trust me, Princess, the only thing I want to spend my time taking care of is a woman in bed."

I couldn't help it.

I laughed.

Hayes looked *horrified*. "What, you don't believe me?" he asked.

I held all my items in my arms, still managing to shrug. "You're just an awful lot of talk, that's all." I was playing with fire. The flames dancing in his eyes told me so.

But then those flames licked my skin as he pulled the items from my arms, stalked me like prey until I was backed up against his wall. Nowhere to go with his body mere centimeters from mine, arms bracketed on either side of my shoulders.

He leaned in until his lips brushed the shell of my ear. "Tell me, Princess. Would you like me to be more action?"

19

────

DELLA

A SILENT GASP passed my lips at what Hayes was saying.

Was he offering... I glanced up, looking at him from under my lashes, and found his mouth dangerously close to mine.

My heart was galloping ahead of my mind, desperate to get lost in Hayes Madigan's special brand of danger. To forget his rules, even if it was in my heart's best interest to stay away from the man who swore my dreams were unrealistic.

I tipped up my chin, inching closer to his lips.

His gaze flicked from my eyes to my mouth.

He leaned ever closer.

And just when our lips were bound to touch, he pulled away. "I... I can't." His eyes pressed closed like he was in physical pain at the thought of kissing me.

Hot, painful embarrassment went searing through me.

He stepped back. "I'm sorry, I—"

I shook my head, not wanting to hear his apology or his reasons for shying away when he had me on a platter before him. "I'm sorry, I shouldn't have come here," I whispered, hot tears threatening to fall.

Maybe running away was in my cards after all, because I turned tail and left his house, hurrying toward my car and wishing I'd have parked closer after all.

Suddenly, I felt stupid for dressing this way. Acting this way as a grown woman. Pranking a grown man who had no intention of making me his, all the while knowing I had a date with Bennett this very evening.

Shit.

My date with Bennett!

I lifted my arm to check my smartwatch.

Luckily, I had just enough time to get home and change. But my mind was so gone with thoughts of Hayes, I would have stayed and spent the night with him, Bennett Smith long forgotten.

How terrible of me.

Who even was I anymore?

I wasn't this girl, the one who threw caution to the wind. Who forgot about my dreams of having a story-book romance, a family. Children who would look at Mom and Dad and think *I want a love like that.*

Hayes wasn't that kind of guy.

There was nothing wrong with him. Only me for forgetting who I was.

I finally reached the safety of my car and got in. The touch of a button was all it took to turn it on. My headlights illuminated the street ahead of me, made brighter by Hayes's pickup pulling onto the road. He looked over at me, caught in my headlights.

I didn't know if he could see my face, but if he could, I wonder what he thought.

Did he see a foolish girl, easily caught off guard with a simple sentence?

Or did he see something more?

Instead of answering my silent question, he continued driving back toward Madigan Auto. With a heavy sigh, I put my car in gear and drove home. Toward *reality*—toward a practical man who would soon be coming to get me.

Once I pulled up to my driveway, I quickly went inside and changed out of my stupid black clothes into something more *me*. A flowy white dress with flowers embroidered up the skirt, my favorite pair of nude ballet flats, and a soft pink cardigan.

Then I quickly weaved my curls into a braid, hoping that I would finish plaiting before the bell rang.

Bennett arrived exactly at seven thirty, like we'd agreed. That was another thing I was coming to learn about him; he was dependable to the core.

He stood at the door, dressed in nice jeans and a plaid shirt. No flowers this time, but he had a big smile on his face as he greeted me. "Hey, Della. Ready to go?"

I nodded. "Let me grab my purse." Once I had the bag looped over my shoulder, I followed him out to his truck, and he opened the door for me, offering his hand for me to step up.

I took it, grateful for the chivalrous gesture. It was so different from how Hayes had acted that day in the tow truck, telling me to find a way up. But for some reason, Bennett didn't have my heart pounding.

What on earth was *wrong* with me?

I tried to ignore my swirling thoughts, get my head in a better space, as Bennett walked around the front of the truck and got back in.

"How was your day?" he asked amicably as he pulled out of my driveway.

Before getting caught in Hayes's living room dressed in all black? "Uneventful. You?"

"About the same," he replied, then launched into a story about welding pens at a ranch north of town. It was clear Bennett cared about his work a lot, and he was an easy talker, filling our ride to the diner.

We went inside and sat at an open table. It seemed to be a little slower tonight with only a few people dining. When Agatha came over to take our orders, we got two milkshakes and a basket of fries to share.

Hayes would never do this, I thought. He wouldn't be caught dead on a date with a woman. Much less one as sappy and nostalgic as milkshakes at the diner.

I used that thought to be grateful for Bennett sitting across from me. Both his hands were on the table, and I noticed the dark hair on his knuckles, winding up the back of his hands until it was covered by his shirt sleeves.

What were we going to talk about? I wondered.

Apparently, Bennett didn't know either because we sat in an awkward silence until Agatha brought our milkshakes and fries to the table.

He got strawberry, and I had chocolate. She even put whipped cream and a cherry on top.

"Thank you, Ms. Agatha," Bennett said warmly.

I smiled at her. "Yeah, thank you."

He was nice to servers too? That was always something I looked for on dates. Being rude to a waitress was a major red flag. But my stomach sank, because I wasn't getting the feeling like there was enough chemistry here to warrant me staying.

Hiding my disappointment, I took a sip of my shake, and Bennett asked, "How is it?"

"Good," I said. "Yours?"

"The best." He took a fry from the basket and dragged it through his shake, bringing it to his lips.

And that gave me an idea. Maybe what I needed to get that feeling, that *spark*, from Bennett was as simple as a kiss.

I promised myself that if he didn't make a move when he dropped me off tonight, I would.

20

HAYES

I DROVE BACK to the garage, unable to pry my mind away from Della. She looked ridiculous, covering her curves and her pretty red hair in all black. But that frumpy outfit did nothing to dampen my attraction to her.

If anything, her playfulness made me that much more interested.

Fuck boring women who acted like fun was beneath them.

I wanted a woman who could play with me. Challenge me. Tease me.

It was a miracle I managed to hold back when she lifted her chin like that to kiss me. Her lips had been so close to mine. I'd been so close to giving in.

But Dad was right about growing into the man she deserved. Sex had always been one of my favorite activities. But the thought of Della considering me a one-night stand was enough to make my stomach turn. And the version of me that would be more to her? I had no idea what the fuck he would do. And that was the problem. This was all new to me, and I was liable to fuck things up with the only woman I'd ever really cared about.

With that lovely fucking thought stabbing at my brain folds, I reached the garage, where all the guys were sitting around one of the waiting room tables playing Texas Hold'em. My dad, Fletcher, and Knox were there, along with Rhett and Tyler Griffen—two guys who had grown up on the farm next to ours.

As I walked in, I could feel all their eyes on me, hopefully just because I brought refreshments. I set a few six-packs on one of the side tables for them, then grabbed a bottle and took my seat at the table. "Deal me in."

Fletcher bridged the cards easily, eyeing me. "What's wrong with you? You haven't made one joke about my shirt yet."

I glanced at his t-shirt that said, Hi Hungry, I'm Dad.

"Hi Dad, I'm hungry."

He studied me, waiting for my answer to his initial question.

Damn him for being so perceptive. "Can we just pretend it's nothing?"

Dad chuckled before taking a swig of his beer and tossing a couple chips into the middle pile. We both knew that Fletcher, with his need to solve every problem we had, would never let it drop.

Rhett gave me a skeptical look under the brim of his black cowboy hat. "It's gotta be a woman."

I gritted my teeth. Of course he would recognize the signs when he went through his own playboy phase before settling down with his wife, Maggie.

Knox teased, "Is she inflatable?"

I glared at him while all the other guys whooped with laughter.

Then Knox's eyes widened with surprise at my expression. "Woah now, are you dating someone?"

Tyler looked just as shocked. "I don't know that I've seen you in a relationship since you were sixteen!"

Rhett dipped his head, his cowboy hat catching shadows as he did. "And that one only lasted a week if I remember right."

I wasn't the kind to get embarrassed, but all the attention was making my cheeks feel hot. I muttered, "And now I'm regretting saying anything."

"You've given us all so much shit over the years, you can take it," Dad replied, chuckling as he threw a chip in the center of the table.

I shot him a look of betrayal. "Should we talk about you and Ms. Agatha at the diner then?"

He quickly brought the beer bottle to his lips. "Nope."

But my attempt at a diversion didn't distract the interrogators from grilling me. "Who is it?" Fletcher pressed. He was worse than a dog with a bone.

"It's Della, okay?" I said, suddenly nervous for their reactions. Della wasn't just some woman in town—she was practically family.

Everyone fell into a stunned silence. It might be the quietest this poker meet-up has ever been. Fletcher shifted uncomfortably. Knowing he was married to Della's best friend, his hesitation made my stomach curdle. "Della?" He shook his head. "Hayes..."

"Don't say it." My throat felt tight, but I swallowed down the emotion. "I know I'm not good enough for her. I know we want different things. But I can't get her off my mind. It's like every fucking morning I wake up hoping her car will break down. Every day, I wear that stupid helmet, hoping it will make her smile when I drive by her office. Every night, I can't even think of having another woman in my bed because *it's not her.*"

My chest heaved with the force of my breath, the weight of my admission. I thought getting it off my chest might make me feel better, but instead I had an oh-shit moment. Because this wasn't nonsense running around my brain. It was real, and these feelings weren't going anywhere... even if it would make my life easier for them to go away.

They all gave each other looks until finally Knox said, "Wow, you've got it bad..."

Tyler chimed in, "Does Della know that?"

"Fuck no!" I practically yelled back. "I wouldn't even know what to say. 'Hey, Della, I want to fuck you more than once'?" I was only half joking, but the guys took pity on me and laughed along.

Dad said, "Why don't you just ask her out to dinner?"

"Just dinner," Fletcher added in that bossy, big-brotherly way.

I raised my eyebrows. "And then what?"

Fletcher said, "You go to dinner again!"

"And then?" I asked. "How do you go from acquaintances to... what you all have?" Relationships didn't make any fucking sense to me. All I knew was I liked talking to her. But eating dinner with her every day didn't seem like enough.

Knox tilted his head, making his blond hair sweep to the side. "It's not as difficult as you're making it out to be. You keep showing up and see where it goes."

My heart thundered at the thought. Not that I'd admit that to anyone. But they must have seen the frown on my face because Fletcher said, "Della will tell you what she wants and what she doesn't. You have to respect that."

I didn't like what he was implying. "I wouldn't force myself on her. If she doesn't want to date me, then... good. That might make my life a little easier."

It was a false bravado. If I put myself out there with Della for more than a one-time lay and she turned me down, it would gut me six ways to Sunday.

Dad said, "When are you going to ask her out?"

They all watched me, waiting for my answer, cards long forgotten on the table. "Tonight."

Dad raised his eyebrows. "We're playing 'til late. You'll have to call her now, or it'll be too late for today."

My stomach squirmed. "Now? With all you fuckers watching?"

Dad nodded. "That way we know you didn't chicken out."

Knox agreed enthusiastically. "We'll be quiet. Just call her."

Rhett gave me a shit-eating grin. "Unless you're too chickenshit."

I glared at him. "Fuck off," I said and pulled my phone from my pocket.

Looks like I was doing this...

I scrolled through my phone, embarrassed for the first time for how many women were in there. Their information seemed like a waste of space when all I wanted to find was Della's name.

When I found her, my thumb hovered over her name, just a tap away from dialing her. But... "This isn't right," I murmured.

They all burst out in protest, telling me I should buck up and give her a call. But I shook my head. "I should ask her in person."

Dad grinned. "Atta boy. Now get out there and ask her out. Can't wait to hear how it goes."

Feeling a flurry of nerves in my chest, I got up from my chair and walked out to my truck.

This was happening. Tonight.

21

____

DELLA

A MOTH FLUTTERED around my porch light as I stood across from Bennett at the end of our date. Usually, I liked living in such a safe, small town where I didn't have to worry about locking my doors or anyone breaking in.

But right now, I really wished for keys I could fumble with to give him a sign that I was ready for a kiss goodnight.

Instead, I stood on my mat that said HELLO SPRING and told him, "Thanks for the milkshakes."

"Of course," he replied. "Glad you liked it."

He turned to walk away, but I said, "Bennett?"

He faced me again, and before I could talk myself out of it, I launched myself forward to kiss him.

But instead of planting a kiss, I smushed our faces together, bonking my nose against his. "Ow!" I said, my hand going to my nose. Looked like his hurt just as bad because his large hand was covering his own.

"Oh, I'm so sorry!" I cried out. "Are you okay?"

"I'm not sure... How does it look?" He pulled his hand away from his face, and a trickle of blood fell from his nose.

"You're bleeding!" I said. As if this could have gotten any worse. "Come inside, I'll clean you up."

I held his elbow to guide him into my house while he pinched the bridge of his nose. I was so embarrassed and thinking this would probably go down for both of us as the worst date ever. "Here, you can sit in this chair." I tugged out a chair from the table and helped him sit before hurrying to my cabinet for a wet rag.

Once I brought it back to him, he moved it to his bleeding nose. Utterly humiliated, I said, "Let me bake some cookies or something. So the nose isn't the last thing we remember about tonight."

He chuckled low. "That's my life motto."

"What's your motto? Stay away from Della or get a busted nose?"

His laugh was warm, albeit muffled by the rag. "Never say no to cookies."

Some of the tension in my chest eased at the comment. Grateful, I said, "I can make peanut butter cookies really easily."

"Sounds great," he replied.

Thankful to have something for my hands to do, I pulled the ingredients out of my cabinets and started combining them, thankful for the simple recipe my mom had taught me. One cup of peanut butter, one egg, and one cup of sugar, in the oven for twelve minutes at 350 degrees.

I held the bowl against my waist, mixing it together and trying not to stare at Bennett while he checked to see if he was still bleeding.

He pressed the rag back to his nose. Looked like it was.

With a frown, I pulled out a cookie sheet from a lower cabinet, lined it with parchment paper, and started dolloping spoonfuls of dough onto the pan. Once it was in the oven, I turned back to Bennett. He was folding up the rag so the blood wouldn't show.

"Has it stopped bleeding?" I asked hopefully. Although my hope might have been misplaced. How did you come back from something like this?

He tipped his chin back to show me. "All clear."

"Great." I must have been coming off adrenaline because my hands were shaking as I put the ingredients away. I fumbled with the sugar canister but finally got it back in the cabinet. Unfortunately, I wasn't so lucky with the eggs.

The carton slipped from my shaky fingertips, opening on the fall and landing half a dozen eggs on the floor. "Crap," I muttered. "*Crap, crap, crap.*" Could this night get any worse?

"Can I help?" Bennett asked.

At least I didn't have to pick up this mess on my

own. I glanced over my shoulder while I tugged at a roll of paper towels. "Can you get my steam mop? It's in the closet over there." I pointed at the closet in the corner of my living room and then bent down to wipe up what I could of the mess.

I carefully carried the pile of paper towels, eggshells, and the innards to my trashcan and then made another swipe at the liquid before I realized Bennett hadn't come back with the mop.

I turned around to see what the holdup was and found him staring at the easel. He'd pulled it out of the closet and was now looking at the list my friends made labeled SINGLE GUYS IN COTTONWOOD FALLS.

My face instantly grew hot, and my vision tunneled. "Bennett..." I could only imagine what this looked like to him.

He turned back to face me again, utter betrayal marring his expression. "Is this some kind of hit list?" His tone was full of disgust.

"No, it's not, it's..." But my voice trailed off. How did I explain that he was part of some last-ditch, wine-induced effort to find my soulmate and stay in Cottonwood Falls? It would sound just as pathetic as I felt right now. "It's not what you think," I finally managed.

He shook his head. "I'm sorry, Della, I'm not real interested in cookies anymore." He walked to my front door, yanking it open only to reveal Hayes Madigan standing there, hand raised.

Bennett gave us both a disgusted look, and I'd never felt so guilty before in my life. He might not have given me butterflies, but he didn't deserve to feel like a reject. I knew that feeling all too well and wouldn't wish it on anyone.

"Bennett, wait," I said, but I couldn't find anything to follow up the request. Not that he stuck around to find out. He walked to his pickup while I stood on the porch awkwardly with Hayes, watching him go.

To Bennett's credit, he didn't spew any foul words or flip us the bird, he just slowly drove off in his truck and used his turn signal at the empty intersection at the end of my street.

I let out a sigh, knowing this would probably get out, and I'd be the topic of the town's gossip. Poor single Della, desperate to find a man.

"Is now a bad time?" Hayes asked.

I gave him a look.

He smirked. But when my features didn't lighten, his expression sobered again.

"Did you come by to yell at me for sneaking in your house?" I asked, suddenly exhausted. "Because it's really not a good time for a lecture." My eyes stung with embarrassment, and I blinked back the tears while a pair of moths plinked against my porch light.

Not only had Hayes caught me in childish antics, but he'd also seen my only romantic prospect in this town walk right out the door without a backward glance. He probably thought I was as pathetic as I felt right now.

But instead of looking down on me, he tipped his head to the side. "What if I was here for something else?"

I raised my eyebrows, folding my arms protectively across my chest. "Would you like another throw pillow to match the first?" I retorted, trying to act more carefree than I felt.

He let out a low laugh at my wry joke. "No, Della. I'm here to ask if you'll see me at the spring festival."

My eyebrows drew together, surprised at the question. Surprised he'd come here to ask. "I'll be at the festival... So I should see you there." Where was he going with this?

He gave me a pained expression and raked his hand through his hair. "I meant can we go *together*."

My lips parted in a mix of confusion and surprise. "Together?" Was he speaking English? Because Hayes and me together at the festival did not compute.

"For a date," he elaborated. The words sounded foreign on his lips.

"You want to go on a... date? With me?" But Hayes Madigan didn't date. Everyone in town knew it. He'd told me so himself. He also made it clear I was in a no-fly zone where he was concerned.

Nevertheless, he nodded slowly, shadows rising and falling along the angles of his face.

It all seemed so strange. "You're not just asking me

out to hook up with me?" I asked. That was the only language Hayes spoke with women as far as I knew.

He lifted his chin defiantly. "What if I'm asking because I enjoy your company?"

I snort-laughed.

But his expression was dead serious. "Della, will you go out with me or not?"

"This isn't a joke?" I asked skeptically. "A prank to get me back?" He couldn't be asking me out. That didn't make sense. Especially not when he had his pick of countless women who, I'm sure, would like more with him than casual sex.

Hayes frowned. "Do I look like I'm joking, Moonshine?"

"What about not 'shitting where you eat'?" I asked, parroting the crass phrase back at him. "What about trying to stay away from me?"

"Sometimes I'm stupid." He raked his fingers through his hair. "Which you should probably take into consideration when answering my question."

When I didn't speak right away, he reached out, holding my hand gently in his. Something about the callouses on his palms contrasting the gentleness of his touch had my skin warming, my heart pounding. "Will you go out with me, Della?" he asked.

My heart answered before my head could get in the way. "I'd like that very much."

22

———

HAYES

I WAS on top of the fucking world for all of two seconds until I realized I had no idea how to go on a date.

The outing had to be special—especially with someone like Della. But how?

I thought maybe I could learn something online—that's how I learned a lot about my motorcycle. But that was not helpful. There were a million different pieces of advice, and I wasn't sure who to believe. None of the people writing those articles knew Della.

But I knew someone who did.

So I got on my motorcycle and drove out of town to the white farmhouse where my brother was living in marital bliss with Della's best friend.

I left my motorcycle in the driveway, propped on its kickstand, and walked toward the front door, knocking a few times.

Graham, Maya's dog they found on the side of the road several years back, let out a few warning barks. Then a baby started wailing.

I cringed.

A few moments later, Fletcher came to the door holding Mira in his arms. Her hair was all mussed, and her cheeks were red. But she twisted and reached for me.

I took her in my arms, saying, "Sorry for waking you up, sweet girl. I didn't know this was naptime."

Fletcher said, "She's been fighting them lately." Then he stepped back to let me in. "What brings you by? Because we'll definitely take some babysitting."

I chuckled, bouncing Mira in my arms. "You know I'll babysit anytime." Graham sniffed my leg, then looked up at me like he was greeting an old friend. I bent a little to scratch his ears and then stood back up. Once the attention was gone, he scuttled down the hallway leading to the bedrooms.

"Tuesday?" Fletch asked, plopping onto the couch in his living room. The other girls must have been in their rooms or something because no one else was around.

"Sure." Then I said, "I need some advice. Is your wife available?"

"Ha ha, where's the injury?" Fletcher started looking me over, ready for a cut or scrape he'd have to stitch together like he'd done dozens of times before. But I shook my head.

"I'm serious."

Understanding dawned in his eyes. And then he chuckled. "You've really got it bad."

"Shut up," I muttered.

"Uh huh," he said. "This way."

I followed behind him, Mira beginning to doze in my arms, feeling like he was taking me into the lion's den instead of his en suite bathroom. The whole place reeked of hairspray. Liv, Maya, and Leah were all in there doing hair and makeup.

They all looked at me in the mirror, in various states of preparation. Maya had a curling iron twisted around a strand of hair. Liv had one set of lashes coated in mascara, the other eye bare. And Leah was painting sparkling lipstick on her lips.

Fletcher said, "You've been summoned, Liv."

She gave me a knowing look that had me feeling way too exposed.

Keeping my voice low, I asked, "Can you help me or not?"

"Of course I can." She continued applying her mascara. "She's my best friend."

I shifted to my other foot, bouncing Mira softly in my arms. "*Will* you?"

Maya smirked at me then whispered, "You forgot to say please."

I gritted my teeth together, knowing Liv was just stubborn enough to make me do it. Probably on my knees and in a tutu if I didn't play my cards right. "Will you *please* help me, Liv?"

"Of course! Why didn't you ask?" she whispered brightly. She finished applying her mascara and said to Fletcher, "Can you supervise?"

"Sure thing," he replied and patted my back on the way out.

Looking down and noticing Mira was now fast asleep, I whispered, "Should I lay her in her bed?"

Liv shook her head. "You're stuck like this for the next two hours." Walking ahead of me into the hallway, she curled her finger over her shoulder. "Step into my office."

I rolled my eyes when she actually stepped into their home office. At least I knew Della was worth all the theatrics.

Liv sat in the high-backed leather chair behind the desk and gestured that I should sit across from her. I gave her a look before sitting down, careful not to wake Mira.

"So," she said, pulling out a yellow legal pad and pen. "What brings you in today?" But she cracked up, giggling on the last couple whispered words. "I've always wanted to do that," she said with humor in her eyes.

"You've sure made it painful to come and ask for help," I said wryly.

She chuckled. "You're cutting it a little close, don't you think?"

"I thought I could do it..." My knee bounced with my nerves. "But the closer I get to picking her up the more I realize that I have no fucking clue how to act tonight."

Liv smiled sadly, a worried tinge to her eyes. "As Della's best friend and someone who knows you pretty well... I gotta ask. Is this real? I don't want to be part of some ploy for you to get her in bed and then leave her."

The reminder of my past stung. I couldn't blame Liv one bit for feeling that way about me and trying to protect her friend. "I wouldn't be coming to you if it was just to sleep with your friend. I'm better than that."

She reached across the desk, patting my hand. "Hayes, you're the best uncle to my girls. You always make them feel special just as they are. Fletcher has told me how many times you gave him great advice on getting Maya through her rough patch. We love you for you."

I swallowed down the lump in my throat, feeling oddly touched at her words. "So why does it feel like there's a 'but' coming?" I only half joked. My muscles felt tense, like they knew I should brace myself.

Liv frowned. "I believe in trusting people when they show you who they are. And you've shown me that when it comes to women... you're around for a good time. Not for a long time."

The words sounded so... gross. But she was right. "I've never been interested in something different until now."

Liv nodded slowly, taking it in. I couldn't tell if she believed me or not, so I pressed ahead, asking, "So what do I do?"

She flattened her hands on the desk and looked at them for a moment. "Here's the deal." She looked up at me, leveling her gaze. "You're going to have to put in some work of your own for me to believe your intentions are pure. If I gave you advice and Della got hurt somehow, I couldn't forgive myself."

My stomach churned at her doubt. Suddenly, I didn't just want to please Della. I wanted to show Liv that I could be a better man.

23

———

DELLA

I WAS STARTING to wonder if agreeing to this date with Hayes was a really bad idea. We weren't exactly friends—although I did enjoy sneaking girly stuff into his house—so it wasn't like there was a close friendship on the line. But I was best friends with his sister-in-law. I counted his family as my friends. Would things be awkward at weekend get-togethers, events at Maya's school, summer little league games, and birthday parties if this went badly?

But before I could back out or overthink it anymore, my doorbell sang its happy song.

Hayes was here.

My heart rate picked up, even as I double-checked my hair in the mirror in all its natural, curly glory, and then continued to the door.

When I opened it, my jaw dropped. Hayes was

holding a colorful bouquet of flowers in a shiny, disco ball vase.

"You got me flowers?" I asked.

His smile had a hint of hope to it. "Do you like them?"

"I love them, and the vase is exactly my style," I said honestly. "Thank you. Let me set this on the table." I carried the pretty arrangement to my table, excited at the fact that I'd get to look at it for the coming week—and keep the vase forever. "Did you have help picking it out?"

His lips lifted slightly as he said, "Bora let me pick."

My heart warmed, and I felt... seen. Bennett had shown up with carnations that I needed to arrange and put in my own vase. But Hayes had gotten me something I'd truly *enjoy* without giving me a chore. I admired the display on my thrifted table runner. It had fake blue dragonflies flitting about the surface, and the flowers matched perfectly. "Thank you, Hayes," I said again.

"You're welcome," he said warmly. Now that I had examined the flowers, I could appreciate his looks. He'd worn a pair of black jeans, a gray shirt, and a denim jacket with the sleeves rolled. Mixed with the smell of his cologne and the spark in his blue eyes, I was already melting.

We walked together out of the house, and I was pleasantly surprised to see that his motorcycle wasn't waiting in the driveway. Instead, he'd driven his pickup.

And he even came to my side of the truck and opened the door for me.

It was strange—this surly guy being all chivalrous. "Who are you and what have you done with Hayes Madigan?" I teased as I sat in the seat.

He stood at the door, leaning his head against the frame. "Today, it's just Hayes."

I lifted a corner of my lips as he shut my door and went around to his side. Over the treetops that framed my house, I caught a glimpse of clear blue sky with white wispy clouds. The weather had given a ten percent chance of rain, but I highly doubted it.

As we pulled away from my house and got closer to Main Street, it hit me what a big deal this date was. Hayes hadn't asked me out and then taken me to some dark and dingy bar the next town over so we could have some privacy. He'd brought me to the busiest event in Cottonwood Falls where *everyone* would see us together.

The thought had my heart racing just as much as his appearance... his smile. No matter how much I'd tried to tamp down my desire for him before today, it was definitely showing up in full force now in this pickup cab.

I tried to steady my nerves while he found a parking spot a few blocks away from Main Street, which had been blocked off and lined with vendors. When we got out of the truck and walked down the sidewalk, I half expected him to keep his distance. Instead, he easily caught my hand in his, lacing his calloused fingers through mine.

I looked over at him, surprised both at the gesture and at the spark I felt, and found him smiling softly back at me. "Is this okay?"

The question, his gentle expression, was so at odds with him—all tattoos and piercings and rough edges. But I was starting to realize there was more to Hayes than met the eye. "I like it," I admitted.

With a pleased smile, he squeezed my hand and said, "What would you like to do?"

I thought that over. I'd been coming to the festival for literal decades now, so I said, "Usually I get my face painted first. The profits go to pay medical bills for people in the community."

"Let's do it," he said.

I raised my eyebrows. "Really?"

He gestured at his arms, covered in tattoos. "You think I have an issue with body art?"

I chuckled. "I guess not."

We walked together toward the tent on the corner of Main and Second that always housed the face painters. The artists were all kids in the high school art classes, and they got extra credit for painting.

The line was already starting to grow, and I was eager to wait in line with Hayes.

As a single gal, you got used to looking for red flags

that hinted at a guy's personality. Being kind to wait-staff was a big one. But so was being kind while waiting in line. I couldn't stand someone who acted like they deserved to be right at the front or grumbled the entire time, making the wait miserable.

I glanced over at Hayes. "Long line," I said noncommittally.

"Yeah." He paused. "You know what I like to do in lines?"

I raised my eyebrows. This was new. "What?"

"I look around and see if I can find the alphabet. It's a game Fletcher used to play with us, although I'm guessing he learned it from Mom."

My heart tweaked at the mention, at the soft look in his eyes. I knew his mom had passed of cancer when he was young. "A game sounds fun," I said.

"Shall we play together?" he asked. "Bet I'll get more letters."

I chuckled. "I don't see why not."

After about ten minutes of racing to find letters and laughing more than I thought I would, Hayes and I were sitting side by side in chairs as the students started painting our skin. I watched out of the corner of my eye while a girl brushed tiger stripes on his cheeks. The poor thing's hands were shaking, and her cheeks were flushed with shyness. Hayes Madigan wasn't an easy one to ignore, even if he was just sitting there patiently.

The girl painting a princess crown on my forehead was chatty and talked my ear off about her art project she was working on for her senior capstone. I could hardly get a word in edgewise, which was a first for me.

Eventually, both our faces were painted, and I stood up, getting a view of Hayes's face. He had a soft pink nose, a white puff of "fur" underneath, and orange and black stripes over his cheeks.

As soon as I giggled, he growled at me, which just made me laugh harder. He paid for our faces and tucked my hand in his while walking out of the tent with me.

So, Hayes was a hand-holder...

He ran his thumb over my skin, making a shiver go up my spine. No one simply holding my hand had ever made me react this way before.

We stalled off to the side of the face painting tent, out of the way of foot traffic. "What now, Della?" he asked, drawing me from my thoughts.

I smiled at the sound of my name on his lips and gestured toward the food trucks lined up farther down the road. "Usually I'd get a cup of cocoa and a funnel cake, but I know how you feel about hot chocolate."

He rolled his eyes as we weaved through people on the sidewalk. "What if I told you that you were right?"

My eyebrows rose, and somewhere in the back of my mind I knew it must have lifted the crown painted on my forehead slightly. "*What?*"

"The mint hot chocolate is the best. Don't make me drink the regular kind."

I shrieked, utterly satisfied that he finally admitted

it. "I knew I was right." A few people stared as they were passing by, but Hayes didn't seem to notice.

He gave me an amused look. "Ah, so you're that kind of girl."

"What kind?"

"The 'I told you so' kind."

I chuckled. "Aren't we all? Not saying 'I told you so' takes all the fun out of being right."

He was smiling, but he didn't argue and guided us through the people mingling about toward our next destination.

Farther down Main Street, there were several tables set up and food trucks pulled into a circle in the biggest intersection. I pointed out a red truck that had been my favorite year after year. This close, I could smell the food coming from the truck, and it made my mouth water as we stood together in line.

Hayes wasn't much for small talk, which was fine. It was easy just to stand hand in hand with him. He only let go of my fingers to pay. And I was feeling a little spoiled by him. I glanced away to keep him from seeing my flushed cheeks, and that's when I noticed my parents together in line at a different food truck.

And they saw me standing with Hayes, our hands linked. Dad looked pissed, and Mom wrung her hands worriedly.

Hayes followed my gaze, a worried look knitting his eyebrows. "Should I—"

"Let me talk to them," I whispered to him. "I'll meet you at a table."

I had to handle this before things got even more awkward.

24

DELLA

I LEFT Hayes waiting for our order and walked quickly to my parents where they stood toward the middle of a long line for the taco truck. What on earth was going on with them? I understood they weren't Hayes's biggest fans, but to be so blatant in front of him...

Before I could say a word, my dad cut in, drawing Mom and me into a family huddle. Even though people were around us in line, they seemed unbothered, chatting with each other or looking at their phones. The dull roar of conversation and country music playing over the loudspeakers would cover up most noise we made.

"What the hell, Della," Dad whispered. "You're here with *him*?"

Mom quietly added, "I thought you were seeing Bennett. What happened?"

Suddenly, I felt five years old again, caught sneaking ice cream sandwiches from the deep freeze when I was supposed to be in bed. But I reminded myself that I was a grown woman—it's not like they could ground me. "Hayes asked me to come to the festival with him, and I agreed. That's it."

Dad looked disgusted. "'That's it? Della, I'm not sure what you've heard about him, but I—"

I held up my hand. "Dad, I am *not* going to argue this with you. Especially not here." I glanced around at the festival still going on around us. At Hayes waiting at the table with our drinks and food, looking at his phone.

Both Dad and Mom seemed taken aback. I didn't cut them off. Ever.

"What does that mean?" Dad finally asked. "You don't care to hear what we think anymore?"

"It means I am here on a date with Hayes," I said with a frown. "It would be rude to stand here listening to my parents speak poorly of him while he's right over there." It took all I had to keep from gesturing at him. I knew Hayes could probably see us arguing, and I didn't want him to feel like we were fighting about him. It was the kind of thing that could scare him away, and even though it was early into the date... it was the first good date I'd had in a long time. I didn't want it to be over yet.

The line moved, and we shuffled forward.

Dad frowned. "I thought you were smarter than this. That boy is a walking red flag."

My jaw gritted together. "I'll see you Wednesday," I replied.

Mom lifted her hand sadly in a wave, and Dad shook his head at me. "Be careful," he warned.

I nodded and quickly turned away before I could say something I'd regret. On the inside, I was *fuming* at how they acted. Did my parents really think so little of my judgment? I didn't live under a rock—of course I knew what people said about Hayes. But I also knew him to be the most honest person in town. He'd never tried to hide who he was with me, on good or bad days. It was better than dating someone for years before finding out their secrets.

With a deep breath, I walked back toward the tables where I found Hayes sitting and sipping on coffee. (Because of course mint hot cocoa wasn't a standard offering around here.)

"Hey there," I said, settling into the seat across from him. The music stopped playing over the speakers, and we both glanced over. A dozen or so yards behind him, I saw a band stepping onto a metal platform stage. Soon, the twang of tuning guitar strings filled the air.

He leveled a look at me. "Your parents are pissed you're here with me," he said flatly.

"No, I—" But at his disappointed look, I nodded slowly. Message received: We weren't lying to each other. I let out a sigh. "Even at my age, I'm still their little girl."

"And I'm the big bad wolf." He managed a smirk, but it didn't quite meet his eyes like usual.

I shook my head at him, rolling my cup in my hands. "What if you're just a sheep in wolf's clothing?"

"Not a chance," he replied, picking up his coffee cup for a drink.

But I shook my head again as I tugged free a piece of funnel cake. "I have a theory."

"You do? I can't wait to hear this," he drawled.

I ignored his sarcasm and popped the funnel cake into my mouth. The mix of bread and grease and powdered sugar was heaven. I chewed it over and said, "I think you're like a porcupine. You're all prickly on the outside, but it's not because you're mean. It's because you're protecting yourself."

He leaned closer, and for a moment, everyone around us, all the tuning instruments and chatter, seemed to disappear. "What would I be protecting myself from? You?"

I bit my bottom lip. Because I didn't know yet. But I was determined to find out if he'd let me close enough.

"That's what I thought," he replied. He ate a piece of the funnel cake. And damn, why did it look so hot when he did it? My eyes followed every movement of his tongue swiping over his lips to catch a stray bit of powdered sugar.

What would it be like if I had kissed it away myself?

"Uncle Hayes!" Maya called, running up to us in a dress reminiscent of the olden days. "Uncle Hayes! It's time to dance!"

I practically jolted up at the interruption—I'd been so lost in my fantasy.

"Oh great," he muttered. He gave me an apologetic look and a quick, "Be right back," while his preteen niece dragged him toward the group of people lining up in the open space between the tables and the band.

An amused smile formed on my lips as I watched them go. Looking around at the festivities, I saw Liv standing off to the side of a forming crowd with her two younger girls in a stroller. There was an open space where children dressed like Maya were gathering with their family members.

When Liv caught my gaze, I gave her a wave and walked her way, dropping the funnel cake in the trash but hanging on to mine and Hayes's coffees.

When I reached my friend, she scoped out my outfit. "You look adorable. How's the date?"

"Really good, actually," I said. I'd told her about the date over text message, and I couldn't get a read on what she thought of it all.

She chuckled. "You sound surprised."

"Because I am," I admitted.

Liv leaned a little closer as the live band counted off a new song. "Can I tell you a secret?"

"Are you finally admitting to your crush on Aaron Carter?"

She snorted out a laugh and then whispered, "Hayes came over to my place earlier freaking out about the date because he wanted to get it right."

My heart melted a little. That was really sweet. But then disappointment washed over me. "So the flowers were your idea? I knew the vase was too perfect."

She raised her eyebrows. "What do you mean?"

I explained how Hayes had picked out the perfect arrangement and vase for me, Liv's smile growing wider all the while. "Why are you smiling like that?" I asked.

"Because that was all Hayes Madigan." She gazed over at him and his brothers lining up for the dance. "Who would have thought?"

The musician up front said, "Please welcome the Cottonwood Falls eighth grade class and their loved ones performing the 'Boot Scootin' Boogie'!"

Clapping for them, I looked out at the group of dancers. Hayes was easy to spot, standing between Maya and Knox, an easy smile on his lips as the music started. He hopped and skipped and scooted along to the beat, matching everyone else's choreography. And I didn't know what he was so reluctant about before because the man could *dance.*

He caught me looking, and a flirty smile graced his lips and lit his eyes. He swung his hips, putting on a show for me. Laughing, I clapped my hands together, cheering him on. "Go, Hayes!"

I could feel Liv watching me, but when I glanced her way, she quickly looked back at the dancers.

At the end of the song, Hayes gave Maya a high five and then walked over to me. The lead singer of the band said, "Thanks for kicking us off! Now this song is a slow one. Grab your partner and pull up some asphalt!"

I shook my head at the cheesy line, but Hayes extended his hand. "Dance with me?"

He was full of surprises today.

I slipped my hand into his, loving his firm grip, and he led me back to the area where everyone was dancing. We stopped somewhere around the double yellow line, and he drew me in close.

One hand holding mine, another settled at the small of my back, he left no room for anyone to doubt his intentions as our bodies pressed close together. This close, I could smell his cologne, feel the heat radiating from his chest, the rough brush of his callouses against my hand.

He guided us in a simple two-step, making it easy for me to follow along, which I was grateful for because this close to him, my brain was quickly turning to mush.

I blinked up at him, nearly breathless as I said, "Who knew you had such good moves."

He gave me a salacious wink and then whispered, "Those weren't even my best ones."

"Is that so?"

He leaned in close so only I could hear. "I can't show you those here."

A small shiver ran down my spine at the thought. I was looking forward to finding out what else Hayes Madigan had in store.

25

———

HAYES

SOMEWHERE BETWEEN SLOW dancing with Della and walking down Main Street eating caramel popcorn, I stopped worrying so much about doing the date right. Because I was having fun with her.

It was confusing—feeling like she was a friend I could hang out with while also feeling like I wanted to do so much more with her, too. Wanting to hear her talk about nothing and everything while simultaneously noticing how amazing she looked in that dress.

She was charming. Magnetic. Fucking magic, as far as I was concerned.

But the darker the sky grew, the more it felt like I was the guy version of Cinderella and my chariot was close to turning into a pumpkin.

I didn't want to go back to my old, ordinary life. Not when just eating funnel cake and walking around with Della had been a hundred times better than any of my regular days.

And then the thought crossed my mind... *I'm going to marry her one day.*

I stopped abruptly on the sidewalk, inadvertently jerking Della's hand, and then someone behind us bumped into me, making the bag of caramel corn spill from my free hand.

"Shit," I muttered. "Sorry."

The person behind us walked around while Della and I bent down to clean up my mess. While cleaning, I glanced up at her, catching her pale-green eyes for a moment, getting a closer look at the dusting of freckles across the bridge of her nose.

That's her. She's the one.

She caught me looking, so I glanced down again, making quick work of the rest. My heart was pounding as we stood up. She must have been able to tell something was off, because her gaze was full of genuine concern. "Everything okay? You look like you might be sick."

I might be, I thought. Why the fuck was my brain thinking about marriage on a first date? "I'm fine," I said, trying to make my voice sound casual. Never mind the fact that my heart was about as casual as a fucking impact wrench.

Where had that thought come from?

I'd never even considered marriage before. And here I was on the first date with Della, a sense of knowing spreading through me just as surely as you could feel rain falling from the sky.

Wait... *Rain was falling from the sky.* I looked up, in utter disbelief, and then over at Della. Her curly hair was growing bigger by the second.

"It's raining!" she cried.

Everyone around us was shouting similar statements, scurrying off toward their vehicles while vendors rapidly packed things under their tents.

"Any chance you have an umbrella in that bag of yours?" I asked.

"No, they said it was only a ten percent chance," she said to me, frowning. "I can't believe I didn't bring it."

"Come on." I took her hand, leading us back toward my truck. But it was no use. We were still three blocks away when a complete downpour let loose. Instead of running the rest of the way, we ducked under the flower shop's awning. It seemed like everyone else had found shelter under a tent or in their vehicles as well.

"I'm soaked," Della said, holding up a thick strand of her red hair and twisting it. Drips of water fell from the strands, and she giggled at the sight.

The sound warmed my chest, causing me to smile right along with her. Until I saw her shiver. She rubbed her hands over her bare arms, doing nothing to quell the gooseflesh there.

"Let me warm you up," I said, drawing her into my

arms. I rubbed my hands up and down the soaking fabric covering her back.

"Mmm," she hummed, linking her fingers behind my waist. "That's better." Her temple leaned against my chin.

I closed my eyes, savoring the feeling. Something about having her in my arms just felt right. With her hair damp, the scent of her mixed with fresh rain was amplified.

She looked up at me, and the light from a street-lamp filtering through the rainfall caught her eyes. They were now beautiful shimmering pools somewhere between light gray and washed-out green.

I reached up, cupping her face in my hand. The tattoos across my skin seemed so at odds with the pale, delicate freckles on her face. I stroked my thumb over her damp cheek, feeling my heart rise and fall with the motion.

And I couldn't hold back. Now that I knew my future, there was no point in waiting. This was it for me. *She* was it for me.

I lowered my mouth to hers, knowing this was my last first kiss. Her kiss was soft, plush, tender, cautious. *Everything.*

Never before had I savored a kiss like this, but I didn't want this one to end. Every second that our lips lingered, the more I learned about her. Like how her fingers felt as they fisted my shirt against my back. How her gentle moan of appreciation vibrated my mouth.

How delicately she parted her lips before sliding her tongue against the seam of mine.

I deepened the kiss in response, desperate to taste her, to savor her and the faint hints of caramel on her tongue. She was a cautious kisser, and I loved how each second that passed seemed to embolden her.

I wound my fingers into the damp tangle of curls at the nape of her neck, drawing her closer yet. My reward was her hand teasing at the hem of my shirt, fingertips brushing over the bare skin above my jeans. A simple touch had never been so intense before.

I broke the kiss, pressing my forehead to hers. "We should stop."

Della would be my undoing. And yet, she had no idea she was slicing the strings holding my carefully constructed life together, changing *everything* for me.

"You're right," she breathed softly. "We're not alone."

Old Hayes might have made a comment about taking this somewhere more private. But the guy I thought she deserved said, "Let's get you warmed up." I disentangled my hand from her hair then reached for her hand. It was warm and soft in mine.

She eyed the rain still coming down past the awning and gave a reaffirming nod. "Okay," she said and hustled toward the truck.

"Knees to chest, Hayes!" she tossed my way.

Laughing, I jogged alongside her, easily keeping her pace. "Did you run track in high school?" I teased.

"At least I wasn't hitting on the coach!" she fired back.

I took the jab, laughing, wondering how she could make something like getting caught in a rainstorm so much fun.

We reached my truck, breathing hard, and climbed in on either side. I hurried to turn it on so she could warm up. But since it would take a while for the heater to work, I lifted my arm, the woven seat covers scratching over my skin. "Come here."

Music played softly over the radio, masking the sloshing of her dress as she scooted into my embrace. I rubbed my hand over her arm to warm her up, thankful for the excuse to touch her. I wanted to touch all of her, now. But I also wanted to be the man she deserved.

And the guy she deserved would take care of her in and out of the bedroom.

"Thank you," she said, curling into me, letting me know I'd done right. "I should have brought an umbrella, but I thought that might be bad luck."

"Bad luck? To be prepared?" I asked. "That sounds strange coming from Miss Wear a Helmet Even on Main Street."

She narrowed her gaze at me. "Haven't you heard the parable about the guy who prepared his field for rain *and then got rain*. If I brought an umbrella, it would have been asking for it."

"That's an old wives' tale," I replied.

She folded her arms across her chest, managing to be huffy while curled under my arm. "Just because wives said it, it's not relevant?"

I pinched my brow. "That's not it, its—" I shook my head, realizing I was smiling. Arguing with her was too much fun. "You're crazy," I replied.

She grinned like she didn't mind one damn bit.

"Let me get you home before I pop a blood vessel arguing with you," I said, putting the truck in gear.

She chuckled. "Looks like you just don't want to be proven wrong. Again."

"Again?" I retorted, pulling onto the road.

"But who's keeping score." She winked.

Rain spattered on the windshield as I drove, and I flicked on the windshield wipers. We'd be at her house in just a few moments so she could change into dry clothes and get warm. My stomach dropped as I realized the date would soon be over... and I had no idea what to do next.

26

DELLA

HAYES LOOKED sexy as hell drenched from the rain, illuminated by the dash lights as he drove me home. His shirt clung to his chest, showing every ridge of muscle underneath. The darkness outside cast shadows over his tattoos, and my eyes traced the design, fascinated by every inch. And his hair had that sexy, wet tousled look that made me want to drag my fingers through the strands.

That kiss under the awning had been the best of my life. My heart sped up at the memory just as much as the anticipation of what would come next. The thought made me shiver.

"Are you cold?" he asked. "I think I have a hoodie in the back." He let go of my hand, keeping his eyes on the road while reaching behind the bench seat for his jacket.

My cheeks flushed with embarrassment. "I don't think any of your jackets will fit me."

He pulled up a thick, black hoodie, handing it to me. "Put it over your legs," he replied simply, like it was no big deal. Maybe it wasn't to him.

I did as he suggested, covering my lap with the thick material. It did feel a little better. Especially when he put his arm back around me again.

One downside of living in a small town was the short drive to my house. I was both disappointed to end our cuddle time and excited to take the next step. If he could kiss me like that, imagine what else he could do.

Sure, Hayes was hot when I thought he was a salacious bad boy skilled at pleasing women. He was even hotter now that I'd seen this side of him. The thoughtful, caring side he only showed to those closest to him.

And now, I was one of those people, getting his special brand of warmth. *How had we gotten here?* I wondered.

"Let me get your door," he said, cutting through my thoughts and the steady rhythm of the rain on his windshield. Considering the deluge, I didn't mind a few extra minutes in the shelter of his truck.

When he came to my side, he pulled the hoodie from my lap and held it up as a makeshift umbrella for me, letting the rain pour over him. The simple gesture had my heart melting. Wasn't that another thing I looked for in a man? One who would put my comfort ahead of his own?

Another box checked without even expecting it.

We hurried over the sidewalk and up the steps to my porch. The awning covered us, and the light cast a warm glow to our little nest surrounded by the shimmering dark night. It was still cold though, especially without his arms around me.

I reached for the door handle to let us inside, but Hayes said, "Wait."

I turned back to him, eyebrows drawn together. "Don't you want to come inside? I can make us some mint hot cocoa," I teased.

He smiled, but it quickly faded, and my heart constricted.

I knew that look. The sad one preparing to shelter me from disappointment. Years in the dating world had taught me it came just before heartbreak.

Surprised by the strength of disappointment rising in my chest, I took a deep breath to brace myself. I had thought our night was incredible, but maybe he didn't feel the same. "You don't want to come in?" I questioned, cursing the slight quiver in my tone.

Hayes bunched the dripping hoodie in his hands, looking supremely uncomfortable. "Can I be honest?"

Walls stacked into place around my heart. "Have you been dishonest until now?"

"No," he replied. But he still stood a couple feet away from me. He couldn't reach out and touch me even if he wanted to. "The thing is, I know how to do this." He gestured toward my door. "I know how to take you inside and make you feel good. I know how to lie next to you until you fall asleep and then get up and leave without making a sound..."

My eyes stung. God, I felt like such an idiot. Hayes wasn't the kind of guy to stay. But that was exactly what I wanted—the biggest checkbox of all. I wanted to pull open my door and run inside, but I forced myself to stay put on the wooden boards of my porch and hear him out.

"I don't know how to date someone," he continued. "I don't know how to show a woman how special she is to me. How to show up for more than one night." He closed the gap between us, tossing his hoodie onto my white rocking chair and holding both my hands in his. His eyes were earnest under the porch light, and I could tell how hard this was for him to say.

Suddenly, that hard wall forming around my heart crumbled, because I understood what Hayes was saying. All this time, I'd expected his rejection, but instead... I meant something to him. And he didn't know how to handle his feelings for me.

My lips curled up into a slow smile, secretly thrilled at being his first. "What do you propose we do?" I asked coyly.

His smile lit by the soft porch light was shy, a side to Hayes I hadn't seen before. "I'd like to kiss you good-night. And then I'd like to go home and think about what a great day I had with you. And then I'll stress about how long I should wait before calling to ask you out again."

A happy laugh bubbled past my lips. "I'd like that very much."

The look in his eyes was as gentle as his touch as he reached out and cupped my cheek in his hand. His palm warmed my face, holding me like something delicate and precious as his gaze flicked from my eyes to my lips.

And then Hayes pressed his mouth to mine. His tongue skated across my lips, and they parted to let him in.

But he didn't push. He savored. And after a moment, he let go. There was a smile on his lips as he said, "Goodnight, Della Dwyer."

I tilted my head and said, "Goodnight, Hayes Madigan."

And as he walked away, I reached for my door handle, twisting the cold metal to open my door. I paused in the threshold, glancing back at Hayes as he got into his truck. He gave me a final wave before backing out of the driveway and going on his way, headlights broken up by a torrent of rain.

My heart pattered happily, matching the drops of rain, as I walked into my house smiling.

I'd just gone on a date with Hayes Madigan. And he liked me *back*.

My phone started to ring, vibrating my bag.

I reached into my purse, wondering how Liv knew

to call at just the right time to dissect every second of my date.

But it wasn't her name on the screen. It was Hayes's.

"Hello?" I said, bringing the phone to my ear as I stood in my living room. Had he forgotten something?

"Has it been long enough?" he asked, a smile to his voice.

With a happy laugh, I said, "I believe so."

"Are you free Monday night for dinner?"

"Let me see if I'm available..." I pretended to check my calendar as I walked back toward my bedroom and then bit back a smile. "I'll see you then."

27

HAYES

"MAMA, LOOK!" *I said, holding up a piece of paper with her favorite colors, yellow and orange. I had used leaves and sticks to trace a design I knew she would love.*

She tried to lift her head from the soft white pillows, her brown hair looking coarse and lank around her like an old horse's mane. But she lowered her head and coughed, making her swollen belly shake. Her arms were like bones, but her stomach was big and swollen. I already asked Dad and there wasn't a baby in there.

Her eyes stayed closed, even after she coughed. She didn't even turn her head.

Why wasn't she looking at my drawing? I knew it would make her smile like it always did. Even though she was having more and more bad days when she couldn't eat with us at the table, she always liked my art.

"Mama?" I repeated. "Look!" I held up the paper. Her head rolled to the other side, away from me.

Anger roared up in me like it always did before I hit one of my brothers. But they weren't around making me mad. She was ignoring me. Mama didn't ignore me.

I tugged on her skeleton-like arm, trying to get her attention. "Mama!"

Dad came into the room, tugging me away from her. "Stop yanking on her, Hayes!" Dad whisper-yelled. "She doesn't feel good! You're hurting her!"

I held up my drawing to show him. "I wanted to give this to her!" I yelled back. "She's ignoring me!"

Mom coughed again, and Dad's face formed a hard line. "Can't you see it's not the time?" he asked in a mad whisper. "Let her sleep!"

I didn't whisper back. "FINE!" I yelled and ripped up the drawing. Dad's face fell and I ran from the room, Mama's coughs echoing behind me.

I JERKED up in a cold sweat, my heart sinking from my dream. That was the last time I'd seen her alive, and when I touched my cheeks, they were wet with tears, just like always.

I hadn't had that dream for over a decade. But now my clothes were soaked with perspiration and even my bedding felt damp.

I got out of bed, the air instantly chilling my skin and making me shake.

A glance at the alarm clock on my nightstand showed it was just past three o'clock. And I knew there would be no going back to sleep. There never was after that dream.

Ripping off my T-shirt, I walked to my bathroom, hoping a hot shower could soothe the crazy thrum of my heart, the unexpected reappearance of my darkest memory.

I'm not a little kid anymore, I reminded myself. Even though my childhood brain had thought I'd caused her death by not letting her rest, I knew better now. *I knew better now, damn it.*

My eyes stung as I angrily twisted the knob on my shower. While I waited for the water to heat up, I stripped the rest of my clothes. Kicking them aside, I stepped in. The hot water burned my skin, and I twisted the knob back. It instantly flashed cold.

I let out a string of curse words, angrily adjusting it to the right temperature. But even the release of swearing mixed with hot water and the rough scrape of a washcloth over my skin didn't soothe that uneasy feeling in my chest. It reminded me of that time we vacationed in California and there was an earthquake. At seventeen, I hadn't known when the ground would stop shaking—and each aftershock said maybe it never would.

Fully washed and giving up on feeling better, I got out of the shower and dressed in jeans and a T-shirt. Then I made some coffee, poured it in a couple travel mugs, and headed out to my truck.

Even in the dark, the drive to Madigan Ranch was

as familiar as the back of my hand. The dirt roads flew under my truck, the same as always. And the countryside out the window always changed in predictable ways. Yellow and brown in the winter. Light green in the spring. Lush in the summertime.

That made me feel a bit better as I steered my truck up the driveway to the home where my dad lived. Where I grew up. Where my mother died.

I blinked back the last thought and parked alongside the front yard. A glance at the dash told me it was half past four. Just like clockwork, Dad would be coming outside soon to start his morning chores.

When I was a kid and having those dreams, he would take me to do the morning chores with him, and it made me feel better. Maybe it was stupid to expect the same treatment now as a grown man, but deep down, I knew Dad wouldn't judge.

So I waited, listening to the radio and watching the slowly lightening horizon, almost in a trance until I heard the screen door squeak open. I glanced over to see Dad coming down the sidewalk, just like always. The dim morning light caught the extra lines on his face, marking the change in time. My heart stuttered as I rolled down my window.

"Everything okay?" Dad asked.

I held out the extra coffee for him. "Had another dream."

Dad frowned. "The one you used to have?"

I nodded.

He brought the coffee to his lips, taking a cautious sip, and then said, "Let's get the girls fed."

He got into my truck, and I drove up to the pens where the heifers and their calves were kept. These were the cows having their first calf, so he kept them closer to the house than the more seasoned mothers.

When we got to the feed truck, I turned off my truck and followed Dad into the older, bigger vehicle. The leather seats were faded and torn, patched with duct tape in some places. But with the turn of the key, the engine fired right to life, rumbling steadily under us and making dust rise from the dash.

We were silent while Dad drove under the grain bin with the chute and filled up the back with rations for the cattle. Then, he started driving alongside the cement feed bunks. He alternated between lifting out of his seat to twisting his head out the window, glancing in the mirror, and glancing ahead, all while maneuvering the massive steering wheel. I watched out the window past Dad, seeing the cattle hurry over and dip their noses into the mixture. The morning light caught each drip of snot and saliva building on their snouts. Every so often, their tongues would dart out to clear their nostrils of the feed.

They were so unbothered, unworried. It wasn't a bad life—you know, aside from becoming dinner eventually.

Dust rose in the air from their heavy steps toward the food, catching the rays coming down. It was a beautiful sight, and it made me feel better like it did all those years ago.

We were silent until the feeding was done, and then Dad got back into my truck so I could take him back to the house. But when we arrived, he didn't get out. Instead, he turned toward me and shrugged. "We gotta talk about it," he said.

I rolled my head toward him. "Like hell we do."

He gave me a look.

I sighed. I did get my stubborn streak somewhere.

"Your second date with Della is tonight," he pointed out, leaning back against the door.

I frowned, not wanting him to connect the dots I was trying so hard to avoid. How could Della, sunshine incarnate, be connected to the darkest days of my life?

Maybe it wasn't her; it was me. Who did I think I was, anyway? Trying to date a woman who believed in happily ever after when I had no idea how to be that kind of guy. I glanced out my window. "Should I make a run for it to avoid this chat? I can definitely outrun you."

When I glanced back, Dad had a half-amused smile on his lips. "Your brain is trying to protect you from getting hurt," he said gently, like I was a scared little calf.

Hell, maybe I was.

"But this is different," I protested, thinking out loud. "Della and I are just going to eat dinner." I wasn't sitting by her side, praying a picture could somehow cure cancer.

Dad's voice was rough over his words. "The only woman you've ever loved left before you could even say goodbye. Before you really knew what goodbye meant."

My eyes stung again, and I looked away from Dad, blinking hard. "I'm too old to be doing this now," I said, angry with myself. "I'm not a little kid anymore."

"You're never too old to be afraid," he said softly. "All these years later, and I'm afraid too."

I knew he was talking about Agatha. The woman at the diner we all knew he loved. But he wasn't giving her a chance with his heart. "You're happy by yourself," I reminded him. "Why take the risk?"

His lips wore a wry smile. "I am happy..." He looked down at his hands and then added, "But I could be happier."

I looked at him, saying what we were both thinking. "You could be sadder, too."

28

———

DELLA

I WALKED into my house after work Monday, hanging my keys on the hook by the door—it was a row of golden cats with their tales looping to form hooks. Seeing it brought a smile to my face. Swinging my gaze around my home, I noticed something out of place: a neat stack of boxes on my coffee table.

A pink sticky note stood out against the brown cardboard, and I went to get it, recognizing my mom's perfect cursive handwriting.

Let's fill these up on Wednesday. We need to get started, or it's going to be way harder come moving time. Love you. - Mom

The back of the note stuck to my fingers. I could practically hear her stress through the note, see the way her head would tilt with concern and a little furrow would form between her pale-brown eyebrows.

Sighing heavily and shoving the note in my pocket, I picked up the boxes and brought them to my guest room. I didn't want to think about moving right now. I wanted to think of my date with Hayes tonight. It was a simple meal at the diner, but my heart was soaring with so much hope.

Going to the spring festival with him had made the annual event infinitely more special than years before. Especially with that kiss in the rain. I found myself wanting to experience even more of Cottonwood Falls through his unique lens. How special would a trip to the diner be with him sitting across from me?

A small smile crossed my lips as I brushed my hands together to rid the dust from the boxes. Hayes would be here in an hour. But since I couldn't speed up the clock, I spent some time scrolling through unique sourdough recipes online. And then I went to my bathroom and touched up my makeup, hoping Hayes would like what he saw when he picked me up.

That cliché about women always being late was totally false, because I was ready ten minutes early, sitting on my couch with my phone on my lap. It was taking just about all my strength not to peer out the crack in the curtains to watch his truck drive up.

A message in the group chat with my girlfriends interrupted my scrolling, and I switched over, seeing more texts coming in.

Henrietta: Good luck on your date tonight, Del! :)

Maggie: Send us a pic of your 'fit! Bet you look gorgeous!

Larkin: Hoping you have a great time! Knox says Hayes is nervous! Hayes! Nervous! *mind blown emoji*

I smiled at that message, then held up the phone to snap a selfie. As the image was loading, a new message came through.

Liv: He better be nervous. He's going out with the best catch in Cottonwood Falls. <3

I smiled at the thread, my eyes threatening to water. I had the best friends ever. The thought of leaving them made a lump form in my throat. Swallowing it down, I tapped a response on the screen.

Della: Thank you all <3 I'll let you know how it goes!

I was about to click away to social media, but in a separate text thread, a new message came through.

Liv: Can you call me?

My eyebrows drew together as I tapped on her name to make the call. After a few rings, she answered, and I said, "Hey, everything okay?"

She seemed to hesitate for a moment. While I usually would have heard her children playing in the background, it was silent, like she'd stepped out just for this call.

"What?" I asked, growing more concerned. Was there something she wasn't telling me?

"I know you're excited to go out with Hayes..." She trailed off.

"But?" I prompted.

"He's a great uncle and a good friend. He'd do anything for his brothers." She hesitated again.

"What, Liv?" I pressed. "Just tell me."

"I'm just not sure he'll be a good boyfriend for you. I don't want you to get your hopes up."

My heart sank at her words. She knew Hayes better than I did. But at the same time, going out with him the other night was the best date I'd had in a long time. Something inside deflated. Was there something I was missing when it came to Hayes? I always thought what you saw was what you got when it came to him, but Liv's warning made me worry there was something darker hiding in the shadows.

"Just be careful, okay?" she asked.

I let out a soft sigh. "I will."

But as I hung up, I thought, I didn't want to be cautious. I wanted to go into something with hope, not with trepidation. Still, Liv's words were ringing in my ear when the doorbell rang. Just moments ago, I might have rushed to the front door to greet him.

Now I had to take a deep breath and try to shake my worry before going to answer the door. Hayes stood on my porch, holding a white giftbag. Pasting a smile on my face, I said, "Come in."

As he walked past me into my living room, I caught a hint of his cologne. It sent my ovaries standing to attention. Damn, he smelled *amazing*. "This is for you," he said, passing me the gift bag.

"Thank you," I said, taking it from him. I looked down at the tissue hiding its contents. "You really didn't have to get me anything."

"I wanted to. I got you flowers on Saturday, so I figured you didn't need new ones yet, and chocolates seemed cliché." He scratched the back of his neck shyly. It was *adorable*.

I smiled at him, saying, "You can never go wrong with chocolates. But I'm excited to see what this is. Can I open it?"

"Of course," he replied, an eager but anxious cast to his gaze.

I pulled back the layers of white tissue paper and chuckled at the bag's contents. "Really?" I looked up at him, finding a shit-eating grin on his face.

"It's something I knew you'd like," he teased.

I pulled out the cream-colored throw pillow and cackled at the design sublimated to the fabric. It was a perfect replica of his motorcycle helmet, middle finger sticker and all. He must have gotten Larkin to make the design for him because it looked like something she'd make on her Cricut.

"Way better than chocolates," I said, still laughing.

"Come on," he said. "Hope you're hungry."

"I sure am. But first..." I went to my couch, setting the throw pillow right in the middle. "Perfect."

We walked outside, and he drove us to Woody's. When we got out, I noticed the parking lot was packed, with barely a spare space for his truck. Hayes wasn't soft launching our relationship one bit—but I suppose that had already happened at the festival. Even my boss, Edna, had asked me about my "new beau" at work today.

"Ready?" Hayes asked.

I nodded, and he came around to get the door for me. He even held my hand on the way inside, not letting go until we were tucked safely into a booth. I settled into the pleather seat, taking in the familiar sights and sounds. Agatha expertly flitting around to serve everyone, grease sizzling in the fryers, silverware clinking on plates, conversation, laughter. It felt better than home.

I smiled as I glanced around at so many familiar faces, then froze. Farther down the diner, I saw Bennett sitting at the counter, his back to us.

I expected to feel guilty, being here with Hayes in front of Bennett, considering how things ended, but... I didn't. Even though I'd thought of Bennett as a "good guy," he'd walked away without waiting for an explanation. And I was happy to be here with Hayes.

If he noticed me looking at Bennett, he didn't show it. He passed me a menu across the table, and I looked it over, even though I could probably read it from memory. "Is it bad I always order the same thing?" I asked him.

He glanced over the menu at me. "Not if it tastes good every time."

I laughed. "It does. It really does."

"Then let's get two of them," he suggested with a smile. He tucked our menus back in the holder and said, "How was your day at work?"

I shrugged. "More or less the same." Except the part where Edna offered me yet another raise to stay, but I couldn't tell him that. Not yet. "You?"

He ran his fingers through his hair in a way that made me want to copy him. "Got to work on a European car today. Don't see many of those around here."

I quirked my lips into a teasing smile. "So you got to speak to a hubcap in French today?"

He snorted, like he was surprised at the joke. "Italian, actually."

"Have you seen 'Cars'? I watched it with Maya one time, and now I give all the cars I see voices."

He raised his eyebrows at me. "You're shitting me."

"No. Look at that hunk of junk out there." I pointed at an older truck with a smashed-in bumper and rust working its way over the hood. Making my voice sound old and haggard, I said, "These old wheels just don't turn like they used to... Stay off my asphalt!"

He chuckled low.

And then I pointed at a cute yellow electric car,

putting on a vocal fry. "I'm like, so happy summer is coming! I am *over* all this spring rain. It totally messes with my wax job."

Hayes laughed again. "My motorcycle probably sounds like Magic Mike, then? It's sexy as hell."

I bit my bottom lip, deciding to be brave. "In that case, I think it sounds like you."

29

HAYES

DELLA WAS FLIRTING WITH ME?

Mixed with her silliness and then the nervous glance of her eyes to the table, it was... so fucking cute.

Della didn't play games like a lot of women, doing the coordinated dance that brought two people from strangers to lovers sharing a bed. She was a friend, a comedian, a confidant, and a conspirator all at once.

It made me want to hide her away from the world and keep her all to myself. Take her away from this restaurant so I could kiss her in private, thoroughly. Until she was purring like the pretty vintage Ferrari I worked with earlier today.

But then Agatha interrupted, having the audacity to ask us for our orders. I glanced up at her, almost surprised we weren't alone, like the world outside of Della still existed.

We couldn't place them fast enough for my liking, but once it was all written in that little notepad, Agatha left us alone once again. I had Della all to myself, even in this crowd of people. She kept her phone in her purse, not texting and distracted like most people. Selfishly, I wanted those pretty green eyes, her attention, her thoughts, on me and me alone.

She was getting all of mine. We were in this crowded diner, smells and sounds coming at us from every direction. But I didn't notice any of them. Just her.

"Can I ask about your tattoos?" Della asked, surprising me.

"You just did," I countered.

She gave me an annoyed roll of her eyes, continuing with her question. "What do they mean?"

"Which one?" I replied, stretching out my arms.

She grazed her fingertips over the ink on the back of my knuckles.

I looked down at her fingers tracing the ink. "These mean I was tired of seeing scars from fights when I was young and dumb."

She froze for a moment, and I wondered what she thought of that. I wasn't ashamed of my past, but I wasn't proud of it either.

Instead of pressing for more information about my fights, her fingertips trailed up to the sunflower covering the back of my hand. "My mom's favorite flower." My voice was husky thinking of the dream from earlier that day.

My skin shivered as she moved her fingertips up my arm to a tattoo of a tiger stretching across my forearm. "This one?"

"I was drunk at a friend's tattoo shop."

She frowned. "It's against the law to tattoo inebriated people."

"Inebriated people with big mouths," I corrected with a smirk.

That rewarded me with a twitch of her lips, and she walked two fingers farther up my arm. She had to lean forward, her full chest brushing the table in the most distracting way. I had to draw my attention back to her fingers when she stopped at a tattoo of a bundle of daisies.

"Got that one when Maya was born."

Her fingers traveled toward some more flowers.

"When Knox married Larkin, I needed one for Emily and Jackson."

"I can't reach any farther," she pouted, dancing her fingers at the edge of my shirt sleeve.

So I took her hand in mine and kissed her fingertips. "There are plenty more to ask about later." Some of them had meaning, some of them held stories, and I found myself looking forward to sharing all of them with her. The experience was a mix of old and new—walking down memory lane but doing so with someone new.

And Della had so many opinions. She always made me think of things in a new way, even when she was arguing with me.

"What are you thinking?" she asked me.

I turned her hand over in mine, tracing the soft lines on her palm. "Thinking I should get your name tattooed on me." I dragged my free finger along the blank space from my ear to my forehead. "Here."

Her eyes widened in shock, and I burst out laughing.

"You suck," she said, swatting at my arm with her free hand. But her other hand was still resting in mine.

I smiled back at her—it was fun to get a rise out of her from time to time. "I'll get it somewhere better. Like my co—"

"Here's your food," Agatha cut in, an amused smile dancing in her eyes. As she slid our plates in front of us, she added, "You're about as much trouble as your dad."

I gave Agatha a salacious smirk. "Tell me more about this trouble."

"Hayes," Della said with a roll of her eyes. Even so, Agatha's cheeks were flushing red.

"Let me know when you need something—like a whoopin'," she retorted, walking away.

But I winked at Della. "I think I'll get the whoopin' from you."

Her laugh was deep and throaty. "You're incorrigible."

"Thank you," I replied, reaching for my sandwich. The smell of fried chicken lifted from the plate, and my mouth was already watering. I took a bite, and damn, she was right. "This is incredible."

"As always," she said with a smile over the half of the chicken-bacon-ranch sandwich she held in her hands.

"I think you've ruined me for all other sandwiches."

"That's what every girl wants to hear," she fired back, wiping a bit of ranch from her lips.

God, that had me turned on. Suddenly, I was thankful to be sitting at the table. I ran through a list of engine parts in my brain, and then, when I cooled down, continued the conversation.

"You never told me if you have any tattoos," I said.

She made a show of chewing for a long time, the apples of her cheeks tinging pink. "I didn't," she finally said.

I grinned wide. "You do have a tattoo."

She took another bite.

My smile grew. "It's a butterfly, isn't it?"

"Fuck you," she mumbled over her food.

"Where is it!?" I said, way too excited to see it. "Tell me it's on your lower back."

She glared at me.

"Your ankle?"

She rolled her eyes.

"Your wrist?" Although how could I have missed it?

I'd love to see some ink on that perfect porcelain skin of hers.

"I guess that's for me to know and..." Her words trailed off.

"And for me to find out." I bit my bottom lip, thinking of how I'd worship every inch of her until I found the design.

Her cheeks flushed again.

If she reacted so strongly to my words, how would she respond to my touch?

I closed my eyes again, hunching over. This woman would be the death of me.

Alternators.

Gasket.

Intake manifold.

"You okay over there?" Della asked.

I opened my eyes to find her curious stare. "I'm just fine," I managed.

She shrugged and took a bite of her sandwich. When she set it back down, she ran a napkin over her lips. "What's your middle name?" she asked.

My eyebrows rose. "Random."

"I can't date a guy and not know his middle name." She dragged a fry through ketchup.

My hands were stalled on the table. "But then you'll use it..."

"And?" she countered.

"And I don't like my middle name."

She shrugged. "Guess it's been nice knowing you."

Fuck. "Really?"

She giggled and ate her fry. "Come on, it can't be that bad."

I raised my eyebrows, shaking my head.

She leaned forward, both arms on the table. "Okay, you have me so curious that I will *never* stop asking. So save yourself the perpetual torment and my eventual sleuthing and tell me." She batted her eyelashes. "Please?"

Fuck. How could I turn her down? Especially when she had me smiling already. "It's..." I cringed. "Brain."

"What?" She stalled with a confused look, midway through picking up her sandwich. "Rayne?"

"No, it's Brain." I grimaced. "Like the organ."

Hearty giggles shook her chest. "Brain? *Why?*"

"Because my dad was in charge of filling out the birth certificate while watching my older brothers. He was supposed to write 'Brian', but he got distracted and mixed up the letters. Guess the nurse didn't notice. Thank fuck he spelled my first name right."

Still laughing, she said, "They couldn't fix it?"

"Mom thought it was a hoot, so they kept it."

Della's laughter grew even louder, and even my lips were twitching.

"I think I love your mom," she said, wiping tears from the corners of her eyes.

My smile softened to something liquid, like warmth spreading in my chest. I wasn't sure I believed in signs, but maybe this was one. The fact that my middle name and this story randomly came up while sitting in the diner the night after a terrible nightmare.

Maybe it was Mom saying everything was going to be okay.

God, I hoped so.

30

DELLA

THE CONVERSATION with Hayes was so enchanting, so *fun*, that I hardly noticed when Bennett walked past us, refusing to look in our direction.

But soon enough, the food on our plates was gone, and the milkshakes we ordered after, to extend our time together, were melting.

Agatha came by our table, picking up our straw wrappers. "Sorry, dolls, it's closing time. Want me to put these shakes in to-go cups for you?"

Surprised, I looked down at my watch. It was nearly nine o'clock. We'd been here talking for over two hours. "No, I don't need mine." I started scooting out of the booth to get up.

"Sorry, Ag, we'll square up and go," Hayes said, standing too.

She smiled at him. "Thanks, hon. See you another day."

He nodded kindly at her, and we walked to the front counter. Walking behind him, I was fascinated by the movement of his muscles under his T-shirt, the way ink trailed from under the collar and then disappeared again behind shaggy, dark blond hair.

When Agatha came to the register to check us out, I offered, "I'll pay for my half."

Hayes gave me an incredulous look. "Fuck no."

Agatha said, "Language. There are ladies present."

"Heck no," he clarified and then pulled out a credit card. And that was that.

A warm feeling spread in my chest. Hayes might not be the most polished man, but he took care of me like it was the most natural thing for him to do. And the fact that he wasn't polished made it even better. Like he was unwilling to or incapable of putting on a front. What you saw was what you got with him.

We walked out of the diner, and he said, "Care for a walk?"

I raised my eyebrows. He didn't look like the type of guy to go for a romantic, moonlit stroll.

But he said, "I know you know how to walk."

I laughed. "Sure, that sounds nice." The weather was mild, and there weren't too many bugs out since we weren't in the heat of summer. By the time we made it to the end of the block, I felt perfectly warm. Especially with his hand curled around mine.

This moment was simply perfect, but in the back of my mind, I had to wonder... why? Why me? Why now?

And since we were both too old to play games, since I was supposed to move in less than two months, I spoke up. "Hayes, I have a question, and I know it might sound strange, but I need to know."

He glanced over at me, casually sauntering beside me. "Shoot."

I chewed nervously on my lip, and he stilled, reaching up to tug it from between my teeth. "It drives me crazy when you do that." His thumb was still on my mouth, sending a shiver down my spine. "What's your question?" he asked, trailing his thumb across my lip and then along my jaw. At the tip of my chin, it fell away.

A swoop of disappointment went through me as I mourned his touch. My heart struggled to find its normal pace again. "My question..."

He nodded.

"Right..." I glanced toward the sidewalk because it felt too vulnerable to look at him while asking. "Why date me? I mean, really date me?"

Now his touch was back, a bent finger lifting my chin so I had to look at him. "Are you asking me why I'd want to go out with you?"

My cheeks heated under the intensity of his stare. "That, and... you've never been the kind to date before."

A conflicted look crossed his face that made my heart clench. I tried reminding myself that it was better to know the truth than live in ignorant bliss. Especially when I had life-altering decisions to make.

"It's simple," he said.

That was the last thing I'd expected to hear. "It is?"

He nodded, reaching up to sweep a curl behind my ear. Then he palmed my cheek—I was beginning to love his touch. He gave his caresses so generously. "My time with you is better than my time without you. So here we are."

His words, spoken so plainly, warmed my heart. "My time's better with you too," I admitted. "But what happens when I annoy you?"

With a grin, he retorted, "Who says you don't already?"

I gave him a light shove, laughing. "Seriously, though. Are you just here for the honeymoon period and then you're done when things get hard?" That sinking feeling returned as Liv's warning echoed through my mind. Maybe she was right. I was too old and respected myself too much to just be someone's good time.

A frown made a line form between his eyebrows, and he stepped closer. "My family annoys me, and I'm not getting rid of them... yet."

I laughed a bit. "I know it's too early to promise anything."

Hayes gave a quick shake of his head. "Everyone likes to put a timeline on things, but that's not me. If you're wanting to know where I'm coming from now, I respect that."

And just like that, he'd unwoven years of learned relationship "rules" that I tried to live by. *Don't be too clingy. Don't be too loud. Don't come on too strong.* He was letting me be me in a way I'd never been able to exist in a relationship before.

The thought had me all choked up, so I had to swallow down the lump in my throat before saying, "That means a lot." I took a breath and then pressed on my next question. "Why date now?"

He smiled gently and drew me under his arm, kissing my temple. "Because when it comes to you... I want to be the exception, not the rule."

My mind raced back to that night in his house, at the conversation we had. And my heart beat a little faster, because Hayes knew I didn't want regular. I wanted extraordinary... and he wanted to give it to me.

When he let go of me, we kept on walking the streets of Cottonwood Falls, everything looking a little brighter while walking next to him.

It was late when he brought me home, and we shared another kiss on the front porch. As he walked away, I hoped next time he would come inside.

31

HAYES

I LAY on a rolling creeper underneath my brother's cop car, working on it for my last job of the day since the other lifts were full. Knox waited on a nearby stool, drinking the last of the coffee from the lobby and shooting the shit with me.

We used to hang out a lot more, but now that he had a wife and children, the one-on-one visits happened less and less. A twinge of loss hit my gut at the thought. But I was happy for him, too—he was living the life he always wanted. "When does the sale go through on the land?" I asked him. He and Larkin were buying a plot outside of town to build a new home.

"Hopefully next Friday," he replied. "Do you have any idea how hard it is to get a loan?"

I rolled out from under the cruiser and gave him a side-eye.

"Oh yeah," he chuckled, blue eyes crinkling at the corners. "You got one to buy this place."

"And you wrote a character reference," I said. "Ironically."

"Hey, I was cleaned up by then," Knox protested. "And didn't Dad have to guarantee your loan after all that fuss?"

"He did," I confirmed. It was one of my life's greatest stressors, knowing if I failed at running a business, it would cost my dad the ranch—everything we'd ever known, really. I'd never stop being grateful for his support.

After letting out a heavy sigh, Knox said, "Date with Della tomorrow?"

My lips twitched into a grin of their own accord as I rolled back under the car. "Yeah."

"The third in what? Seven days? Damn."

The way he said it made my back stiffen a bit. I was glad my face was hidden under the car so he wouldn't see my expression. But still I said, "Do you have to sound so surprised?"

"I didn't mean it that way. It's just—I don't want you getting into something you don't want."

My eyebrows drew together, and I rolled out from under the car again and sat up, my back against the side of the car. "What are you talking about?"

Knox shifted uncomfortably in his seat, scratching at the back of his neck. If I wasn't waiting for his answer, it might have been comical, seeing him all dressed in his cop uniform and squirming. But as it was, a tight knot was forming in my chest. I didn't care what everyone in town thought of me, but my family knew me best.

"Spit it out," I said, wringing the shop towel in my hands.

He sighed heavily. "You've always enjoyed your independence. And Della, she's older by what? Ten years?"

I drew my eyebrows together. "Shit like that doesn't matter at our age."

"But it does," Knox replied. He spun the sleeve around his coffee cup. "Guys can have kids forever, but if that's something she wants, there's not a lot of time left for someone who isn't certain."

My stomach clenched at the thought, and I looked down at my grease-stained hands.

"I know Della—she's great. She's a dreamer. I'm worried that her dreams of romance are affecting your wishes for your life. I want you to have what you want, and you've always been vocal about wanting to be alone."

I gritted my teeth. "Can't a guy change his mind? Or am I forever stuck as the guy y'all see me as?"

Knox tilted his head, speaking gently. "It's a big change, you have to admit."

"It's a big change. But you know the cost of staying the same?"

He waited for my answer.

"Della."

Knox nodded solemnly. "I get it. I just don't want you to feel pressured into doing something you don't want. Just because all of us are settling down. Or because there's a time pressure on it for her."

"Thanks for looking out," I said finally, and then I put myself back under the car, thankful for something to do with my hands. Knox's comments and Della's questions from our date Monday night were weighing heavy on my mind.

I did like my life. I liked it even better with Della in it.

What else was there to decide?

32

———

DELLA

MY HOUSE WAS LOOKING BARER than usual as I got ready for my date with Hayes Friday night. When my parents came over for Wednesday night dinner, Mom insisted we started packing while we watched GBBO.

I'd protested at first, but when she asked, "Are you not moving?" I had to say I was.

Hayes and I had been on two dates. It was too early to change all my plans. Especially with everyone I loved and respected being so worried for me. Maybe it would be different if they were as excited about my relationship with Hayes as I was.

But my parents were busy pretending he didn't exist, and Liv's skepticism was clear even when she wasn't warning me about him. For some reason, I always assumed they would adore the person I wanted to be with. And I had no idea what to do now that they didn't.

With a sigh, I sat on my couch to wait for his arrival. Maybe all this stress about their opinions was moot.

It was too early to think about a forever type of love with Hayes—if that was even on the table with him. He'd never been the guy to take a chance on love before, and I had a hard time thinking he'd choose something long-term and monogamous with me when he'd spent most of his adult life with his pick of every other single woman in town.

And I didn't have time for something temporary. Not if I wanted a family.

All my spinning thoughts had me off-kilter when I heard the doorbell ring.

Hayes was here.

And tonight, we weren't staying in Cottonwood Falls —he was taking me to a dance hall in Roderdale. So I tried to focus on that, because I was excited to go dancing with him. After seeing his moves at the spring festival, I couldn't wait to have him spin me around the dance floor.

Maybe part of me thought it would be a good test too. If the dance hall was anything like I remembered, there would be plenty of pretty young women there dressed to the nines. If his eyes wandered, if his focus drifted, I'd have my answer on his priorities, no matter how disappointing it might be.

I zipped my phone into my purse and then hurried in my heeled boots to the door. My turquoise dress swayed around me as I walked, and my hair brushed over my shoulders, curly and wild.

I'd hoped to take his breath away, but when I opened the door, I nearly gasped. Instead of his usual distressed wardrobe, Hayes had on dark jeans, a black dress shirt unbuttoned to reveal the mural of tattoos across his chest. His sleeves were rolled halfway up his forearms, showing more of the inky designs there. His lip ring glinted under my porch light just like the glittering dance of trouble in his blue-green eyes.

But he looked just as mystified as I was. "Wow," he breathed. My cheeks felt hot under his gaze, and he made no act to hide the attraction he felt as he bit his bottom lip. "Stunning, Della," he rasped.

I smiled at the compliment and how genuine it seemed. "And look who stepped away from the GQ cover shoot to go dancing with little ol' me."

He shook his head as he circled his arms around my waist. "I can't wait." He drew his lips to mine and took my breath away with a heated kiss.

My thighs clenched, and I had half a mind to ask him to stay here and dance in my bedroom with our clothes off or some other cheesy pickup line. But just as I was about to drag him to my bedroom cavewoman style, he linked his fingers with mine and said, "Let's get going."

"Okay," I whispered begrudgingly, still coming out of my kiss-induced daze.

He led me out to his truck, our feet making soft scraping sounds over the sidewalk. It blended perfectly with the sounds of crickets filling the night air. I always loved this part of spring, when the nights came alive with the sounds of nature, even in our small town.

After helping me into his truck, he walked around to the driver's side, backed out of the driveway, and laced our fingers over the middle seat. We'd only been seeing each other for a week, and already we were falling into a rhythm.

He drew my hand to his lips. "I missed you."

I giggled. "We saw each other Monday."

"And now it's Friday. Such bullshit."

I laughed. "Don't worry. I'm sure my hunk of junk car will bring me back to your shop soon." I shook my head. "Maybe it's time to look for something new."

"Your car isn't a hunk of junk," he countered. "It's one of the more reliable brands."

I raised my eyebrows. "It's broken down twice in the last month, and it's still under a hundred thousand miles. I wouldn't call that reliable."

His jaw tensed for a moment, and I wondered what was behind it. "What?" I asked him.

"Nothing," he said too quickly, staring hard at the road.

"Hayes Brain Madigan," I warned.

He let out a heavy sigh, a smile threatening at the

corners of his mouth. If it was a little lighter in the car, I'd have sworn he was blushing. As it was, I was about eighty-five percent sure he was.

"So that night your car broke down before your date with Bennett..." he began.

"Yeah?" I asked. "Did you overcharge me? I swear, people always say you need to change your filters when you don't really."

"No, you need to change your filters," he said. But he hesitated again.

"Hayes! Tell me!" I pressed.

"I may or may not have... disconnected your car battery while you were working so you couldn't go on your date."

My. Jaw. Dropped.

"You made my car break down?"

He cringed. "I fixed it for free too. I haven't sent you the bill, if you haven't noticed."

I used my free arm to hit him. "Hayes! That's so messed up!" And kind of sweet, too, in a twisted sort of way... not that I was going to tell him that.

With a grimace, he said, "It wasn't one of my finer moments. But I never said I was smart. Actually, I'm kind of a dumbass sometimes. Like letting that fucker take you out when I knew damn well that I wanted to. I'm sorry I played games, Della. I promise I'm done with that."

Okay, at least he's moving in the right direction. My

heart warmed a bit, and I said, "You're fired as my mechanic."

"Like I'd let someone else touch your car," he growled.

"Maybe Ethan?" I teased, knowing how he felt about his coworker. "He's not as hot as the boss, but he'll do."

"Fuck off." He rolled his eyes.

"So romantic," I teased.

"I like to keep you guessing," he countered with a smirk.

I chuckled and then unbuckled so I could slide into the seat next to his. He draped his arm around me, and after buckling back up, I leaned my head on his shoulder.

Hayes wasn't a knight in shining armor.

He made mistakes. He wasn't always good at saying how he felt. He was rough around the edges and cussed more than my parents would ever approve of.

But against all odds... I was falling for him.

Would he catch me? Or was falling for the town's bad boy a terrible idea?

MUSIC MINGLED with the scent of alcohol and sweat as we made our way into the dance hall. My brothers and I used to come here when we were single to meet new women. But now, with Della on my arm, it was clear just how much had changed.

I wasn't interested in the buckle bunnies in cut-off denim and knee-high cowboy boots. I was obsessed with the curvy, proud, bubbly woman with a mane of red curls and a smile that had me doing stupid shit like making her car break down.

She was captivating.

Even against the noise and flashing lights, I couldn't look away. She grinned at the bartender and chatted with a waitress while we got drinks. She sang along to every song that played on the speakers, regardless of whether she knew the words. Her shoulders swayed, inspired by the beat but not in pace with it.

"You're staring," she said over the rim of her glass as we stood at a table near the dance floor.

"And?" I grinned at her before taking a drink of my whiskey.

She rewarded me with one of her smiles. Little lines formed at the corners of her eyes, and the strobe lights on the dance floor caught her perfect teeth save for a small chip on her canine.

I took another drink, even though no amount of liquor could compete with the buzz I got just from being near her. And still I wanted more. "Let's go dance."

She looked wistfully over the dance floor. "You should probably know I'm liable to step on your toes."

"You still wouldn't be close enough," I replied, feeling the low ache of *want* I experienced every time we were together.

Her cheeks heated and she failed at fighting a pleased smile. "Is that so?"

I nodded, my hands aching to hold her. To feel the soft curves of her body. "Let me prove it to you." I took the drink from her hand, setting it on the table. A new, bouncy song was playing over the speakers, something that reminded me of Della. I linked my fingers with hers, leading us toward the dance floor opening.

"But you shouldn't leave a drink unattended!" she argued, ever worried about the risks while my thoughts were already on spinning her around.

"I'll get you a new one," I said, "Come on!"

Laughing, she followed along, and when we reached the parquet flooring where all the couples were dancing, I pulled her to me.

She was right; she didn't have rhythm, but that didn't matter with a good leader. I used my grip on her hand and her waist to guide her along as she made little exclamations of joy and completely butchered the words to the song.

I loved having her this close, feeling the brush of her chest over mine, being enveloped by her sweet perfume.

Sweat shimmered on her forehead by the time the closing chords played over the speakers, transitioning to a slow song. Della made to move off the dance floor, but I shook my head, taking her even closer.

My fingers intertwined over her lower back, and I leaned my temple against hers. "Let me dance with my girl a little longer," I breathed.

Her cheek lifted against mine, indicating her smile. And she wound her hands around my shoulders, tangling her fingers in my hair as I guided her to the song's slow, tender notes. The soft swell of her chest pressed against my front, and her toes bumped into mine as we slowly twisted our way around the floor in the best dance of my life.

An overwhelming feeling of *rightness* rose over me, and I kissed her temple. Her curls brushed against my cheek. I never wanted to let her go. Never wanted to be farther apart than this.

It was like holding my world in my arms. And in that moment, I knew I was gone.

I wasn't my own anymore.

I didn't fucking care about spare bedrooms or pink throw pillows or plushy rugs on the bathroom floor.

I cared about this. About *her*.

About the way she scratched her fingertips over the back of my neck and sighed against me like she didn't want anything more.

It was the happiest I'd ever felt.

And I never knew I could feel this way with a woman.

And I'd never been more scared. Knox had warned me she didn't have time to waste when it came to relationships.

What if she didn't feel the same way about me?

What if she only saw me as the carefree bachelor and not as a partner, an equal?

What if I was falling for her, only for her to eventually leave me?

34
____

DELLA

ONE SLOW DANCE was all it took for my heart to pound out of my chest, to feel like I couldn't get close enough to Hayes Madigan. To feel like I needed *more* of him.

So when the song faded into the next, I looked up at him and said, "Take me home?"

Like he could read my thoughts, he swallowed, making his Adam's apple move under tatted skin. And then he nodded, linking his hand with mine.

Forget the drinks.

Forget the dancing.

I wanted Hayes Madigan. All of him.

We walked out into the cool evening air, the breeze pricking at my sweat-dampened skin. I released his hand to lift my hair off the back of my neck, and his eyes followed like he was just as captivated by me.

Once we reached the parking lot, I let my hair fall

again. Because even though the breeze helped with my body temperature, my skin was still sizzling with the heat of desire. And I couldn't hold myself back when he opened the truck door on my side.

Instead of sitting on the bench seat, I reached up and kissed him, holding on to his neck with one hand and fisting my other in his shirt.

His skin was hot under my touch, the sweat of dancing still lingering at the nape of his neck, just like mine. It made me think of what was to come and turned me on that much more. He wound his hands around my waist, sliding them over the swell of my ass like the handfuls he had weren't nearly enough. Using his knee, he parted my legs so I could straddle his thigh, and thank God, because the pressure against me felt just as intense as his kiss.

With a tug of my hair, he had my head falling back so he could nip and kiss along my neck.

I shivered at his touch, overcome with the need to have him closer still.

But he broke apart from my neck and growled into my ear, "Let me get you home before I fuck you right here."

My skin hummed, my thighs clenched, and I nodded quickly. Anything to get closer to that moment. To express this overwhelmed emotion humming through my chest. I got into the truck, scooting to the middle because I didn't want to be apart from him, and then he got in.

And I couldn't help myself. I kissed him again, running my hands over his thigh, up to his hard length straining against denim. Thirty minutes home was too far. "I can't wait that long," I gasped against his ear.

His eyes glittered in the darkness, and the light shined off his teeth as he said, "I can help with that."

My heart skittered along. "You can?"

"Give me a second." He put the truck in drive and curled his hand around my bare thigh under the skirt of my dress. As he pulled onto the road, he stroked his thumb over my inner thigh. City lights passed around us, blurring at the edges of my vision, and I clutched his arm. I'd never been this turned on in my life. And we hadn't done anything more than kiss.

I leaned over, nipping his shoulder. "Hayes," I whined.

"Almost there, baby."

We reached a road on the outskirts of town where he pulled off and killed the lights on his truck. Without the engine rumbling underneath us, my skin was still thrumming. I could feel myself already wet for him. I wanted to feel him inside me, to sate this aching need in my core.

But he only said, "Lie down."

Everything in me wanted to obey.

I lay back on the seat, hyperaware of my dress falling over my thighs, showing the lace of my lingerie worn especially for him, for this night.

"Fucking beautiful," he said softly, looking right at my feminine parts.

Usually, I was shy to leave myself on display like this, but Hayes never made me doubt myself. He left no room for interpretation when it came to his feelings. Within seconds, he had my knees hooked over his shoulders, my dress falling to my stomach.

Using his teeth, he dragged my panties aside and ran his tongue along my slit while his hands gripped my sides.

I let out a whimper. It already felt so good.

A hazy look in his eyes, he reached up, parting my folds so he could place his tongue on my clit, and I moaned loudly. I clenched my legs on his shoulders to support my weight and reached up to lick my fingers and tease my nipples under my dress, imagining his mouth could be two places at once.

He continued licking, sucking, and even lightly biting me, and just when I felt like I was going to fall over the edge and come apart, he pulled back, licking my entrance.

"Hayes," I whimpered. I'd never come with any of my past boyfriends without the help of a vibrator, but he was pushing me to the edge with just his mouth.

"It'll feel better the longer you wait," he promised, teasing a finger around my entrance.

I moaned. "How could it feel better than this?"

"Just wait." I felt him smile against my pussy before continuing to please me. The rhythm was savoring, punishing, teasing, and torturing until I couldn't hold back anymore. I reached up, winding my fingers through his hair and holding him in place.

"Make me come," I begged.

At that, he stopped teasing me with his fingers and slid them inside me. A feral sound came through my lips, driven purely by pleasure. And then he curled his fingers toward himself to hit my G-spot while his tongue continued the most amazing oral of my life. Now I wasn't holding his head in place; I was bucking against him, taking everything he was willing to give me.

Because I was falling apart under his touch. Shattering around his fingers and onto his mouth. And even when the waves of my orgasm slowed, he took his time tasting my release.

My breaths were still coming in gasps when he pulled back and gently lowered my hips to the seat, my exposed skin extra sensitive to the rough seat cover.

My eyes had adjusted to the dark, and I watched as he drew his fingers to his lips and sucked, not wasting a drop of *me*.

I shuddered.

Hayes Fucking Madigan.

35

HAYES

DELLA LOLLED against me in the passenger seat, thoroughly sated. And as I drove, I could smell her arousal on my hand. It kept my cock painfully hard and aching for release. She wanted me to take her right there in the truck, but Della was a romantic who deserved more.

Besides, how could any release compare to feeling her fall apart under my tongue? The way she'd called out my name? Held at my hair and bucked against my face, showing just how much she liked how I made her feel?

I kept my arm wrapped around her shoulders, and she reached up to hold my hand, as if being held in my arms wasn't even close enough for her.

I'd thought I'd had a heart before. But I'd been wrong. Now I could feel it—the need it had to hold Della close. How buoyed it felt at her smile. The fear it held of her walking away. It all radiated from the fist-sized organ in my chest I used to completely ignore. Now I knew it had been waiting for this moment. For her.

I was gone for her, no chance of saving me now.

My headlights panned over her house, and a deep sense of loss came over me at the thought of going to my own place. Of spending the night somewhere different from her. Nevertheless, I turned off the car and walked her to her front porch. She reached for the door to lead us inside, but I halted. "Wait," I managed.

I couldn't believe I was doing this.

She turned, eyebrows knitting in confusion. "Let's talk inside."

But I shook my head, tugging her back to me, holding her in my arms even though I knew it wasn't enough. "I can't come in."

Now her head reared back. "Excuse me?"

Her indignation had me smiling despite myself. "What happened earlier, I didn't do that to get anything in return."

She opened her mouth to argue, but I captured her lips in a kiss. One that made my pulse speed and my cock strain against my pants. When we broke apart, breathless, I said, "When you lie down tonight, I don't want there to be a doubt in your mind. I'm here for *you*. Not what I can get from you."

Her lips tipped into a defeated smile. "You're going to be the death of me."

"Funny, I was thinking the same thing." I kissed the tip of her nose. "When can I see you again?"

"Tonight?"

I chuckled.

"Tomorrow?" she suggested. "I don't have any plans."

"Good, because I have an idea." I kissed her again quickly because if I lingered any longer, no amount of my fading self-control could keep me from going inside with her. "I'll pick you up around seven?"

"At night?" she asked.

I shook my head. "AM."

She tilted her head to the side, making her hair fall. "You're one of those people, aren't you?"

I settled my hands on her waist. "What people?"

She made a sour face. "A morning person."

That had me chuckling. "That's not a good thing?"

"The only thing mornings are good for is cuddles and pancakes."

I smiled. "Then I'll be here at seven with both."

What Della wanted, she would get.

She smiled up at me. "See you then."

I didn't want to leave, so I walked backward, drinking in my beautiful girl standing under her porch light. Her hair was wild from earlier, and her cheeks still had that post-orgasm glow.

"Hayes Madigan," she said, a hint of awe in her voice. Like she didn't know she was the amazing one.

"Della Dwyer," I called before getting in my truck and driving away.

I smiled to myself as I pulled out of the driveway, feeling like I'd found something I hadn't even known I was looking for. And judging by Della's smile, maybe I wasn't as bad at relationships as I'd initially thought.

Even so, a sinking feeling competed with that sense of *rightness* the closer I got to home.

I pulled into the driveway, my gray stucco house looking so fucking cold compared to the home I'd just left. My chest tightened, knowing I'd be going inside by myself.

Sighing, I got out of my truck and walked through the front door, looking around. The dark leather couches felt cold. The glass table staunchly sharp.

I walked back to my bedroom.

Too fucking empty.

And then a new worry crossed my mind. If I had a flashback dream after planning a date with Della, what would getting even closer to her do?

The thought kept me away from my bed, taking my time to shower, to get dressed for bed, to plan the following morning and set my alarm to make sure I'd be at her place when I said I would.

But finally, I couldn't avoid my bed anymore.

I lay down under the covers, heaving a sigh. Of worry, stress, of not wanting to have a bad night of sleep when the day had been so fucking perfect.

But soon my thoughts of Della turned to my mom.

Most of my memories of her were so fuzzy. I couldn't really remember her when she was healthy. But I did remember one thing. A song she used to sing.

Rolling over, I grabbed my phone from the side table and went to my music player, finding the song.

"Red River Valley."

I put it on repeat and closed my eyes.

When I woke up, a smile touched my lips.

I hadn't dreamed at all.

36

DELLA

I TAKE back everything I said about no one waiting on me. Because when the doorbell rang at seven in the morning, I was just barely getting out of the shower.

Wrapping a towel around me, I got out my phone and dialed Hayes's number.

A few rings later, an amused voice came over the phone. "Did I wake you?"

I rolled my eyes. "No, but I'm not ready yet. You can come in and wait in my living room. There's coffee brewing in the kitchen too."

"You sure? I can wait outside," he said.

"Don't be silly," I replied. "I'll be out in five."

"I don't know that anyone has ever described me as silly," he replied, and I heard the doorknob turning in the background.

I had half a mind to drop the towel and strut to the living room, demanding to finish what we'd started the night before. But then Hayes said, "Take your time. I'll have breakfast ready out here when you are."

Smiling to myself, I said, "Thank you."

"Of course."

We hung up, and I set my phone back down on the vanity, smiling at myself in the foggy mirror. For the first time in a relationship, I felt like I was with someone who truly listened. All it took was me saying I liked pancakes in the morning, and here he was with pancakes. I said helmets were safe, and I had a smarmy helmet pillow on my couch.

Relationships were a give and take, and Hayes seemed so much more focused on the giving part.

Eager to see him—and the breakfast he brought—I went through a quick morning routine, twisting my curls into a knot atop my head, putting on tinted sunscreen and mascara, and dressing casually in jeans and a T-shirt I'd gotten from donating in a blood drive.

When I came out of the bathroom, I could smell a mix of coffee and syrup, and my mouth watered. Then I rounded the corner and found Hayes setting the table for us.

A smile tilted my lips. Something about seeing him in my kitchen just felt right. "Hello, trouble," I practically purred.

He glanced over his shoulder at me, blond hair falling across his forehead, and his smile could have competed with a sunrise. "Della." The way he said my name had my heart turning to liquid gold.

He came to me, wrapping an arm around my waist and kissing me, the taste of coffee on his tongue. When we pulled apart, he nipped his nose over mine. "Let's eat before it gets cold."

Begrudgingly, I agreed.

There were two plates on the table with pancakes, bacon, and eggs, along with a bottle of syrup, two cups of steaming coffee, and silverware. "Hope you didn't mind me going through your cabinets," he said. "Thought you'd like this better than Styrofoam."

I nodded, feeling seen again. "Thank you."

We both sat at the table, and I took a bite of pancake, immediately recognizing them as coming from Woody's Diner. "So good," I said.

He smiled. "Just missing the cuddles."

With a chuckle, I said, "Guess you can't have it all."

But then he scooted his chair closer to mine so our shoulders brushed.

My heart warmed again, and I dropped my head to his shoulder for a moment. "Perfect."

He kissed the top of my head, completing the moment, and then we went back to eating our breakfast.

"So what's on the agenda?" I asked. "You never said last night."

"I didn't, did I?" He shrugged, then drew a bite of pancake to his mouth.

I hit his shoulder, and he pretended to be wounded.

"Tell me," I said with a laugh.

"It's something I think we'll both enjoy," he finally replied.

Realizing he was just as stubborn as me, I gave up, eating my breakfast and sipping coffee instead. It felt nice to have him in my kitchen, seeing him first thing in the morning. It felt right, somehow.

"Did you sleep okay?" he asked.

I nodded. "Is it lame to say my bed felt lonely without you?"

He shook his head. "Not when I was thinking the same damn thing."

The answer made me chuckle, and then I took my last bite of breakfast, feeling full. I made to get up and clear my spot, but Hayes said, "Let me." He took my plate and his, clearing them in the trash and then hand-washing them in the sink and putting them in the strainer. I stared at him, so impressed.

Was he naturally this thoughtful? Or was this him putting his best foot forward?

I wish I had more time to know. More time to decide before choosing a job and a move that would change my life forever.

"Ready?" Hayes asked, drawing me from my thoughts.

I took a last sip of my coffee and nodded.

We walked out to his truck, and as he drove, I watched our surroundings curiously, looking for clues as to where we were going. But then he pulled out onto the highway leading away from Cottonwood Falls, and I really had no idea.

"We're going to another town?" I asked.

"Not exactly..." We were a couple miles from town when he pulled onto a dirt road. "So there was this older woman who wanted her late husband's car looked after, even though she couldn't drive it. It was sentimental. So I went out there a couple times a month to turn it on, drive it around a bit, and make sure it stayed in good condition."

I leaned my head against Hayes's shoulder, thinking of him making time for a sweet older lady and a car that mattered so much to her. "That's really nice of you."

He squeezed my shoulder a bit. "She passed away a few weeks ago."

My heart constricted. "Hayes... I'm so sorry."

"Me too. But she had been telling me for months she was ready whenever God was. She wanted to see her Herbert again."

The thought of them being reunited had tears pricking at my eyes. That was the love I wanted—one that transcended earthly responsibilities and hindrances. One that would last forever. "You're going to make me cry."

His soft chuckle wasn't derisive, but appreciative. "There's a shoulder here if you want."

I smiled, leaning into him. "Please tell me we're not going to a funeral."

He laughed. "Let me finish my story, woman."

I shook my head at him calling me woman. But he continued, "Her son lives in Dallas, and he was so thankful for what I was doing, he said I could come to the estate sale before they opened it to the public. And I thought you might enjoy it too."

I sat up straight, staring at him in surprise. "You're taking me to an estate sale?"

He nodded, glancing my way. "You like antiquing and thrifting, right?"

An excited little hum went through my veins. "I don't like it. I *love* it."

He grinned, turning off the dirt road toward a beautiful, well-kept country home.

37

HAYES

SEEING Della's face light up at the prospect of an estate sale made the whole trip worth it. We got out of the car and walked into the house where Hudson told me he and the estate sale company would be setting up.

It was strange, seeing the perfectly kept home arranged with all of Mrs. Walker's items on display for sale. As we walked through the door, Hudson came around the corner from the living room, limping a little with each step. "Hayes, good to see you." Then he smiled at Della. "This must be Della."

I nodded, and Della extended her hand. "I'm so sorry for your loss."

Hudson responded with a wry smile. "She lived a good life, you know? I'm just happy she's with Dad again."

Della held on to my hand a little tighter at that.

"So as you can see, we have the house set up with

everything." He gestured around. "And then if you go outside, the Quonset has most of the machinery. There's something out there I think you might like." He gave me a wink.

And then a yipping sounded, followed by the sound of skittering claws over linoleum.

Hudson groaned while Della got down on her hands and knees. "Who's this little guy?" she asked, petting the overly excited puppy. It looked like a little white poodle with curly hair and floppy ears.

"A stray my daughter picked up," Hudson explained. "She found him wandering the streets near her apartment, and of course she can't keep him. Said I'd hold on to him until we found him a good home." Hudson raised his eyebrows expectedly. "Interested?"

"Fuck no," I said at the same time Della said, "He's so cute..."

I could see the war raging in her features. It was like there was an angel on her shoulder screaming PUPPY and a devil on the other saying BAD IDEA.

"Let's go look around," I said, hoping to spare her.

"Okay," she said, pushing up from the ground. The puppy danced around her feet.

"What's his name?" Della asked.

Hudson said, "I've been calling him 'We're Not Keeping You' so my wife wouldn't get any ideas."

Della laughed, the sound warming me just as much as her fingers twining with mine. "Should we look around outside first?"

"Sure," I said.

We left the little puppy inside, going out the back door and walking across the gravel path to the Quonset hut, a big metal building with a garage door leading inside. There was everything inside, from tractors to mowers and a couple cars that could make cool project pieces. Della asked questions about them, seeming interested just because I cared about it.

Most women didn't bother getting to know me beyond what I could do for them. Not that it ever bothered me before, but now I was grateful to share this piece of me with her. There was an old dirt bike toward the back that would be fun to restore, and I made a mental note to ask Hudson about it later.

Then we went inside, wandering the room. I wasn't much of a knickknack guy, but I watched Della, seeing what caught her eye. She flitted about the room while We're Not Keeping You trailed at her feet and eventually found his way into her arms as she browsed every item. His fluffy white head lolled in the crook of her elbow while his big doe-brown eyes slowly blinked shut.

I smiled at the two of them, shaking my head. Was I about to get a dog?

Hell, I'd get a slug if it made her smile like that.

As we browsed the room, Della pointed out things for me to carry. A lamp with a stained-glass shade. A crock she said would be great for holding her sourdough starter. She seemed thrilled with each piece.

"Ready to go?" she asked. "I'm getting a little hungry."

I nodded, leading the way back to the living room, where Hudson was sitting, flipping through an old photo album. At the muted sound of our footsteps on plush green carpet, he looked up. "Find any goodies?"

"So many," Della said with a smile. "Your parents had excellent taste."

The wrinkles around Hudson's eyes crinkled. "Looks like you found a friend, too." He gestured at the dog in her arms.

"Hope you don't mind me hogging him all morning," she said, a little guilty expression on her face. Then she glanced down at the sleepy puppy with a dejected look. "It's going to be hard to say goodbye."

Hudson pushed up from the chair, walking over to the cash register set up on a card table. "You can have him for free with all this stuff you found."

"Oh, I don't know..." Della said, looking down at him. "I'm not sure I have the time for him. I would hate to leave him at home all day while I'm working."

"I'll take him," I said.

Both Della and Hudson gaped at me.

"What?" Della said.

I shrugged. "He could hang out with me at work. I'm sure the customers would love him too. And training him would be a good part-time job for Maya if she's up for it." It was making more and more sense by the second.

While Hudson totaled up all the items, Della leaned closer to me. "Are you sure about this? You really don't have to for my sake."

My eyebrows drew together. "Why else would I do it?"

That earned me an exasperated smile. "Hayes Madigan," she whispered.

I leaned in and kissed her temple. "Della Dwyer."

38

DELLA

AS WE DROVE down the road, I looked down at the little white fluffball in my arms, contented to just be scratched behind his ears. I was in *love*. And not just with the dog.

I glanced over at Hayes, one arm on the steering wheel, forearm muscles forming a delicious pattern of lines and ridges. And I couldn't believe it. He'd gotten me a dog just because I wanted one. Committed to caring for it when I couldn't.

And it had been so *easy* for him to do something just to make me smile.

Without glancing my way, Hayes said, "You're staring."

I chuckled softly, looking back at the dog and shaking my head. "You're just different is all."

"What do you mean?" he asked, lifting his chin.

I shook my head, looking down at our new puppy.

"Other guys I've dated, it felt like it was a fight to get what I wanted." I thought of my ex from a few years prior and how when I mentioned wanting a pet to share between us, he'd acted like my simple desire was such a *nuisance* to him, even though he worked from home.

"Kyle, right?"

I was surprised he knew or even remembered the name of my ex, but then again, we did live in a small town. "Yeah," I finally said, stroking the puppy's back. "He nearly lost his mind when I told him I wanted a kitten. And asking for a marriage with children was the end of us..."

Hayes's arm stiffened, and my stomach clenched. "Sorry," I rushed out. "I didn't mean to throw the kid conversation out there. I know it's still early."

But instead of brushing me off or changing the topic, Hayes flicked his blinker on and then turned off the dirt road, pulling along a level side of a ditch. "It's important to you, it's important to me."

The noon sun streamed in through the windows and filtered through the dust slowly drifting away from his truck. It was just the two of us, out here in the country, surrounded by miles of barbed wire fences and lightly green fields. But we were hardly alone, with the puppy and such a heavy conversation in the pickup cab with us.

I looked over at him, nervous, knowing this conversation was what ended things in my last relationship. I wasn't ready to say goodbye to Hayes. "We really don't have to do this right now."

Concern knitted his eyebrows, and he pulled the puppy from my lap, setting it on the floorboards. It curled up on my feet, letting out an annoyed sigh.

Then he took my hands and said, "Look, Della, I know I'm new to this dating thing, but I'm not dumb."

My chest tightened. "I didn't mean to say you are."

"I know," he confirmed, stroking the back of my hand with his thumb. "I also know we can't avoid the conversation either. We can put if off if you want, but I don't like it hanging over our heads."

His gaze was so intense, I had to look down for a moment, focusing on the puppy laying contentedly at my feet. His white fur was sure to have a coat of dust soon, but the thought just made me smile, if only for a moment.

When I looked up at Hayes, I had to take a shaky breath. Because I cared about him. I didn't want this to end. But he was right... We needed to talk about it.

Fear flooding through my system, I tried to stay strong while voicing what I really wanted, what I'd held out for all these years. "I do want children. At least one, but probably two or three if my partner's up for more."

The seconds before his response played out like hours. My heart fluttered, a jolt of pain marking each beat as I braced myself for Hayes's rejection.

He was the town playboy.

The rolling stone that gathered no moss.

The one who never dated, much less fell in love. How could a family be in the cards?

But there was nothing but truth in his eyes when he said, "I've never thought of having kids, until I met you."

The hope blossoming in my chest was nearly as painful as the fear.

"I don't want to be a dad right this second, but if this thing between us keeps going, I'm willing to see what that would look like. I'm just..." His throat seemed to close around his words, and he looked down for a second, gathering himself.

Then he looked up at me again, fear shining in his eyes for the first time. "My mom died when I was young. I know we can't control things like that, but if we move forward in our relationship, having a plan in place for our kids... I think that would really help."

Seeing the vulnerability in his features, the grief in his voice, it nearly undid me. He didn't share this with everyone, but he was letting me in. I shifted in the seat so I could hug him, waking the puppy again. Hayes held on to me like he needed me, like I was a rock for him too.

"Of course we could do that," I said softly into his shoulder.

He held on tighter, taking a steadying breath. "Thank you."

I smiled against him, overcome with gratitude. All these years, I'd seen the same side of Hayes everyone else did, but now I knew better. And I felt so lucky that he chose to let me in, that he saw something in me too.

The puppy whined at my feet, and Hayes pulled back, giving him a weak smile. "Guess we better get some supplies for the little guy."

I nodded. "I'm so excited. He'd look so cute in a little sweater."

Hayes clapped his hand over his forehead and dragged it down. "You are not putting a sweater on that dog."

My eyebrows rose. "Watch me."

His smile was chagrined, and he leaned down to speak to the dog. "I'll do my best, but you gotta know... she's stubborn."

I shoved his shoulder, laughing. "You should also know that Hayes is frequently wrong."

Hayes snorted and put the truck into drive, and we headed toward town, discussing names for the puppy, feeling closer than ever.

But my job still hung over my head. I was running out of time to make a decision, and I didn't want to choose wrong.

39

HAYES

MY CHEEKS WERE hot as we pulled up to my dad's house, Della and the fluffball, Chopper, sitting in the passenger seat in... matching T-shirts. The woman was a wizard because she had me in a matching shirt, too.

It made her smile too much to say no.

Thank God Dad had just invited Della and me over for dinner, because if my brothers saw this, I'd *never* hear the end of it.

Della squeezed my hand and said, "Nervous for me to meet your dad?"

"No, I'm nervous for him to see me in this shirt," I retorted, gesturing at the light blue tee that matched Chopper's. "And he already knows you."

Della shook her head. "He knows me as Della, a family friend and insurance agent. Not as Della, Hayes's girlfriend."

My lips quirked at the sound of that. "Girlfriend?"

Her cheeks flushed in the cutest way, making her freckles fade amongst all the red. "Sorry, I didn't mean—"

"Don't apologize," I said, turning to her. "I like the sound of that."

She smiled. "So I should call you boyfriend?"

"Call me anything you want," I replied, kissing her cheek. "I'm yours."

She smiled sweetly. "Aw, I like sentimental Hayes."

Now my cheeks were getting hot again. "Don't tell anyone. I've got a reputation to maintain."

She scooped Chopper in her arms, reaching for her door. "I think the shirt already took care of that." She laughed wickedly, and I reached to tickle her side, but she escaped, running toward the front door of the house as I chased her.

Damn, when did she get so fast?

"I'm around here!" Dad called from the patio on the side of the house.

Della let out a peal of laughter and darted around the house with the dog. "Hey, Gray!"

I caught up just in time to see Dad grinning at her and waving his spatula. Then his eyes slid over to me, and he snorted out a laugh.

"Dad!" I protested.

But he shook his head and said, "Who's the little guy?"

Della waved his little white paw. "This is Chopper."

Dad's eyes crinkled with his smile as he leaned in

and scratched the puppy's neck. "He's so cute. Why give him such a tough name?"

I said, "So the other dogs don't bully him for his shirt."

Della gave me a look while my dad snorted with laughter. That was the agreement—I picked the name and she picked his outfits, and by extension, *our* outfits.

Della said, "Let me test that theory and introduce him to your dog, Gray."

She took him out to the yard, gently getting the puppy acquainted with dad's older dog. When she was far enough away, I looked to Dad and said, "Don't say it."

He flipped the steaks on the grill and then shut the lid. "Say what?"

I gave him a look. But he smiled gently, looking between me and my woman, sitting in the yard with the two dogs.

He clapped my shoulder and said, "I was going to say that I've never seen you so happy."

I smiled at that because despite the stupid shirt, I was happy in a way I'd never thought I could be or even thought to hope for. I didn't know this kind of happiness existed before I gave in to my feelings for Della.

"I am happy," I said. "She's the one."

Dad nodded, a glistening smile on his lips. "I see it in your eyes."

My throat felt tight as I nodded. But I was also

terrified. She held my heart, my happiness, in her hands. Something I'd never given another person. And I somehow had to trust that she wouldn't let me go. Wouldn't look at me with all my flaws and my past and decide she deserved better or wanted different.

"How do you walk around every day with your heart outside your chest?" I asked Dad.

He offered a wry smile. "I don't think you get a choice not to."

Della pressed up from the ground, leaving Chopper and Dad's dog playing an admittedly cute game of tug-of-war. She came up to me smiling and said, "They'll be BFFs soon."

Dad chuckled, saying, "I'm surprised the old boy is playing along. He's a crotchety old bastard."

"Chopper has special powers. He even warmed this guy's iron will." She patted my chest, and I easily slipped my arm around her waist. It felt as natural as breathing.

"It wasn't fair," I muttered. "Not with the both of you giving me puppy-dog eyes."

Dad checked the steaks again and determined it was time for us to eat. We spent the rest of the evening sitting on the patio, eating, drinking, and chatting. It didn't feel like bringing a girlfriend home—it felt like spending an evening with family.

In that moment I realized that Della was becoming family to me, our lives fitting together like the gears of a newly built engine, one we had to custom make to be just right for the two of us.

When she started yawning, we left Dad's place, and she insisted that we get Chopper set up at my house.

I wanted her to stay at my place, wanted her in my bed, but I also cherished this time of getting to know her without sex. And that's when it hit me, the reason I'd been holding back. Yes, I wanted to take things slow, but it was more than that.

I didn't want to have sex with Della. I wanted to make love.

I had to get the courage to tell her how I felt first.

Because knowing how I felt and saying it out loud were two completely different things. Especially when I didn't know if Della felt the same way about me. Or if all this trust I was placing in her would be the end of me.

40

———

DELLA

MY PARENTS MADE their monthly run to the bulk purchase store in Dallas the next day, and I always tagged along to pick up things like toilet paper and the protein bars I liked to keep stocked at my desk.

But I was thinking about Hayes all day, my mind consumed with thoughts of him and our day together. It felt like each time we were together, we got closer, and all I was seeing on the road ahead with him were green flags.

When I got home that night, I texted him and we made plans to go out to dinner Monday evening after I got off work.

When I walked into the office Monday morning, I was already looking forward to it, glancing at the clock and wishing it was five.

Edna was already inside at her desk, so I walked over and said, "Good morning, sunshine."

She smiled up at me. "How was your weekend?"

I let out a happy sigh. "The best. How about you?"

Her response was a shrug as she took off her glasses and rubbed at the bridge of her nose. "It would be better if I didn't have to find a replacement for my right-hand woman. But I think I finally have a job description written up. Will you read it over if I email it to you?"

My chest twisted at the thought of my replacement, and I resolved to talk to Hayes about the move and what I was thinking. How I was feeling. But I said, "Sure, I'll read it over. I'm sure it's great."

Edna made prayer hands, and I chuckled.

"Can I get you a coffee?" I asked her.

"Yes, please." She held up her cup already covered on one side with bright red lipstick stains. I grabbed it from her, taking it to the break area and making us both a cup like I did every day.

It struck me how much I'd miss this part of my routine. I liked making her a cup exactly how she preferred—two Splendas and one sugar with a splash of dairy-free creamer. It was something I could do to feel like I was taking care of her in return for how she'd looked out for me all these years.

I'd miss her just as much as I'd miss my parents and friends once I moved away. If I moved away.

With the weight of indecision heavy on my shoulders, I brought her the mug and set it down.

"Thanks, doll," she said, winking at me over her computer.

I smiled. "Anytime." And then I went to my office, imagining what it would be like to stay in Cottonwood Falls and continue working this job, knowing I would get to continue my relationship with Hayes. Maybe even move in together one day and get to see him every evening when I clocked out.

It was as blissful as being a little girl and writing my first name with my crush's last name surrounded by hearts in my notebook. I could practically envision the curly letters in my head. Della Madigan.

It didn't sound bad.

Would Hayes feel the same way?

I WALKED across the street to the diner to meet Hayes for supper just in time to hear the roar of his motorcycle coming down Main Street. Pausing on the corner, I watched him, head covered with a helmet, T-shirt fluttering in the wind, strong arms holding on to the handlebars.

He looked so hot like that. But it was even hotter when he pulled into a spot and took off his helmet, awarding me with his messy, dirty-blond hair and heart-melting smile.

I grinned back at him, feeling my whole body react

to his presence with pure joy that competed with the radiant sunlight streaming down from a cloudless sky.

He got off the bike, setting his helmet on the seat, and I noticed there was an extra one there. My eyebrows drew together. "Have you had a passenger?" I asked as I walked closer.

"I'm about to," he said, drawing me in for a breath-taking kiss. My head was so foggy with lust, I almost forgot what he'd said.

I stepped back, blinking back the fog, and said, "I'm not riding on that."

He reached up, catching a curl between his fingers and then twirling it. "Not even if I promise a surprise where we're going?"

I bit my bottom lip... Why was it so hard to say no to him?

"And if I promise to drive twenty or less?"

I tilted my head, considering.

"And if I say pretty please with a cherry on top?"

That had me chuckling. "Okay, okay, you convinced me."

He pumped a fist in the air. "Victory!"

I rolled my eyes, laughing at him, and we went into the diner together. I loved sitting and eating dinner with him, chatting about our days and getting to hear about Chopper's first day at the shop. He said all the customers adored seeing the puppy in the waiting room, and Chopper lapped up the attention.

I smiled, saying, "Maybe I can swing by on my lunch break tomorrow to give him some pets."

Hayes pouted out his lip. "Can I have pets too?"

I laughed. "I think we can manage that."

After we finished eating, Hayes paid for our meal, and we walked out to the parking lot, seeing the setting sun was starting to cast orange and pink rays over the sky. I eyed his bike again, thinking I should be more worried than I was. But last time on his bike had been fine. Better than fine, considering it was an excuse to wrap my arms around him and feel his warmth against me.

He passed me the helmet, and I pushed it over my head. He reached out, tenderly helping me clip the strap under my chin. When it was in place, he brushed his finger over my chin like he relished the chance to touch me. And yet again, I felt precious in his presence.

We both got onto the motorcycle, and then he kicked the bike to life. It purred underneath me, and the mix of its vibrations and Hayes's closeness was a painfully erotic reminder that we hadn't had sex yet.

I was starting to get desperate to experience it with Hayes, to get closer to him. But then he edged the bike forward and I held on, focusing more on staying upright and off the pavement flying beneath us.

He steered us down Main Street first, and then we continued heading down a dirt road out of town. The more comfortable I got on the bike, the more I could enjoy it and see why he loved it so much.

There was something about having the sun on your skin, feeling the air rushing past, and seeing the beautiful countryside that surrounded Cottonwood Falls.

Hayes kept his promise, not driving too fast. And then he turned the bike off the dirt road, taking us into a pasture and down a country trail that was rutted down from years of vehicles driving over the same spot, leaving their marks in the ground.

I saw something up ahead and realized there was a blanket laid out on the hilltop with a cooler beside it. When he stopped the bike and got off, I realized we had the most incredible view from here—miles and miles of farmland and pastures containing the black, red, and white dots of cattle.

"Wow," I breathed, tugging off my helmet. I took it in a moment longer before turning to Hayes, seeing him set his helmet on the bike seat. "This is quite the surprise," I said.

He grinned at me. "I thought you might like wine and a sunset better than closing out the diner." He walked to the blanket and opened the cooler.

I smiled at him, thinking that any way I spent the evening with him was fine with me. "Thank you for doing this. It was so thoughtful of you."

He smiled gently before coming to me and pressing a gentle kiss to my lips. "It was worth it, seeing you smile like that."

My heart thudded with love for this man. For his thoughtfulness. For how he continued to put himself out there and try new things to make me happy. The words tugged at my lips, begging to come out. But how could I say such powerful words when there was still so much to decide? When my decision could tear us apart?

Hayes gripped my hand and said, "Let's sit."

I swallowed down my emotions, going to join him on the quilt spread out on the grassy ground. He poured us both a glass of Cupcake wine and then offered me a piece of chocolate to go with it.

With a smile, I took the square, biting off a piece. Sweetness flooded my mouth, matching the beauty of the landscape before me and the actions of the man sitting beside me.

For a moment, we were quiet, watching the display of hues painted before us.

"Sometimes, when I've had a long day at work, I come out here to clear my head," he said quietly. "Something about this sight, seeing the sun set, reminds me that there will always be another day, no matter what happened today."

I turned to look at him, seeing that the sunset was casting a beautiful orange glow over his skin.

He smiled at me, brushing curls away from my face and tucking them behind my ear. "I think the sunset's even prettier in your eyes."

My lips twisted in a small smile. The words were on the tip of my tongue.

I love you.

I'm falling for you.

I think you could be the one.

But then Hayes said, "I love you, Della." His voice was raw, scraping over the words. And I felt the depth of them in his tone.

I looked at him in wonder. How could we be in lockstep? Feeling the same way about each other at the same time?

I used to doubt fate. Wondering if it existed, if it was working for me. But looking in Hayes's eyes, seeing just how much he meant those words, I didn't have a doubt.

Fate had been by my side all this time, waiting for Hayes and me to be ready at the same time. To give each other a chance.

Fate had brought me here.

"I love you too," I said, my eyes stinging with the admission. "I really do."

He held me close, brushing the tears that had fallen. And then he pulled me closer, sitting with me in silence as the sun sank and the clouds changed from orange to pink to purple to gray and the sun was just a memory.

I looked up at him and said, "Come home with me?"

41

HAYES

I MAY HAVE SPED, just a little bit, to get back to her house.

But how could I not, knowing that everything I was waiting for had finally come true?

I'd never been happier in my life. It was one thing to love Della. Another still to know *she loved me too.*

Nothing had ever felt more right than being with her, in love. I couldn't wait to worship her body, knowing I had her heart and soul as well.

It was sacred.

So I handled her like the precious woman she was, helping her off the bike, setting her helmet on the seat beside mine, and walking her into her home. Back to her bedroom, where we got lost in kissing each other and the promise of what would come next.

I walked us slowly back to her bed until I could lay her down. We lay atop the covers, kissing until our breaths were coming as pants. Until her lips were red and swollen from my touch.

I imagined spilling my cum past those lips and nearly came undone. But I held back, saying, "That dress. Take it off."

She reached shyly for the hem and pulled it up, showing her pale legs, the curve of her hips and stomach. The swell of her breasts straining against a white lacy bra. "I love this," I said, teasing at the strap with my fingertips. "Almost as much as I love this." I kissed her breast right over the lace. "And this." I kissed her stomach. And then I applied pressure at her mound, making her squirm. "You know I like this." Crawling back up her body, I smiled against her neck, kissing her more.

"I want you naked, too," she said in an almost whine. "It's not fair I can't see you." There was a little pout to her lips that was cute as hell. I couldn't deny her that, so I stepped back, standing at the foot of her bed so she could watch me tug my T-shirt over my head and toss it aside.

Her eyes weren't just hungry. They were *reverent*.

I'd undressed for dozens of women, but none of them looked at me like Della did. They all saw me as a means to an end, and that was okay because I'd felt the same. But Della drank me in like each piece of me was important information to tuck away. To appreciate.

Feeling seen under her gaze, I took off my socks and then jeans, kicking them aside into a careless pile.

My cock strained at my black underwear. The wet spot from my precum caught the light, shimmering darkly like a promise of what was to come.

And when I tugged my pants down, Della's lips parted. "You're... You have..."

I wrapped my hand around my cock, pumping it while doing nothing to ease the need of being inside her. "I'm pierced."

Her eyes shone with curiosity. "It's pretty."

I chuckled. "That's not why I got it."

At her curious look, I explained, "It makes it feel better, for both of us."

She smiled shyly at me. "I've never tried it before."

"There's plenty of time for that," I replied, getting back on the bed and crawling toward her. Kissing her skin to skin was so much better than before. I could feel the hard spots of her nipples scrape against my chest. The softness of her stomach against mine.

I slid my fingers between her thighs, finding her just as wet as before. "You're so wet for me," I hummed.

She moaned and then pulled back slightly. "We should talk."

I swore my cock softened. "Is everything okay?" I asked. That was the last thing a guy wanted to hear in bed.

She bit her lip nervously. "I've never come with a partner. I don't want you to feel like you're doing anything wrong."

Smiling slightly, I caught one of her hands. "Are you telling me that last week was the first time?"

She glanced down while she nodded, like it was something to be embarrassed of. "I think there might be something wrong with me. I read it just doesn't happen for, like, ten percent of women. I'm kind of..." She bit her lip. "I'm wondering if what happened then was a fluke because I've been wanting to jump you so bad."

That brought a smile to my lips, even though I wanted to tell her exes how shitty they were for prioritizing their pleasure over hers. For being too lazy to learn what she liked. I would have spent all night with my mouth between her thighs if that's what it took to have her calling my name.

"You're frowning," she said nervously. She reached for a throw pillow to cover herself up, and my stomach sank. She'd been so confident moments ago.

I placed my hand on her knee, holding her gaze as I said, "I'm thinking of how shitty it was for them to make you think there was something wrong with you because they weren't willing to put in the effort." I smoothed my hand over her soft thigh. "I'd like to explore with you and figure out what works for you if that's okay. No pressure on an orgasm. I just want us to enjoy each other."

"You would?"

I nodded and gave her a salacious grin. "And if you

only come on my tongue…" I shrugged. "I guess I'm okay with that."

She gave a happy laugh, and I smiled because my girl was back.

"And while we're talking," I said, "I think you should know I was recently tested, and I'm clean. Do you want me to wear a condom?"

She shook her head. "I have an IUD."

My cock hardened at the thought of being in her, nothing between me and her soft warmth.

"Now move that pillow and let me see you," I said. "I want to see you."

Shyly, she withdrew the pillow, showing me her soft skin, her curves. And since we were much too far apart, I drew her to me, kissing again. But this time, it was better. Like a weight was lifted from Della's shoulders for sharing her fears. And from mine too, because now I knew what she needed even more than before.

She needed someone patient. Caring. Willing to listen to her cues and respond. I could be that guy.

Our kisses grew increasingly heated, and then she reached down to my cock, boldly taking it into her hand and pumping.

It felt too fucking good.

"God, you're so hard," she whispered while caressing me. "I want to feel you inside me."

I wanted the same. God, I wanted the same.

And it wasn't just the heat of desire. I wanted to be closer to Della. I wanted to explore her. Discover what she liked, what she didn't. To find our own rhythm and explore how our bodies fit together.

I laid her back on the bed, her red curls wild against the white pillowcases embroidered with dainty flowers. And I wondered what the fuck I ever had against flowers. Against pink. Because they brought Della joy.

I looked into her soft eyes, saw the freckles dashed across the bridge of her nose as I hovered over her, as my tip slid against the slickness of her folds.

I gave her a questioning look, and she nodded.

And I was done holding back. I pressed into her, my cock surrounded by her warmth.

"Oh God," she breathed.

"You feel so good," I replied, hovering over her, grinding my hips against hers because deep wasn't deep enough.

She moaned. "More."

I pumped into her again, beating a steady rhythm that made her tits shake in the most mesmerizing way. She looked so hot, lying back like this, her hands working up and down my sides, fingernails digging into my back. And her eyes met mine. Trusting. Loving.

And I realized this wasn't sex. It wasn't fucking. It wasn't a release.

It was love.

We were making love.

The thought pushed me dangerously close to the edge, but I couldn't, not yet.

"Your piercing," she whispered, eyes crinkling. "It feels..." she gasped. "Oh, I'm..."

She tightened around me, and pride swelled in my chest.

Della was coming for me. And I was coming for her.

As I released into her, I was giving her more than my cum. I was giving her my heart. My everything.

There was no going back.

Not with Della in front of me.

42

DELLA

AFTER THE BEST sex of my life, a tiny, terrified part of me expected Hayes to walk away. That used to be his MO, after all. He'd told me so himself.

So I gave a surprised, happy giggle when he tugged me close into his arms, unbothered by our sweaty bodies or the mess of his spend. He held me like I was the most important person in the world.

I looked into his eyes, searching for some tell that this was a game to him. That it wouldn't last. Because my heart was thinking crazy things, like giving up my new job and staying in Cottonwood Falls to discover what could happen between the two of us.

Could this relationship be something real? Something that would last?

He brushed my hair away from my face, saying, "You're beautiful you know."

I smiled back at him, fighting the urge to dismiss his compliment. I knew Hayes was too honest to lie to me. "Thank you," I whispered. It was like talking might break this blissful bubble between us.

Tracing his thumb over my cheek, he said, "I still haven't seen that tattoo."

A small laugh bubbled past my lips. "I was hoping you'd forget."

He shook his head. "Not a chance."

Knowing Hayes was almost as stubborn as me, I rolled over to my stomach and said, "My lower back."

He pulled up the covers, and I cringed, wondering what he would think of the orange and black butterfly resting along my spine. My skin sizzled as he traced his fingers over the design. "I like it." He lowered his lips to my back, kissing there.

I looked over my shoulder at him, curls tickling my skin. "You do? I was kind of thinking I should get it lasered off."

"Fuck no," he said, putting the blanket back. "Don't change a thing. Anything."

I couldn't help but smile back at him, and I twisted into his arms again, resting my head on his shoulder. "I'll keep my tattoo if you keep your piercing."

His lip ring glinted as he smirked. "I knew you'd like it."

I laughed happily.

He kissed my temple. "Where do you keep your washcloths? I'll help you clean up," he said.

"He's thoughtful and good in bed? An impossible combination," I teased, feeling happier than I ever had. I liked how he took care of me. "They're in the hall bathroom."

He kissed my forehead and then walked away, still completely naked. I noticed there were tattoos that covered his back, his shoulders, and on the back of his thighs, though they were sparser there than the other parts of his body. I wanted to ask him about every single one. Especially the tattoo below his heart that said, "Lead with love."

I'd spotted it earlier when he was undressing, but his cock quickly distracted me from asking further questions. I was excited for him to return so I could find out more.

But instead, I heard him call from the hallway, "Della? Can you come here a sec?"

My eyebrows pinched together. "Everything okay?"

"I'm not sure." His voice was uneven.

Feeling my chest squeeze with fear, I grabbed my dress and tugged it over my head, feeling the remnants of our pleasure slide down my leg. "What's going on?" I asked, heading that way. "Is there a leak?"

But I stopped in the hallway, seeing him standing in the doorway of the guest room. The one with all my packed boxes and stacks of boxes waiting to be used.

His eyes were fully guarded, absent of the light that was usually there. "Are you moving?" he asked, not a hint of emotion to his voice.

My chest felt so tight I nearly doubled over with the pain. I could feel myself losing him. "Let me explain," I said.

"I'm waiting." He was still naked, but he folded his arms over his chest like he couldn't wait for simple things like getting dressed. But I was glad I'd thrown on my dress because I'd never felt more exposed.

"I got a job offer in Dallas, and I'm supposed to move there in a month."

His jaw hardened, a muscle in his cheek flexing. "You weren't going to tell me," he accused.

"I—" How could I explain to him in a way that would remove that stony expression from his face? It was so opposite from the warm, caring man I'd lain in bed with. "I was lonely here!" I cried. "I thought I was going to waste away in this small town, never having someone to love me."

"So what were you doing with me then? Passing the time until you could leave, move on and find someone serious?" Hurt leaked through his tone but only for a minute.

"Hayes," I said gently, going to put my hand on his shoulder, but he flinched away. I had to steel myself against the ache growing in my chest. "Of course that's not it. I love you. I just didn't know where you stood or if you really wanted something long-term."

When he didn't speak, I said, "What do you want, Hayes?"

His jaw shook, but only for a second. "I don't know if I want *this* when I know your plan all along was to leave me behind. When were you going to tell me? When you put the for-sale sign up on your house? When you had the moving truck loaded? Or were you going to let the rumor mill make its way to the garage to let me know how pathetic I was for thinking you were the one?"

My mouth fell open at his words. But before I could question him, he brushed past me, going to my bedroom. When I caught up, he had tugged on his jeans and was sliding his shirt over his arms.

"Hayes, stay. We can talk this out."

He shook his head sharply, sliding on his boots without bothering to button his shirt. "I need time to think."

"How much time?" I asked. I didn't want him to leave. We were so happy just moments ago.

"I don't know."

He walked past me, going toward the front door, and anger flared up in me.

"This is what you wanted, isn't it?" I called after him. "An easy out so you could go back to your old ways?"

He paused on his trajectory and slowly turned around. I backpedaled at the pain I saw in his face. "This isn't about what I want. I didn't *want* to love you. I didn't have a choice. But you are my every thought when I'm awake and my every dream while I sleep. You can leave me, but I can't escape you. Why the hell would I want that?"

His words hit every part of my heart. But before I could reply, he was out the door.

43
___

HAYES

MY HANDS WERE SHAKING on the handlebars as I drove out of town. I knew I couldn't be by myself, or I was liable to do something stupid. Especially with whatever mangled pieces remained of my heart feeling like they were being ripped out of my chest.

I couldn't think clearly. The second I saw those boxes, I panicked. I was five years old again, showing my mom a drawing in the hopes of making her smile. I'd thought my drawing was good enough then, just like I thought my best was good enough for Della now.

I knew I could never trust a woman to love me, to stay.

With the lights of Cottonwood Falls in the rearview mirror, I felt stupid for thinking I was enough for Della. She knew I wasn't worth staying for, even when I was giving her my all.

My dad had told me to give love a chance. That I could be happier than before. But for the second time in my life, the woman I loved was leaving me. And unlike my mom, this was a choice—Della's choice.

I drove, almost in a trance, only the sound of wind raging past my helmet and the dirt road under my tires until I reached the big white house out in the countryside. I got off my bike and pulled out my cell, dialing Fletcher's number. His girls were asleep—hell, he might be too—but I needed to talk to him.

After a few rings, he answered, groggy. "Hayes. Everything okay?"

"No," I uttered. "Can you come outside?"

"You're here?"

"I am."

He hung up, and a few seconds later, the front porch light came on and he walked outside in pajama pants and a crumpled white T-shirt. His hair was a mess, and there was the imprint of a blanket on his cheek. I was pacing his front sidewalk, feeling like a caged animal. How could my body hold all this pain? It felt like it could split me apart, rip me to a thousand ragged pieces at any second.

There was a worried look in my brother's dark eyes. "What happened?" he asked.

"Did you know Della was moving?" I asked.

His hesitation was all the answer I needed.

The panic welled up making my legs weak. I

slumped to the ground, too overwhelmed by my emotions to even stand.

"Hayes!" he uttered and rushed to me where I'd fallen. "Where does it hurt?"

"Everywhere!" I whimpered, keening and holding myself. "It hurts everywhere."

Fletcher tugged me into his arms like I weighed nothing. "You're scaring me. Did you take something? Are you wounded?"

I held on to him. "I love her, and she's leaving." Now the sobs came. It felt like I couldn't stop, couldn't catch my breath. It was worse than any injury. Instead of my body failing, it was like the world was coming apart. Everything I'd hoped for, the future my mind had dared to picture for Della and me—it was all gone, broken down like those moving boxes waiting in her spare room.

Fletcher said, "I'm here." He rubbed my back and waited until I couldn't cry anymore. "Let's go to the guesthouse. Get you inside."

Even though I didn't see the point in being inside or outside, I let him tug me up and leaned on him heavily as he helped me stand on legs that didn't feel like my own. And we walked slowly across the gravel path to the guesthouse in his backyard. He opened the door for us and flicked on the lights. "Sit at the counter," he said, "I'll make us some coffee."

Never mind the fact that Fletcher always pressed

that no one should drink caffeine after noon. "I'm not drunk," I told him.

"I know," he said, his back to me as he pressed a filter into the pot.

I watched while he started the pot brewing, slowly and methodically. "She told you about the move tonight?" he asked, his face still turned away from me.

"No, I found the boxes packed in her guest room after we..."

I could see the sympathy in his eyes as he asked, "How did it go after that?"

I relayed the story to him, almost like I was an observer instead of a participant. And when I was done, he had two cups of coffee. He stood on the opposite side of the counter, sipping his drink while I just stared down at the dark liquid and the few bubbles sitting on the top.

"I need you to text her and tell her when you'll meet up again to discuss this," Fletcher said in his official doctor tone. He'd used it on us all the time as the oldest of five brothers.

"Why?" I asked.

"You can't just leave her waiting and worrying about you."

I looked up at him. "What makes you think she's worried about me?"

His lips twitched slightly. "Because she called Liv before you even got here."

The irony hit me like a punch to the chest. "Liv

said I was going to hurt Della. She didn't want me dating her friend. Turns out she didn't have to be worried about me at all." The sight of moving boxes flashed back through my mind, and I had to rub my temples to ease the ache forming there.

Fletcher said, "Della cares about you, Hayes. And if you want a chance with her, you need to do the right thing and text her so you can handle this when you cool down."

A dangerous spark of hope lit in my heart at the idea of fixing things. I took a sip of coffee to tame it. But still, I got out my phone and sent a message to Della, following my brother's guidance.

Hayes: Can we meet up tomorrow night to talk? We can have supper at my place.

I showed Fletcher the screen. "Done."

"Good... Look." He pushed the phone back to me on the counter. Della had already replied.

Della: I'll be there.

That spark of hope started flickering, growing stronger. "What do I do next?"

Fletcher said, "You need to think about what you want. Now that you know she's moving, and she kept it from you, do you want a relationship with her?"

My throat felt tight.

"If you do," Fletcher continued, "what do you want that relationship to look like? Are you okay with long distance?"

His questions weighed on me as he continued. "And if you decide to stay together, what do you want out of a relationship? How do you want a partner to behave in conflict? In good times? In some ways, you're grown, but in others, it's like you're seventeen with your first girlfriend, trying to figure out how all this works. It's okay that you don't have all the answers right now, but you do need to think about them."

I nodded slowly. He was right. Of course he was right. But underneath it all, the only thing going through my mind was that I just wanted Della. Any piece of her I could have. "How do you decide?" I asked.

Fletcher set his coffee on the counter, looking pensively down at it. "Here's the thing about relationships. Most people think about what they want, not what they're willing to give. You should do both."

I looked down at my own coffee as I mulled it over, eyes trailing a spiral of steam.

Fletcher drained his coffee in the sink. "Why don't you stay in the guesthouse tonight? We can talk more in the morning when you've had a chance to think."

He knew me better than almost anyone else. And I was grateful for the time and space to process.

I got up from the counter, embracing my brother in a hug. "Thank you." It wasn't lost on me that I could show up here in the middle of the night and know that he'd be here for me, no matter what.

And I mentally added something to my list of desires.

That's the kind of man I wanted to be.

44

———

LIV

I TUGGED at the blanket strings on my quilt as Della told me what had happened between her and Hayes just moments ago. She sounded so upset, and my heart hurt for her. I hated that she was going through this, even more so because I saw it coming. I wanted to throttle Hayes for getting into a relationship with my best friend when he had no idea how to be in one.

Yes, Della could have told him about her job offer sooner, but that didn't mean he should run away when things got hard.

But then my husband's phone started ringing and he rolled to the side, blearily looking at the screen. He showed me the incoming call. Hayes.

I pursed my lips.

Fletcher whispered, "I'll go handle this."

I nodded, and once he left the room, I shifted the

phone to my other ear and said to Della, "Looks like he turned up here."

She sniffed. "I guess that makes me feel better. At least he didn't turn to someone else..."

Part of me thought it was just a matter of time before he went back to his old patterns. Someone couldn't just spend their entire adult life going to bed with a different woman every night just to settle down and devote themselves to only one.

"What are you thinking?" Della asked me, then sniffed.

I gritted my teeth, knowing I couldn't lay all my feelings on her. Not when she was feeling like this. "I'm pissed that he just ran out on you," I said. "For starters."

"He said he needed time," Della replied.

I frowned at her defense of him. It was hard to see Hayes through her eyes when I'd known him all my life. He was six years younger than me and grew up on the neighboring ranch. When Maya Madigan died, he seemed to soak up all the oxygen in that family. He threw tantrums. Destroyed things. Was constantly in the principal's office at school. And then when he got older, it was all about fast cars and women. I watched a parade of women go in and out of his driveway on my way to work every morning.

He was nothing like I'd pictured Della's person would be.

But I let out a sigh and said, "I know he was upset,

but you've been dating for such a short time. How could he expect to know all your future plans off the bat? That's not fair to you."

"We said I love you," Della whispered sadly.

My heart clenched for her and all her pain. "Oh, Della…"

"I know." She sounded so heartbroken.

I kneaded my brow. "Do you really think Hayes could be your person?" The doubt was clear in my voice. But Della was like a sister to me, and I worried about her like one. She didn't have a hint of cynicism in her heart, and that was both a power and a weakness.

"Liv," Della said sharply. "You're the one who was so desperate to keep me in town you were setting me up on dates! Now the guy I love isn't good enough to meet your expectations?"

She'd never spoken to me like that before, and I instantly wanted to fix things. "Della, I—"

"No, I'm sorry he's not a doctor, and I'm sorry he doesn't have a past you approve of, and I'm sorry he's not a good-natured bump on a log like Bennett!" Della's voice was rising with each word, growing with her emotions.

I gritted my teeth, feeling guilty. "Della, you know I love Hayes. He's my brother-in-law and a great uncle to my kids. He's just the last person I expected for *you*. I think you deserve a prince. I have always thought that."

"Maybe that's the problem," Della whispered,

almost like she was speaking to herself. "I've spent my whole life waiting for Prince Charming, waiting for a relationship that looks like my parents'. But I haven't thought about what actually makes *me* feel good."

At the truth in her words, I tugged a little too hard on a thread and a small hole appeared in the quilt. "It's your life," I finally said. "You have to decide for yourself and deal with the consequences too." I hated the truth in those words. I wanted to save her from all her pain.

"It is my life." Her voice only shook a little. "But you're my best friend. I want you to support me."

"I can support you, but I can't always agree with you," I said. "We promised we'd always be honest with each other. Even when it was hard."

Della's voice shook as she said, "If I'm being honest, I wish I wouldn't have called you at all tonight. I didn't need you to say I told you so."

"Della—"

"Goodbye," she said and hung up. I stared at my phone in disbelief. Della had to know I was just trying to protect her. And she had to know how it looked for her to be dating Hayes—she'd grown up in the same town!

The front door of the house opened, and I hoped Hayes wasn't coming in or I'd be taking out some frustration on him. Instead, my husband walked into our room, a troubled look in his eyes.

"Did you ream him out?" I asked. "I can't believe he ran out on Della like that."

Fletcher gave me an incredulous look. "You've got to be kidding me. He's *devastated*. I'm worried about him. And I'm pissed Della didn't tell him sooner."

"*He's* devastated? What about my friend crying on the phone because Hayes couldn't handle a hard conversation?"

Fletcher gave me a disappointed look. "There's more to it than that, and you know it."

Maybe he was right, but I was also frustrated. "Fletch, *you* know it was a bad idea for them to date. I told him so in March!"

With a frown, he said, "I disagree."

"That's it?" I asked, incredulous. "You disagree?"

Slowly, he walked over to our bed and pulled back the covers on his side, sitting down. "I think it was a great idea for them to date."

My eyebrows crept up my forehead. "You do?" How could he think that?

"I've never been prouder of Hayes than I have here lately. He's put his heart on the line, thought consistently of someone else, communicated his feelings. I would be torn up too if I were in his shoes. The woman he loves is about to leave and didn't even tell him."

Fletcher lifted his legs under the covers and then tugged them up to his waist while I sat there in disbelief...

"He's in love with her?" I asked. "Really?"

Fletcher nodded. "He's so far gone, you'd need a map to find him."

I frowned, trying to reconcile it in my mind. I knew Della said they exchanged I-love-yous, but I wasn't sure Hayes understood what that meant in a romantic relationship. "But he ran out on her," I finally said. "He found out the truth and didn't fight for her to stay."

"He held it together just long enough to fall apart," Fletcher said, his voice raw. "You should have seen him out there. If they break it off, I don't know if he'll ever recover."

My heart ached with guilt and regret. If this thing with Della and Hayes is something that lasts, I might have ruined my friendship and hurt my relationship with Fletcher's family.

"I think I really messed up," I admitted to him, tears pricking at my eyes. "I love Hayes, you know I do, but I just couldn't believe he was in so deep, for real. And Della... she deserves the world."

Fletcher scooted over, taking me under his arm. "It's ironic, isn't it?"

I rolled my head on his shoulder to look at him. "What is?"

"That your brother was so nervous about you and me dating because of my past. You were so mad at him, and yet..." He tilted his head at me.

"It's different," I argued.

He raised his eyebrows doubtfully.

I sighed. "Shit."

He kissed the top of my head. "Let them sort it out. And then you and Della will have a chance to talk too."

45

———

DELLA

WHEN I WOKE up the next day after hardly sleeping, I really didn't feel like going into work. But staying at home and stewing with nothing to distract me from what happened the night before sounded like torture.

I kept replaying the night in my mind—how close Hayes and I were. How happy I felt. And then the anguish in his voice. The way he shut all the softest parts of himself away from me, leaving only the rough stony edges I used to know.

My heart ached as I went into the office, wondering what our conversation tonight would bring. Was last night my first and last time with him in my bed? How could we move forward when he felt so betrayed by me? I couldn't blame him for being upset and needing space. Putting myself in his shoes, I would have felt the same way.

I went back to the break area, making coffee for

Edna and me, then brought it to her desk just in time for her to breeze into the office. Today she had on a pair of white capris, a teal-blue shirt and a gauzy neck scarf held in place with a golden brooch.

"Looking good," I told her.

She smiled. "Look good, feel good."

I dipped my head in acknowledgement.

"I sent that job description to a few candidates last night. I know they won't be as good as you, but fingers crossed they'll be half as good." She set her purse down on a chair in the corner of her office and then sat at her desk. "See you for our huddle in fifteen?"

I nodded despite the painful twist of my heart. Time was running out for me to ask Edna to keep my job, but with any luck, I'd have more clarity tonight.

I FELT dizzy with nerves as I pulled into Hayes's driveway. I couldn't see into his home, but his truck was parked outside along with his motorcycle, carefully stored under a cover to protect it from the elements.

My heart raced a jaunty pace at the sight as I wondered if this would be my last time coming to his house.

Was this the part where we turned into strangers?

I'd been there before in past relationships, but I really didn't want that to happen with Hayes. Even with my best friend's doubt. Even with my parents' disapproval. Something deep inside of me knew this thing with Hayes felt right.

Taking a deep breath, I got out of my car and walked toward his house, praying this wouldn't be the end.

I was about to knock on the wooden door with the diamond-shaped window up high, but it opened before I could. And Hayes was standing there in ripped-up jeans and a baggy white shirt, his hair slightly damp from a shower.

Just the sight of him made me want to fall into his arms and let him hold me, but he simply stepped back and said, "Come on in." Nothing in his expression gave away what was to come.

I followed him into his place, noticing the savory scents coming from his kitchen. He'd cooked for us as promised, but I didn't have much of an appetite.

"You can sit at the table," he said, "I'll serve you."

"Thank you," I replied.

It all seemed so stiff, so formal.

That wasn't us.

Where was Hayes's joke about serving me a piece of meat? Or the roll of my eyes in return?

A small scuffle of paws on hard floors sounded, and I looked down just in time to see Chopper launch himself at my knees. "Hi, sweetie!" I cooed, picking him up.

Oh God, I thought as I stroked his soft, curly fur. *Was this my last time seeing Chopper too?*

My heart sank as Hayes said, "Would you like something to drink? Water? Lemonade? Tea?"

"Lemonade, please." The words felt like cotton in my mouth.

He brought me a glass half full of ice and topped off with lemonade. Then he said, "I made spaghetti and a salad. Are you okay with that?"

I nodded, finding it hard to speak. My throat was feeling tight. After taking a drink, I focused again on Chopper, trying not to cry. The dog was looking at me with big, brown, shiny eyes. As if he could feel my mood, he ducked his head to my chest. It took all I had not to sob.

Hayes set a heaping plate of spaghetti and red sauce and a fresh salad in front of me. "Is there anything else you'd like?" he asked.

I looked up at him, trying to see how he was so calm. "Honestly, Hayes, my stomach is in so many knots I don't know how I'm going to eat before we talk."

"Same here." He sat down across from me, hand shaking as he reached for a spiral notebook I hadn't noticed on his table. Our plates were completely forgotten as he began speaking. "I'm sorry I ran out like that last night. I wasn't in a good head space."

I nodded slowly. "I understand. I would have freaked out too."

His lips formed a sad smile that quickly fell.

"So what's in the notebook?" I asked, trying to keep my voice from shaking.

"Well, I went to my brother for advice, and he pointed out that since this is all new to me, I'm still figuring things out. He told me I needed to think about what I wanted moving forward. What I was willing to give."

I searched his eyes, hoping for a hint of his answer. I'd spent my whole life dreaming of what I wanted in a man. This really was all new to him.

Hayes cleared his throat and flipped open the notebook where I could see the pages lifting and wrinkled from pen indentations. "I know I'm not done yet, but when I thought of what I wanted, I thought... I want Della."

My lips trembled, because I'd been around long enough to know that wasn't always enough.

"I thought, I want to argue with her about trivial bullshit just to see how happy she is when she finds out she was right all along. I want to dance with her and her two left feet—as long as I'm wearing steel-toe boots. I want to look at her from across the room at a family party and see the blush on her cheeks when she notices me looking. I want her to believe in love, and I want to be someone she can believe in."

"Hayes..." I said, even as a tear slipped down my cheek. But he continued reading from his list.

"I want to trust and be trusted. I want no secrets or surprises. I want to be a provider to my woman—and my children if they come. I want to learn to stay through the hard stuff instead of running away." And then he set the notebook down.

This time, he didn't read from the book but looked in my eyes as he spoke. "I want a chance to see if this relationship is something that will last... but not at the cost of your dreams." He reached over and grabbed Chopper and set him on the floor. Then he grabbed my hands, squeezing them lightly but with purpose. "I don't know much about this job you're moving for, but I know it must be a good opportunity for you to uproot your life here. If that new job is something you want, I could never stand in your way. But my life is here. I can't go, and I won't ask you to stay."

I took one of my hands from his and swiped at the tears falling down my cheeks. "Did you mean it?"

"Mean what?" he asked.

"What you said last night, about loving me?"

His eyes were tortured as they stayed on mine. "I meant every word."

My lips trembled as I took it in. Hayes loved me. And not in the tentative, shy way of a new relationship. He'd gone all in with me, just like I had with him. "The job was never about needing more money or to move up in my career," I said softly, afraid my voice would fail. "It was about thinking I could never find *this* feeling in Cottonwood Falls... But then I found you. And you were here all along." My voice cracked. My heart did too. "All this time we've missed out on..."

Hayes shook his head, wiping away my tears with both his thumbs. "We weren't late. You and I were right on time."

He seemed so confident, I had to ask, "What do you mean?"

"I needed time to grow into the man you deserved, to see you for the incredible woman you are."

More tears flowed at the compliment, this time happy and relieved. "This isn't going to be easy," I warned. "My family, my friends, their support means a lot to me. You've shown me how amazing you are, but you'll have to show them too."

He rested his forehead against mine. "I'll be here as long as it takes."

"And no more making my car break down," I teased.

He chuckled, the corners of his eyes crinkling. "But how am I supposed to get you on the back of my motorcycle?"

I leaned back, hitting his shoulder.

Laughing, he pulled me in. I held on to him, thankful to be in his arms. It felt like right where I belonged.

46

HAYES

AS WE LAY in my bed, naked under the covers, Della traced her fingertips over the ridges of my stomach and then stalled on one particular tattoo.

"What does this one mean?" she asked, tracing the letters. *Lead with love.*

"It's my first tattoo," I said. The ink wasn't as sharp, the letters slightly fuzzy at the edges, but it was still my favorite one.

"Really?" she asked, turning her green eyes on me. And instead of asking, she waited—because it was so different from my other tattoos.

"You want to know the story?" I asked, covering her hand on my chest. Her warm palm flattened against the tattoo, and I held it there.

Her voice was soft as she replied, "Only if you want to share."

"I do." I buried a kiss amongst her wild curls, closing my eyes to savor the moment, to gather my strength. "This one is for my mom. It's what's written on her gravestone."

"Oh," Della breathed.

"I'm not sure if I remember her saying it or if it's just a memory my brain filled in. But according to my dad and my older brothers, it was her life's motto."

Della leaned her head against my shoulder, her weight a comfort. "What does it mean?" she asked. "I mean, I can guess, but..." Her words trailed off, leaving me to fill in the blanks.

"Mom said that there were a lot of unknowns in life and no one was ever handed a manual with instructions. And Dad said even if there were instructions, the men wouldn't read them." We both chuckled at that. "So Mom said that when you were in doubt of what to do next, you should always lead with love. When you're lost, ask what love would do, and do that. She said that love could never steer you wrong."

My throat grew tight, thinking of the night before. "Fear led me away from you last night. And love brought me back."

Della looked up at me, her green eyes shining. "That's beautiful, Hayes."

DELLA

He gripped my fingers and brought them up to his lips before placing them over his steadily beating heart.

I realized I had been letting fear lead me too. I'd fallen for him but held back the news about my job because I was worried about what he'd say. The loving thing to do would have been being up-front with him. I promised myself that would change right now. "Hayes, I love you."

The hope in his eyes was nearly my undoing. But then he asked, "You do?" and my heart melted for him. Some part of him worried if he was worthy, just like part of me worried the same.

I wondered how much better the world would be if we could just say how we felt. To be bravely honest like Hayes.

"I love you," I repeated. "So much that it scares me. But I want to lead with love like your mom... like you."

Emotion pooled in his eyes, and he brought me in again for another kiss that showed exactly how he felt for me.

♥

HAYES and I spent the rest of the evening in his bed, savoring each other and the time we had. I think we were both shaken by the fact that we could have been spending this night very differently, depending on how our conversation went.

I hardly got a chance to look at my phone, but once during a bathroom break, I checked my messages.

Liv: Can we talk? I don't like how we left things last night.

My shoulders tensed, and my chest ached, because I didn't like it either. But I also didn't want to argue with my friend about the man I loved.

Liv: Can I come by your place tomorrow?
Liv: I'll bring food too.

She was making an effort, which helped me feel better. And when you were friends for as long as we were, you were bound to have some ups and downs. So I typed back my response, hoping for the best.

Della: 7 work?
Liv: See you then.

I walked out of the restroom in my dress, holding my phone to my chest. There was a commotion coming from the other side of the house, though, and I could hear several masculine voices speaking.

"Hayes?" I called out. "Where did you go?"

"Over here," he called out, the other voices silencing.

It sounded like he was in the hallway. I walked out of his room to find the hallway empty, but the door to his guest room open. There stood Hayes, Ethan, and another one of his employees while Chopper danced around their feet.

"What's going on?" I asked them. It was past seven o'clock, and Hayes hadn't mentioned company.

Ethan looked over at me, eyes stalling on my mass of tangled curls. I tried not to flush at the fact that I definitely had sex hair. "We're moving these boxes to the garage," Ethan said. "Dane, why don't you carry the smaller ones and I'll get the dolly?"

"Sure thing..." They continued strategizing, but I couldn't hear them over the buzzing thoughts in my head. Hayes met my eyes, and I gave him a questioning look.

He simply offered me a gentle smile.

Hayes was making room in his home... for me.

With the guys set up, Hayes brought me back to his bedroom, closing the door to give us privacy. "Sorry," he said. "They're a little earlier than we planned."

I shook my head and gave him a hug. Emotion was threatening to spill from my eyes at the depth of what the gesture meant, but I blinked it back. "It's okay. I should go anyway. I slept like shit last night."

He chuckled wryly then kissed the top of my head. "Call me before you go to sleep?"

"I will."

As I walked out to my car and drove home in the dwindling evening light, everything about life seemed better. The grass was greening up in everyone's lawns.

Some people even had their hanging planters out with fresh new flowers, making the whole town look brighter.

Or maybe that was just me seeing life through love-colored glasses.

I was excited about the future for the first time in a long time. And that was all thanks to Hayes.

47

DELLA

ONCE I GOT HOME, I showered and changed into pajamas, tired from the emotional toll of the day. But I still couldn't wait to call Hayes and hear his voice again. It was hard to leave his house when his bed was just big enough for the two of us.

So as soon as I was under my covers, I did as promised and called Hayes. Leaning back on the pillows, I listened to the phone ring until his voice came over the line. "Hey, beautiful."

I smiled at the greeting. "Hey there."

"How was the drive home?"

I chuckled at the comment. "Short. Is the guest room all empty now?" I asked him, lying down and looking up at the ceiling.

"Completely. I think these dust bunnies are at least fifteen years old. They're practically sending their baby dust bunnies off to college."

I giggled at the visual. "They must be so proud."

"Nah, college is a waste of money."

I sat up on my bed, surprised by the statement. "*What*? Your brother's a literal doctor."

"I think it's fine for something like that," he explained. "Like if you have to get a degree to do your job. But let's be honest—most people don't."

My eyebrows rose. "You know I have a degree, right?"

"And could you do your job now without it?"

I shifted uncomfortably in my bed. "Probably, but I wouldn't be the same person. I learned a lot at college."

"Like how to do a keg stand?" he needled.

"I'm glaring at you," I replied.

He laughed. "I'm just saying, I don't like the thought of going into debt to do something you could learn another way, like through an apprenticeship or at a trade school. Or hell, even YouTube."

I thought about what he was saying, and it made sense from his perspective. He'd taken on an entire business with a trade school education. "But what if you had kids one day? What would you tell them?" I always thought I'd encourage my children to go to college. I even kept a savings account for that purpose.

"I want my kids to do whatever the fuck they want after graduation, but they also need to handle the consequences of their decisions either way."

I chuckled at his answer—it was totally in character for him. "Well, I'd want my children to go to college. I feel like you learn so much being on your own and keeping your own schedule, being accountable to your professors."

"You learn a lot living on your own and being accountable to a boss too," Hayes countered.

"True." I lay back in my pillows. "You have a lot of opinions, you know."

He laughed at that. "I guess that makes two of us."

I smiled, knowing he was right, but I wouldn't admit it. I bit my bottom lip, gathering courage to ask my next question. "What does your family think of us being together?"

"My family? They all love you, but that was before we even started dating."

I chuckled. "What about now?"

"My family's the kind of people who will support you 'slong as you're doing what makes you happy. At first they were worried that I was losing part of myself."

My heart clenched at that. "Were they right?"

"Maybe... Maybe I was just losing the stupid part that kept me away from you."

I grinned. "Hayes Madigan, you do have a way with words."

"Even without a college degree?"

I laughed at that.

But then we quieted, and Hayes's voice almost sounded nervous. "Did you mean it when you said you'd stay in town? I could do long distance if you wanted."

"Yeah," I said, nearly whispering. "I did mean it. I just need to tell Edna tomorrow morning. She's going to be thrilled."

"If you're sure that's what you want," Hayes said. He sounded doubtful, and that worried me.

"I always wanted to stay in Cottonwood Falls. And if this doesn't work out between us, there will be more jobs in more cities. But there's only one Hayes Madigan. The world couldn't handle two."

He chuckled at that with me. "So... I was thinking."

"Oh boy," I teased. "Even without a college degree?"

"Oh shush." He laughed. "I was thinking this Wednesday... maybe we could invite your parents to my place?"

I sat up again, my heart beating its nervous drum. "You mean it?"

"Yeah. I need to start winning them over, like we said. Why not start now? Or Wednesday, I guess, since that's when y'all usually hang out."

I smiled. "I love you."

"So that's a yes?"

"It's a yes."

"Great. And I love you too."

We said our goodnights and got off the phone. Setting it on my nightstand, I lay in bed thinking life couldn't get any better. I was going to stay in Cottonwood Falls with all my friends and family. Hayes was loving me exactly the way I'd always dreamed. And I'd get to keep working with the boss and clients I loved. I couldn't wait to tell Edna tomorrow morning.

IT WAS STILL morning time when Della called me the next day. I smiled because she'd been on my mind since I woke up. Being on her mind too felt so damn good.

"Hey, beautiful," I answered, holding my phone to my ear as I filled out a purchase order for new parts while Chopper slept in his doggy bed in the corner of my office.

"Hayes." She sniffed, and my heart instantly plummeted.

I got up, shutting the door to my office. "What's going on?"

"I talked to Edna this morning and..." Her voice cracked, and I heard her sniff again. "And she already offered my job to someone else. They accepted, and she said she doesn't feel right going back on her offer."

My heart, which had dropped to the floor, now had

boot prints all over it. "You're kidding me. You've worked for her for twenty years."

"Eighteen," Della corrected with a cracking voice. "But I understand where she's coming from. She's a woman of her word. And she offered me several chances to stay. I just didn't take her up on it soon enough." She took in a shaky breath that made me want to wrap my arms around her.

I hated that she was losing her job. And that she was in so much pain.

And that she might not have a choice to stay.

"I can try and find another job around here, but..." She broke down in a fresh round of sobs. "I'm so sorry."

"Where are you?" I asked.

"I'm fine, I—"

"Della, where are you?"

"In the parking lot behind my work," she managed to say.

"I'll be right there." I hung up and told the guys I'd be back soon. Then I hopped on my motorcycle and drove down Main Street to her office. Chopper rested in a carrier bag around my chest.

I never thought I'd be the kind of guy bringing a lap dog on my motorcycle, but it's funny how life changes. And how happy you are for that change when you find the woman you love.

Within a few minutes, I'd parked my bike beside

her car, cut the engine, and was opening her passenger door.

She wiped her eyes as she looked over at me. Black makeup streaked down her cheeks and puddled around her eyes, which were already red from crying. "Babe..." I whispered, reaching across the console to hold her. But it was in the way. "Sit in my lap."

A skeptical look was her response.

"Come on," I said. I took Chopper out of his holder and put him in the back seat.

Begrudgingly, she unbuckled and crawled over the console to settle in my lap, her feet still resting in the driver's seat. It felt so much better to hold her close like this. She wrapped her arms around me and cried on my shoulder. "I'm sorry," she whispered. "I tried, but I couldn't make it work."

"Don't apologize," I said, brushing my hand over her head, her curls contained in a low bun. "We'll figure this out."

"But how?" she asked, looking at me again. "It's not like there are a ton of people hiring—especially for office work."

A thought popped into my mind, but I didn't want to say anything until I knew for sure. So I held her close, breathing in the smell of her perfume mingling with her shampoo. I couldn't lose her, not now that I finally had her. "When's your last day?"

Her answer came out muffled. "Three weeks from Friday."

"Can you trust me to figure something out by then?" I asked.

She pulled back, searching my gaze, makeup smudged around her eyes. "What do you mean?"

"I mean, we'll find you a job. A good job. The best job only second to a breast job."

She cracked a smile and smacked me.

"Kidding," I said with a smile. "About the last part, not the first. We're keeping you here, baby."

She nodded slowly. "I trust you. But I'm wondering how you're so confident, Hayes. I mean, it's a small town. It's not like there are dozens of jobs just waiting to be filled. I'd be lucky to get a job at the diner."

My heart twitched at her despair. I wished I could take it away. "You forget you're with a Madigan," I said, brushing back her hair. "That means you have me *and* my crazy, overprotective, very motivated family on your side. All my brothers, their wives... we're going to figure this out, because we're all here for you."

Her spirits seemed to lift. "Can I admit something? I was always a little jealous of Liv marrying into your family. I always wanted something big and close-knit like that, but it's just my parents and me."

"Not anymore," I said, holding her tight. "So you get your cry out, and then we'll take you home and clean you up, and we'll figure this out. Because giving up on us is not an option."

49

DELLA

A SENSE of peace settled over me after talking with Hayes. Even though I wasn't sure how things would turn out, it was a relief to know I had the world's most stubborn man (and his entire family) in my corner.

But as I let my thoughts drift on my drive home from work, I knew the coming weeks and months wouldn't be easy. I'd be starting a new career, likely in an entirely new field. The three people who mattered the most to me weren't Hayes's biggest fans, which would surely make any gathering awkward.

With any luck, Liv's visit tonight would clear up at least some of that awkwardness. Doing my best to stay hopeful, I went inside and got in the shower to clean up before Liv arrived with dinner. I was sitting on my couch, letting my hair air dry while watching a rerun of GBBO when my friend knocked on the door.

My chest tightened. She usually just walked right

in. This rift between us might be even bigger than I thought.

"Come in," I called.

And she did, carrying a plastic bag loaded with to-go boxes and Styrofoam cups tucked under her arm. "Hey, Del," she said with a tentative smile.

"Let me help you," I replied, getting up and retrieving the drinks from her. We set up all the food on the coffee table so we could watch TV while we ate like we had so many times before—especially when we were both single.

But now she had a family of her own, and life was starting to change for me too.

"Before we eat, I wanted to tell you how sorry I am," Liv said quickly.

My heart twisted because a simple sorry wouldn't fix how badly I felt after our conversation the night before. I owed it to our friendship to be honest. So I shifted on the couch, my knees nearly touching hers, and looked her in the eyes. "Liv, I've always supported you, even when I didn't totally agree with your decisions, because I trust that you know what's best for you."

"I know." She looked down at her lap, thumb tracing the lines on her opposite palm. "You're a great friend, and I haven't been a great friend or a great sister-in-law."

The hurt in her voice hurt me. I hated seeing her in pain, even if I was as well. "Liv..."

She shook her head. "Fletcher pointed out that my brother Rhett and I may be more alike than I thought... We fight fiercely for the people we love, even if the fight isn't needed."

"It's really not," I told her. "Hayes is a great guy. I wish you could see what I see in him."

She rubbed her palms over her jeans. "The thing is, I don't need to see what you see in Hayes. Because I know you, and I trust you."

I blinked quickly, trying to fight the stinging in my eyes.

"Whatever happens, I want to be here for it. If you're willing to risk the hurt, I'm willing to eat a hundred tubs of frosting with you until we paste your heart together like a gingerbread house. If he's your happily ever after, you bet I'm holding your wedding dress when you have to pee. Because Fletcher might be the love of my life, but you're my soulmate."

Tears started falling down my cheeks, so much so that I was wondering if some type of magic was turning me into a water spigot, I'd cried so much lately.

"Don't cry," Liv said sadly. "I didn't mean to upset you."

I shook my head. "These are relieved tears. It's been... a lot these past couple days."

Liv nodded and passed me one of the drinks. "A milkshake should help."

I let out a teary chuckle, taking it from her. She was

right, of course. The smooth, creamy drink felt amazing as I swallowed it down.

"How did the conversation go with Hayes?" she asked.

I smiled—I couldn't help myself. And I was still smiling when I finished telling her all about it.

Her mouth fell open at the last part. "Hayes is cleaning out his guest room?"

I nodded.

She reached over to me and hugged me tight. We squealed happily like the giddy teens we once were together.

"I'm so happy for you," she said, eyes shining with joy.

I smiled back. "Thank you." I just hoped my parents would be as easy to convince.

"So is it just issues with Hayes and my stubborn ass, or is there something else?"

I frowned, setting my drink back down. "It's my job too. Edna already offered my position to someone else, and if I stay in town, I'm out of work."

Liv's features sank. "Oh, Della..."

"I know." My voice cracked. "Hayes said he's going to help me figure it out, and I trust him, but I also know there aren't a ton of options here."

I reached for a napkin from the bag and wiped at my eyes. "Sorry, I didn't mean for this visit to be a big cry fest." I bunched up the napkin in my hand, crumpling the scratchy white tissue.

"We've both shed plenty of tears over the years—don't start apologizing now." Liv bumped my shoulder.

I shook my head at her. "I just don't know what to do."

"Whatever it is, we'll find the solution together," she promised. "Once we've eaten our weight in mozzarella sticks."

I chuckled and hugged my friend. Just like that, a little bit of my life felt right again.

50

FLETCHER

WITH THE YOUNGER TWO girls in bed and Maya finishing up homework in her room, I went to the home office to file paperwork for the practice. It was the least favorite part of my day, but it had to get done.

I was so much in the zone, I didn't notice my wife coming into the office until her pregnancy bump knocked over a picture frame on my desk.

"Shit," she muttered, picking it up and then brushing her hand over her belly. "I'm never going to get used to this."

I looked up at her, amused. "You okay?"

"Fine," she grumbled. "Enormous. When's this baby coming out again?"

"You've got a few months, I'm afraid," I said with an apologetic smile. "How was Della?"

"Great, but there's something I want to talk to you about."

I closed my laptop and rubbed my eyes. "I'm all ears. Let's head out to the kitchen?"

"Sure."

I went around the desk, putting my arm around her waist. I loved the way her stomach rounded with our child. Her hand covered my own, and she walked with me to the island, sitting at one of the barstools.

"Care for a mocktail?" I offered, grabbing a couple glasses from the cabinet.

"Sure." She leaned forward on the counter, resting her chin in her hand. "It's funny they call them virgin drinks, since all us pregnant whores are the ones drinking them."

I nearly snorted. "Liv."

She grinned. "You know how I got pregnant. Or should I refresh your memory?"

My cock twitched. "Damn, woman, let me make your drink first."

She replied with a wicked giggle, and I went about cutting a lime in half, pulling a few leaves from the mint plant above the sink, and adding sparkling water.

"So I had an idea I think could be really good," Liv began tentatively. The last time she talked like this, I ended up with a puppy she and Maya found alongside the road. So when I turned to face her, it was with a heavy dose of skepticism.

"I—"

We heard the sound of a loud engine along the

road and growing closer in the driveway, then gave each other a look.

"Hayes," we said at the same time.

She gave me a smile. "Better mix an extra drink." She pushed up from the stool, going to the front door, and I may have stared at her ample curves as she walked away.

A few seconds later, I heard her greeting Hayes and the tread of his boots as he came inside. He got to the counter, and before he even said hello, he declared, "You've got to give Della a job."

Liv and I both stared at him in shock.

"Hey, that was my idea!" Liv protested.

Now I was staring at both of them, absolutely confused. "Okay, what the hell is going on? Della has a job."

My wife and my brother sat at the counter, filling me in on how Della actually couldn't stay at her job. How her timing was off in deciding to stay, and it left her in a bad position, having to find another job or stick with her plan to move out of Cottonwood Falls.

Hayes said, "Brenda's old as dirt—she can't work with you forever. And Liv's complained to me about you working at night."

I gave my wife a look, but she lifted her chin. "It's true. I would love to get my husband back at night and keep my best friend in town. And didn't Brenda tell you she wants to look at retiring in the next year or two? She wants to spend more time with her grandkids. This way, you'd have the office manager part of the business solid before bringing in a new nurse. You even said you wanted to start offering more aesthetic services, which you can't do if your nurse spends half her time on paperwork and—"

I held up my hand to stall Liv's spiel. She could go on for hours until she got her point across. "Can you both give me a second to think?"

They gave each other a look and then nodded. Without their chatter, I had a second to pour myself a Moscow mule, lean against the counter, and take a few sips. They were making a lot of sense, but I hadn't planned to bring on anyone new. It would be an extra cost and would take time to train her on the job duties, not to mention working with my wife's best friend and my brother's girlfriend could get messy. Someone had to be practical here.

"I haven't even opened a position or interviewed her," I said.

Hayes's brow puckered as he pushed his glass away. "Why do you need to interview her? Edna kept her on for eighteen years, and you know she doesn't deal with dead weight."

Liv nodded in agreement. "Not to mention she's here every week. She's babysat our children for literal days before. You're telling me you'd trust her with the most important humans in your life and not some paperwork she's overqualified to handle?"

My cheeks got hot at the mention, and instead of

responding, I turned to my brother. "Okay, but what if you and Della break up?" I countered. "I don't want you mad at me because I'm working with your ex."

Hayes glowered at me. "Give me a little credit."

I held my hands up in surrender and looked between them, both of them staring me down like they wouldn't take no for an answer. Then I heard my eldest daughter say, "Are you going to work with Auntie Della? That's a *great* idea, Daddy!" She breezed into the kitchen, going to the fridge in her pajamas.

I let out a sigh, rubbing my temples. Now they just needed Rhett to come over, and the four strongest-willed people I knew could all gang up on me. "You planned this, didn't you?" I asked Liv.

She held up her hands. "Maya's a brilliant girl all on her own."

Maya pulled back from the fridge, holding a yogurt. "Thanks, Livvy."

My wife smiled at her. "Of course, babe."

Hayes ran his fingers through his hair. "So are you in or not?"

I let out a sigh, knowing I'd been bested. It was a good idea, even if I hadn't come up with it on my own. "I'll need to write a job description and do an inter-view, but I'll consider it."

Before the words were even out of my mouth, Hayes and Liv were celebrating together. And I had to laugh at this crazy life. Sometimes things didn't work out the way you expected them to—they worked out exactly how they were meant to.

51

DELLA

I'D NEVER BEEN SO nervous to see Fletcher in my life.

In fact, he was a package deal with my best friend as far as I was concerned. Except today I wasn't hanging out with them at their country home or meeting up with them for dinner. No, I was walking up to Madigan Medical with three copies of my resume printed on cream-colored paper.

I hadn't needed a resume since I graduated college, but I'd spent all of my lunch break working on it and told Edna I had to take off early for an interview. Thankfully, she understood.

I smoothed my dress, ran my tongue over my teeth to make sure there wasn't anything stuck there, and opened the front door of the old home turned medical practice.

In the front room, which was now the lobby, Brenda

got up from her desk and said, "Della, right on time!" The woman was in her sixties but looked so much younger with perfect blond hair and an insanely in-shape body. "Great to see you."

Her cheery mood put me a little at ease, and I smiled back at her. "You too, Brenda."

"Come back to the kitchen," she said, waving me over. "Fletcher's waiting back there."

I nodded, walking over the wood floors on my best pair of heels. Each step marked the time that passed until I was back in the kitchen with them, sitting around a heavy oak table, my hands fidgeting anxiously in my lap.

"Thank you so much for having me," I said to both of them. "I'm really grateful to you for giving me a chance to apply."

Fletcher's wry smile was enough to tell me he might have taken some convincing, but he said, "I've been denying for a long time that we might need some extra help around here. But the truth is, Cottonwood Falls deserves the best medical care, and bringing someone on who can specialize in insurance and office manage-ment is a big step in that direction."

Brenda nodded. "And since you know insurance already, it might not be so frustrating to you, all the hoops we have to jump through."

I chuckled at that. "I'm definitely used to jumping hoops. Metaphorically speaking, of course."

That got a polite laugh from them and broke the

ice a bit so we could discuss the position and what they were looking for. When we were done talking about what they'd need at the practice and going over the details, Fletcher said he'd be doing a lot of thinking and would call me back by the end of the week.

I nodded and thanked them, my heart racing nervously. But before I left the kitchen, I turned back to them. "Fletcher, I just want you to know, if you decide not to hire me, I completely understand. I don't want a job because I know your wife or am dating your brother. I want a job because you believe I'm what's best for this practice to help you and your patients, because that's what I'd be here to do. I love this town and the people in it too much to take a job that isn't really needed."

Fletcher and Brenda exchanged a look, and he broke out in a grin. "You're hired."

I WAS on cloud nine as I pulled into the parking lot of Madigan Auto. As soon as I heard the news, there was one person I wanted to tell, and I had to see his face as I did.

Getting out of my car, the first place I checked was the garage, where several cars were pulled in and being worked on. Ethan saw me and said, "He's in the office."

I gave him a thankful smile and passed through the

side door, going back to the office. The door was shut, so I knocked a few times and Hayes called, "Come in," as Chopper gave a warning bark.

I smiled. Even here at the garage, it sounded like home.

I pushed open the door, and Chopper bounded up to me. I scooped him in my arms and looked over to my man, who was pushing back from his desk and standing up. Something about him in that gray shirt with the nametag, tattoos winding down his arms, was so damn hot.

"Della." My name was barely past his lips before he tugged me into a kiss that had me forgetting the news I came here to share. But when he pulled away, he said, "How was the interview?"

I blinked. "Oh, the interview."

He chuckled. "With Fletcher and Brenda?"

"Oh!" I set Chopper down and grabbed Hayes's hands. "I start next month!"

His eyes went wide. "You're shitting me."

Grinning, I shook my head.

The look on his face was pure joy, and he swept me into his arms, kissing me again between words. "I knew you could do it! You're going to do such a good job. He's so lucky to have you."

I smiled against his kiss, so fully happy. "We should do something to celebrate."

Still holding me close, he mumbled, "What were you thinking?"

Reaching between us, I ran my hand over his jeans. "Something to do with this?"

"Fuck me," he whispered.

"Why not?" My voice was breathy. I'd never had sex in a public place like this before, but with Hayes... I couldn't hold back.

He kissed me again, urgently, his tongue sliding against the seam of my mouth. I moaned softly, not wanting anyone to hear us. But then he walked me back until I was pressed against the wall. And he said, "Put your foot on my desk."

My eyebrows raised, wondering what he had in mind. But he lifted my knee until I had one heel placed on his desk, the other solidly on the floor. And then he lowered himself to his knees before me.

"I worship you." And then he was on me, tugging aside my panties and placing his mouth to my sex.

I let out a surprised whimper, and then he hummed. "Bite on a pen."

Following his guide, I fumbled for his pen holder. It spilled over his desk in my haste, but I grabbed one, bringing it to my lips and biting down while he continued lapping, nipping, and sucking on my sensitive parts.

My head lulled against the wall. "Hayes," I moaned around the pen.

A knock sounded at the door, and I clenched, but Hayes called back, "I'm busy!"

And then, just like that, he was on me again, adding

fingers this time. Filling me and teasing me until I was panting for air, fighting for any thought beyond how good he was making me feel.

And then I was tumbling over the edge, nothing existing in my mind but Hayes and the way he made my body crumble at his command like no man ever had before.

"That's my girl," he said, standing up and fumbling with the belt at his pants.

I barely had a chance to catch my breath before his cock was in me, and he was fucking me against the wall, holding my leg in his elbow. Bending his head next to mine, he spoke in my ear as he filled me with his cock.

It was all so overwhelming that all I could do was hold on to him, digging my fingers into his back just to keep myself upright.

"Hayes," I moaned quietly.

"I know, baby," he breathed into my ear. And as he filled me with an unrelenting pace, he said, "You are everything."

"My sunshine."

"My undoing."

"My love."

"My life."

"Hayes," I cried, on the verge of coming again.

"I love you," he said, voice husky. "I love you so fucking much."

And that was *my* undoing.

Right there.

Not just what he said, but how he showed it with every stroke into me. The careful way he held me.

The way he refused to give in to his own release until I was shattering around him, giving whatever pieces of me I'd held on to and making them wholly *his*.

52

HAYES

DELLA and her parents were coming to my place to watch their cooking show and eat dinner. I'd met them before, done work on their vehicles, but it was the first time I was meeting them as Della's boyfriend.

I'd never been a nervous hurler, but that might change today.

My house had never looked cleaner. Even Chopper's dog bed in the corner of the living room was clear of any stray hairs. He curled up in the bed, resting without a care in the world. Lucky bastard.

Unlike the spoiled dog, I had things to worry about, like the lemon herb chicken breasts cooking in the oven. Della said it was her parents' favorite meal, and I wasn't above scoring brownie points in any way possible.

Literally, considering I was currently mixing

brownie batter. This was from a box because I knew I couldn't screw that up.

A knock sounded on my door, and I called, "Come in!"

The knocking came again.

With a sigh, I set down my mixing spoon and walked over to the door to open it. Della stood holding a glass pan with two hot pink oven mitts. "Sorry," she said. "Hands were full."

I chuckled, standing back to let her in. "Was the sourdough a success?"

With glee in her eyes, she said, "You *have* to try this focaccia. I think it's the best thing I've ever tasted."

She set the pan on my counter and peeled back the foil. Sure enough, there was a corner of the cheesy, crusty bread missing. Della got a butterknife from my drawer and handed it to me. I cut myself a piece and put it in my mouth, ready to tell her it was the best damn thing I'd ever tasted, regardless of whether or not it was true.

But then a burst of garlic butter flavor mixed with mozzarella and tangy bread took over my taste buds, and I accidentally moaned. "You made this?"

She nodded, making her red curls bounce.

"And it didn't come out of a box?" Dang, my brownies may not be as impressive as I thought.

This time she shook her head.

"Pretty and talented too?" I went to her, taking her in my arms and dipping her for a kiss. She giggled as she stood up. "How did I get so lucky?" I asked.

She reached up to kiss my cheek. "I'm the lucky one. Thank you for braving dinner with my parents."

"Don't thank me yet," I cautioned. "I might just fuck it all up." Real fear hid behind my joking tone, and I went back to stirring brownies to hide my anxious expression. I didn't need her worrying about my feelings.

"Even if it goes badly, we have time to change their minds," she reminded me, hugging me from behind.

Just that little gesture eased some of the tension in my shoulders, and not for the first time, I wondered why the fuck I was so against relationships before. Sure, I was stressing about her parents liking me, but I also got Della. She made all the worry more than worth it.

I turned away from the brownies, looping my arms around her. "You're distracting me." I brushed my nose over hers.

She pressed a soft kiss to my lips. "And?"

I smiled against her kiss. "Just thought you should know." Our kiss deepened, and the brownies were completely forgotten. Winding my hand around the swell of her ass, I pulled her closer to me.

She tangled her fingers in my hair and nipped at my bottom lip. I shuddered at how sexy it was and trailed kisses down her throat. "Do we have time for a quickie before your parents get here?" I asked. "Please?"

She giggled. "No, they're always——"

The doorbell rang.

"Early," she finished with a sigh.

She stepped back, straightening her dress, and I cursed my semihard cock. Nothing could soften it like her parents standing at the door, though. Adjusting myself in my jeans, I followed her to the front door, pasting a smile on my face.

My dad had given me tips on making a good impression on her parents, and I followed every one.

Keep eye contact and smile.

Unfortunately, I hadn't planned on Chopper. He burst up from his bed, darting toward the front door and jumping on Della's dad. He stared in horror at the little thing.

"What's this?" he asked.

Della scooped up the dog and said, "Our puppy."

Her parents shared a worried look.

"Welcome to my home," I said quickly, stepping back to let them inside. Then I shook her dad's hand, nice and firm. And I told her mom she looked lovely.

But then Chuck said, "Are you coming on to my wife?"

The blood drained from my face.

Della said, "Dad, you're going to give him a heart attack."

Chuck laughed, but it didn't quite meet his eyes. He was testing me. So I forced out a laugh and said, "Is it working, Nora? The flowers on the table are for you."

Nora pressed a hand to her chest. "Why, that's sweet of you. Isn't it sweet, Chuck?"

He grunted his acknowledgement.

Della cut in and said, "I have to show you my focaccia."

I breathed a sigh of relief because that gave me a second to gather myself while I got all the food ready to bring to the table. I'd made rotini pasta in a cream sauce, chicken, and green beans to go with Della's pride and joy.

And soon we were all sitting around my glass table, Chopper lying in his bed once more while we ate off black and red plates. Della said, "Hayes, this chicken is so good. You made it just perfect."

I smiled at her compliment. It seemed a little forced, but I knew tonight mattered a lot to her. "Thanks, babe," I replied, squeezing her hand under the glass table.

Her dad stared at our hands like he wished his eyes could produce laser beams.

I was glad he couldn't.

Nora said, "It's delicious."

After a quiet moment, she broke the silence, asking, "So, how did you two start dating?"

Della and I exchanged a glance. That was a good question. Especially since Della used to annoy me with her sunny personality.

Like she could read my mind, she said, "Actually, I used to annoy him." I barely held back a snort.

Her dad shot me a thinly veiled glare as he wiped his mouth on a napkin.

Della continued. "And it was really fun to annoy him, so I kept doing it."

Now I really did snort, and even her dad's lips twitched.

Her mom said, "Sounds like happily ever after."

I chuckled. I was starting to like Della's mom—she was clearly where Della got her warmth from. "I had a crush on Della," I admitted, and all eyes swung to me.

"You did?" Della asked.

I nodded, setting my silverware down and wiping my fingers on the napkin in my lap. "Actually, I was hanging out with my brothers and telling them I liked you but thought you would never be interested in me. So they practically shoved me away and forced me to man up and talk to you. Tell you how I felt. It was the best thing they ever did for me."

Della gave me a grateful smile. "For both of us."

Her mom made a small, "Aw."

But her dad wasn't as convinced. "The whole town knows of your history with women, Hayes. Even knowing that, knowing how *good* she is, your family pushed you toward my little girl?"

53

DELLA

OH SHIT.

Dad was generally mild-mannered. Sweet. But he was also fiercely protective, and he wasn't giving Hayes an easy time.

"Dad," I hissed. "That's so inappropriate. We're in Hayes's house right now, and if you can't respect him—"

Hayes quieted me by squeezing my hand. "It's okay."

"Seriously?" I asked him. Because I wasn't okay with how Dad was treating the man I loved.

But Hayes nodded and faced my dad again. "Look, I'm not gonna pretend I was ever a saint. Because I'm not one—but I'm not stupid. Della's as good as it gets. If I fuck this up, you have every right to come over here and kick my ass. Hell, I'll be kicking my own ass if I do something to lose her."

He paused, taking a breath. "I know how incredible she is, and I plan to be around as long as she'll have me. I know it would mean the world to Della—to both of us—if you'd give me a chance."

I nodded, trying to blink back tears. Hayes may have cussed, but he'd also stood up for me and my desires. He'd put me first. "It really would mean a lot," I echoed, looking between my dad and mom.

Mom covered my hand with hers and then squeezed Dad's hand on her other side. "Of course we will," Mom said. Then she gave Dad a look. And since my dad's only weakness was my mom, he said, "We will give you a chance. But I'll take you up on kicking your ass if you hurt my little girl."

"Chuck!" Mom said, shocked at my dad's language. I was surprised too; I could count the times he'd cussed in front of us on a single hand and still not use all my fingers.

But Hayes beamed at my dad. "Thank you."

Instead of responding, Dad took a bite of his chicken. "This is pretty good."

I felt relief like it was air releasing from a balloon. Thank God.

We finished eating supper, and then we all went to Hayes's living room to sit and watch TV. I sat tucked under his arm on the love seat while my parents sat beside each other on the couch.

And I realized I didn't have a relationship like my parents. I never would, because that was their unique coupling. But I had a man I loved, and he loved me. It wasn't what I pictured. Somehow, it was even better.

After we finished watching our show, it was dark outside. Hayes and I walked my parents to the door and said goodnight. Mom even gave him a one-armed hug goodbye as she carried her flowers.

Once the door shut, Hayes and I turned to each other. His smile widened as he said, "I think we pulled it off!"

I took his hands, jumping up and down excitedly. "We totally pulled it off!"

He chuckled at me and pulled me into a hug. His lips pressed to the crown of my head, and he took a deep breath. "I love you," he whispered.

I smiled against his chest, feeling warmth radiating from him. "I love you too. Thank you for fighting for us."

"I'll never stop," he promised, still holding me tight.

I knew he meant every word.

I reached down, grabbing his belt and beginning to pull it apart. "Now, to celebrate all of that hard work," I hummed, lowering myself to my knees.

He gave me an incredulous grin. "How did I get so fucking lucky? Celebrating twice in one day?"

I freed his cock and licked his piercing, making him shudder. "Might have something to do with this," I purred.

He tossed his head back and laughed, even as his fingers wound through my curls. "Is that so?"

I gave him a sultry smile and took him in my mouth. The smooth skin of his head was velvet under my tongue. Just tasting and feeling him was already turning me on. But then he gathered my curls in his hands, holding them away from my face.

"You take my cock so fucking good."

I looked up at him to find him gazing down at me, fire in his eyes. I nearly shuddered at the intensity I found there. It was all I needed to pull him deeper into my mouth, shaking my head until he was at the back of my throat.

"Take me deep, baby." His voice was husky. "You know how to make me feel good."

His encouragement had me holding as long as I could until I had to pull back and gasp for air. Seeing his lips curl into a wicked smile had me spitting on his cock and taking him again, licking up and down his shaft, then teasing his piercing with the tip of my tongue while I cupped his heavy sack with my hands.

He'd made me feel so good with his mouth, and the way he moaned told me I was making him feel just as good. The tang of precum spread onto my tongue, and I lapped at it.

"Fuck, Della," he grunted, gripping my hair tighter. The way his fingers tangled in my curls was an aphrodisiac all its own.

I took him in my mouth again, bobbing my head on his cock, and he said, "Your pretty lips look so fucking good on my cock."

God, his dirty talk was so hot. Most guys I'd been with just moaned, or worse, put their hands on my head to guide me into what they wanted. Even when I was supposed to be on my knees worshiping him, Hayes treated me like the goddess in charge.

"I'm getting close," he warned. "We can take this to the bedroom."

I'd never been the kind of girl to swallow. But I'd also never had Hayes Madigan standing over me and telling me how amazing I was either.

So I held on to his hips, refusing to let him pull away from my mouth, making sure he came all over my tongue, and I swallowed every drop as he uttered my name and tangled his fingers in my mane.

"God, Della," he whispered, lowering himself to his knees to kiss me. "Are you trying to kill me?"

I smirked. "Didn't work. Guess I'll have to try again."

54

HAYES

ONE YEAR LATER

I DROVE down the street toward my house, warm air wrapped around me, making my shirt ripple. The air wound over my muscles, stinging the fresh tattoo right next to the one dedicated to my mom.

I'd gotten a butterfly for Della. Every stroke the artist made reminded me her ink was on my skin forever, just like she'd imprinted herself on my soul. I wasn't the same guy as when we first started dating; I was better because of her love, changed forever just like this tattoo altered the canvas of my skin.

There was just one more step to take to make her mine for just as long.

I pulled up to my house and walked in, thinking just how different it looked now to when I first met Della.

The leather furniture stayed—since I owned a garage and grease was bound to find its way home. But there were now throw blankets layered over the back of the chairs and throw pillows for resting on. A bookshelf stood by the TV with framed photos of Della and me and even some of my family.

There was a photo hanging in my hallway of Della and me on our first vacation to Galveston, where we spent hours upon hours hiding under an umbrella on the beach so her pale skin wouldn't burn.

My house was fine before. But now? Everywhere I looked reminded me of her in the best possible way. Even the shampoo bottles she kept in my shower for when she stayed over. We hardly spent a night apart but hadn't yet decided where to make our home together.

All in due time.

I showered up and got dressed, then grabbed the supplies I needed from the kitchen and put them in a cooler. Then I gave Chopper a quick pet goodbye and drove back to the garage, finding her car parked and running in the empty parking lot.

I watched through her window as she sang along to a song I couldn't hear, her head bobbing—no doubt out of sync with the beat. Her fingers tapped against the steering wheel and red curls fell across her face with the performance.

I grinned at the sight, and when she turned to see me, she smiled back.

Over the last year, I'd gotten so many of those smiles. I wanted to keep seeing her smile forever.

I got out of the truck, grabbing the cooler, and met her at the front door to the garage.

"What is this?" she asked, glancing at the cooler as I unlocked the door.

"A surprise," I said with a small smile.

"Ooh, what is it?" she asked, her eyes wide.

I pushed the door open then carried the cooler to one of the tables as she followed me. "Turns out our favorite brand released three new flavors of hot chocolate."

"They did?" she asked excitedly. "What are they?"

I pulled one thermos out of the cooler and read the label. "Fruity cereal. Sounds terrible," I said, setting it on the table.

She laughed.

"And this one is... dandelion. What the fuck?"

Her giggle warmed my heart. "Maybe they read about the medicinal effects of so-called weeds."

"Or you called and told them about it?" I teased. "Multiple times?"

She shook her head at me. "It wouldn't kill you to drink a dandelion tea once a day."

"I'm not willing to chance it," I retorted, which earned me a roll of her eyes.

"Okay, what next?" she asked.

"The last one is my favorite," I said. "Can you read the label for me while I get our cups?" I held out the thermos for her. She took it, and I reached for the "mugs" in the cooler before watching her eyes trail across the letters I'd carefully written on the label.

Her pink lips parted. "Hayes?"

I lowered myself to one knee, holding open a white velvet box I thought looked like a marshmallow. Inside rested a vintage engagement ring with character and charm, just like Della. The diamond glittered in the light.

"Oh my gosh," she whispered, freckled hands covering her mouth.

"A year ago today, you brought in a cooler of hot chocolate, convinced that you'd find one I liked. Before you walked in, I was convinced neither hot chocolate nor a relationship were for me."

She smiled slightly, shaking her head. The tears in her eyes caught the light.

"But turns out you're great at proving me wrong."

A teary chuckle passed through her hands.

"Della Dwyer... I want to be your sourdough-recipe tester. Your dance partner. The one you bitch at about safety statistics. I want you to be the one I wake up to in the morning with crusty eyes and bad breath and the one you fall asleep next to with that ridiculous mouth tape on your face and those weird things under your eyes."

She wiped tears away from her cheeks. "I told you they're to help with dark spots."

Smiling, I reached for one of her hands, holding it.

"Della, I want to be your husband. Will you be my wife?"

"Of course I will," she said.

I slid the ring on her finger, finding the perfect fit. It

was barely in place before she lowered herself into my arms, wrapping her arms around my neck and holding on tightly.

"I love you so fucking much," I breathed.

"I love you too," she replied. "I can't wait to be Mrs. Hayes Brain Madigan."

EPILOGUE
GRAYSON

I WALKED down the hallway to Hayes's old bedroom in disbelief that my son was getting married today. And to a woman as incredible as Della, no less. Hayes was getting ready in the main bedroom downstairs while the ladies used all the bedrooms and the bathroom upstairs to get ready for the big day.

For a long time, I thought Hayes would be a bachelor forever. But Della was exactly what he needed. It was clear in the way he lived his life now. Before he fell for her, it was like he wanted to live as fast as possible.

Now he slowed down. He savored his life with Della instead of racing it away.

I reached the last door in the hallway and knocked.

Soon, the door opened, my daughter-in-law Liv there to greet me. She looked pretty in a mint-green dress, her hair twisted up into a bun. "Hey, Gray," she said warmly.

I smiled at her. "You look lovely."

"Thank you," she replied with a grin. "You're so handsome in a suit, Gray." She straightened my lapel for me.

"Any chance I can get a second with the bride?" I asked.

Liv peeked back over her shoulder then looked back at me. "Sure thing. I'll give you a few minutes." She walked past me and left the door open, showing Della sitting in front of the desk where Hayes used to do homework. When I could convince him to do it.

My mind flashed back to my little boy who felt everything so deeply. To my surly teen no one seemed able to reach. To the young man who made a life for himself as a mechanic and business owner. God, it had gone by so fast.

It was hard to believe my son had grown into the man marrying this stunner of a woman.

Today she wore a champagne-colored dress with a full skirt that spilled around the chair she sat in. But the dress paled compared to her. She wore simple makeup, her curly red hair pulled into a loose bun at the base of her neck. "How did my son get so lucky to marry you?" My throat felt tight.

Della smiled, getting up to hug me. "I feel so lucky to be with him and to marry into this family." She patted my cheek gently. "You should be incredibly proud of yourself for the men you raised. They wouldn't be who they are without you, Gray."

A ball of emotion formed in my throat, and I had to swallow it down. "Thought I wouldn't cry today," I managed.

Her eyes shone as she smiled. "I got you something just in case..." She walked to the corner of the room where a tote bag sat on the nightstand. Then she reached in and pulled out a folded piece of fabric.

Passing it to me, she said, "A handkerchief for you."

I took it in my hands, studying the sunflower embroidered in the corner next to a blue heart.

I gave her a watery smile, wishing yet again that my wife could be at her son's wedding. "Maya would have loved you."

Now she pressed at her eyes. "Oh, Gray..."

"I know," I said roughly. "Before we get to the ceremony, I wanted to tell you how grateful I am to have you in our family. You are exactly what Hayes needed. And you've made our family so much fuller with your presence, Dell. I can't wait for you to be a Madigan."

She smiled up at me and then hugged me, pressing a kiss to my cheek. "Thank you, Gray."

"Of course," I replied. "I'll let you get to it. I'm sure other people want their time with the bride."

At her wave goodbye, I let myself out to find Liv waiting in the hallway with Della's parents. We exchanged a few kind words, putting me on the verge of tears again, and then I made my way downstairs to see my son, tucking the handkerchief into my jacket pocket.

It was almost time. And even though I knew Hayes loved Della with his whole heart, part of me worried he would take up his old ways and run.

So I took a deep breath before knocking on my bedroom door, not quite sure what I would find with the seconds ticking down.

"Come in," Hayes called.

I walked in, seeing Fletcher adjusting the black tie at Hayes's neck. Hayes wore an all-black suit with a black tie, and it looked damn good on him. Especially when Fletcher stepped back, revealing the perfectly straight tie.

"You look so grown up," I uttered.

Hayes gave me a pained look. "I'm over thirty, Dad."

"You're still my little boy," I managed, reaching for the handkerchief.

"Oh boy," Fletcher said, coming to my side and wrapping his arm around my shoulders. "You don't want to show emotion in front of groomzilla."

I raised my eyebrows in surprise as I dabbed at my eyes. "Groomzilla?"

Hayes shot him a glare. "Just 'cause I want Della to have a good fucking day, all of a sudden I'm a groomzilla. Bah." Hayes turned back to the mirror, adjusting his jacket.

Fletcher leaned closer to my ear. "Turns out the company wanted to send a *new* limo instead of the vintage one Hayes picked out months ago. Hayes had words for them."

"Yeah," Hayes chimed in. "And they're sending the right fucking one. With free champagne."

I chuckled. "Atta boy."

Hayes smiled slightly, and I walked up to him, rubbing his shoulders through the suit jacket. "How are you feeling, son?"

He lifted a shoulder in response, looking at me in the mirror with a weary expression. "I'm thinking I'll feel a hell of a lot better once Della says 'I do.'" He turned around to face us. "Why the fuck didn't we go to Vegas the second she said yes to marrying me?"

Well, I guess he was still my son. "Because you wanted to make her happy. Like a good husband does."

Hayes's lips twitched. "Fucking stupid of me."

Fletcher and I both laughed.

Hayes fiddled with the sleeves of his shirt, adjusting the cuff links. "I knew I wanted her to be my wife on our first date... I thought *she's the one*. Scared the hell out of me."

I smiled. "I thought the same thing about your mom the first day I met her."

Both Fletcher and Hayes looked at me in surprise. "You did?" Hayes asked.

I nodded. "Of course, it took me four years to stop running from it." I shook my head. "Turns out you're a smarter man than me."

"We already knew that," Hayes cracked. But there was a hint of his usual playfulness missing from his voice, and he looked down and turned back to the mirror.

Fletcher looked between us and said, "I'm going to make sure everyone knows it's about time to start."

He left the room, and Hayes and I were alone with only Chopper for company, lying on my bed like he thought he was king of the house. To be fair, he looked the part in his little black doggy suit.

I walked up to my son in the mirror, looking at him but seeing the little boy his mom and I loved so very much. Maya always had a soft spot for him. Days like today were harder without her, even decades later.

"You know what your mom always said about you?" I asked him.

"That I was a hundred pounds of energy in a fifty-pound suit?"

I chuckled. "In addition to that."

Hayes smiled slightly. "Tell me."

"She said, 'Hayes feels so much because he has so much to give.'"

I paused, taking a shaky breath, and Hayes's bottom lip quavered to match.

I gripped his shoulder with one hand and his hand with my other as we looked at each other in the mirror. "She knew all those years ago how *good* you are inside. How great of a friend and brother you would be. How great of a husband."

Hayes turned to me now, his eyes tortured. "I can't lose her like we lost Mom. I can't, Dad, I—"

I shushed him, pulling him into a hug. "I know."

Hayes gripped my back while I held the back of his neck in my hand.

Still holding him, I said, "You're brave, Hayes. To love Della with your whole heart on your sleeve. Even knowing what loss looks like. *That's* the man Della's marrying. The brave, kindhearted man she loves."

Hayes sniffed and stepped back, wiping at his eyes. "Thank you, Dad. For always *seeing* me when most people judged."

Tears threatened again, but I blinked them back. "Always," I promised.

A knock sounded on the door, and Fletcher called, "It's time."

"You ready?" I asked my son.

Hayes grinned at me. "What part of Vegas didn't you understand?"

Chuckling, I took his hand, and we walked out of the room toward his happily ever after.

After walking him down the aisle, I took my seat in the front row next to my best friend. My Aggie.

She looked gorgeous in a soft blue dress that reached halfway down her calves and strappy silver heels that showed the bright red polish on her toes. She patted my knee, saying, "Don't worry, I brought tissues."

I gave her a grateful smile. "Good, 'cause my hanky's already getting full."

"Oh gross," she said with a small chuckle.

I reached down and squeezed her hand. "Thank you for thinking of me." Aggie was my best friend. She was my sunrise after so much pain of losing my wife and raising five boys on my own. Even if we weren't in love, I loved her still.

She smiled over at me, something in her eyes I couldn't quite place. But before I could ask how she was feeling, the preacher said it was time for us all to stand for the bride.

Guitar strings plucked softly as Della came out of the house with her dad, looking even more stunning as the early evening light caught the red shock of her hair.

She walked down the aisle toward Hayes, tears slowly dripping down her cheeks even as she smiled at her groom. And when I looked at my son, he was crying too.

She reached the end of the aisle, her dad shaking Hayes's hand. Their relationship had started off rough, but in the last year, Hayes had shown up for Della like he promised. And her dad started to see Hayes through his daughter's eyes. So he smiled at Hayes, and then he gave Della a big hug before walking to the other side of the aisle and holding his wife in his arms.

A pang of wistfulness, of envy, shot through me. Even though I appreciated Aggie's friendship and cared for her deeply, it should be my wife sitting next to me.

I was lost in a sea of grief as the preacher started talking, but slowly brought myself to shore in time for the vows. They'd written their vows themselves at Hayes's suggestion. He'd told me canned words could never come close to saying how he felt for Della.

She went first, speaking eloquently of her love and appreciation for Hayes. For always being himself and loving her exactly as she is.

And then my son spoke his vows.

"Everyone here knows I'm not the best with words," he began. "I cuss a lot."

A chuckle went through everyone here.

"Turns out, when you find your forever, it's easy to say how much you love them."

Aggie passed me a tissue, and I pressed it to the corners of my eyes.

Hayes gripped his bride's hands, running his thumbs over her freckled skin. "Della, I was so afraid when we first started dating. I was afraid to fuck it up. Afraid to hurt you. Afraid you'd figure out you're an angel too good for a devil like me... But turns out, I should have been afraid of missing out on a love like this."

As Hayes spoke the rest of his vows, I gave up on holding back tears, and they flowed down my cheeks as I wiped at them.

Over the course of the ceremony, my tears changed to a happy smile. They made sure Hayes's sense of humor and Della's contagious joy were incorporated into every bit of the wedding. And when they kissed, I stood up with everyone else, whooping and cheering for their happily ever after.

As people started filing out of their seats, I noticed just how happy everyone seemed. Almost everyone.

To my side, tears streamed down my Aggie's cheeks. She tried to hide her pain by looking away, but I held her elbows, steering her toward me. "Aggie, what's wrong?"

She looked up at me, so much pain in her eyes it shot through my heart. "I'm just... I'm realizing that I might never have a love like that." She twisted from me and joined the group of people walking toward the tent set up for the reception.

But I stayed frozen in place, an all-too familiar ache cutting me bone deep.

I loved Aggie, but I'd loved a woman once before.

I hardly survived her loss, and only because I promised Maya I'd stay strong for our boys. How could I do it a second time?

A cheer erupted as Hayes stopped on the path to the reception building and dipped Della into a romantic kiss.

And then a small voice spoke in my head...

If my son can be brave, maybe I can too.

THANK you for reading Hello Trouble! To get a spicy

peek at what Hayes and Della are up to after the wedding, get the free bonus scene today!

Read Gray and Aggie's story in Hello Handsome!

Get the free bonus story today!

Get your copy of Hello Handsome today!

AUTHOR'S NOTE

I've heard others say that people never change, but I think that's wrong.

People change when they're ready to *and* when the conditions are right.

It makes me think of my garden and how many years I utterly failed at growing anything but weeds until I started learning more. I got so frustrated thinking I would never figure it out and be a black thumb for life.

And then someone told me not to water if the ground felt damp—wait until the dirt is a little dry to the touch.

I was over-watering 99% of my plants.

Nothing would be able to grow when I was just adding water every single day without knowing how it affected the growing environment.

Then, someone told me adding mulch would hold

back the weeds and keep more moisture and nutrients in the soil.

Holy game changer. Instead of my plants fighting against hot, harsh earth on sunny summer days, they had the cooling effect of mulch and didn't have to compete with as many weeds! Plus, I didn't get so worn out and annoyed with weeding that I lost gusto for the garden.

Then, I went down the TikTok rabbit hole about composting and saving food scraps to enhance the garden. My biggest pumpkin vine ever grew from the compost pile.

My plants needed more nutrition to meet their full potential.

Over time, I learned so many things that helped my gardening, like watering in the evening or morning to lose less water to evaporation. How planting certain plants near each other could help or harm their growth. The importance of planting flowers for pollinators even if your goal is a vegetable garden.

And now, with all this knowledge and practice, I consider myself a fairly successful gardener.

The reason my plants wouldn't grow back then wasn't because of faulty seeds or poor equipment. It was because I didn't know how to give them the conditions to *grow*.

Same with Hayes.

The conditions for his life were to live hyper-independently. He wanted total autonomy and to rely on himself only. He'd lost his mom at a young age, his dad struggled to raise five boys as a widower, and his brothers were all dealing with struggles of their own.

But slowly (so slowly he probably couldn't see it happening) his environment changed. His brothers went from being single bachelors to finding happy, loving relationships of their own. His Dad supported him in purchasing a business where Hayes had to rely on employees and customers to keep the lights on. His siblings started to have children and gained children through marriage so he could see more examples of loving family life.

And then there was Della. The final bit of sunlight he needed to *bloom*.

Sometimes waiting on change can be frustrating, whether you're waiting on another person or trying to make a change in yourself. I've been guilty of pressing myself too hard to make a change without really considering my environment.

I can remember a few years ago when I felt like the only time I had to work out was early in the morning. But every day, my babies would wake up before my alarm and crawl into bed with me and give me the best morning cuddles. Sometimes we'd sleep a little extra, sometimes we'd talk about the day to come, and others we'd tease each other with tickles and jokes. It was my favorite part of the day and I remember those as some of my best mornings ever.

Knowing that, it was unfair of myself to expect myself to get up and work out when I loved getting those precious, stolen moments every day before the hustle and bustle started. The conditions weren't right for me to change my behavior of not working out in the mornings.

What I could have done instead was change the conditions for working out. I could looked for alternative times like during my lunch break or coordinating with my partner to get a little bit of time in the evening a few days a week. Or maybe an evening walk with the kids would have satisfied my need for movement *and* connection.

Now that I've learned what it takes to make consistent changes in my life, I love problem solving and seeing how I can better support myself toward my goals instead of mentally beating myself into submission. Not only does it feel better, it also gets better results.

If you're trying to make a change in your life and struggling to stick to it or see any progress, maybe you're not planting yourself in fertile soil. Maybe there's something still to learn or a step you can take to support your change. You're one tweak away from blooming just like Hayes. I believe in you.

ACKNOWLEDGMENTS

Writing a book can feel lonely sometimes, but the truth is that I could never do it on my own. There are so many incredible people in my corner who made this story possible, and I'm thankful to each of them!

Let's start with my husband, Ty. From the first book I wrote to Hello Trouble, he's always believed in me, given me space to write, and been there to brainstorm ideas.

Then my three boys. They love to tell people their mom is an author. I can always count on them to tell me which covers they like and don't like. Plus, they're great sports about watching rom-coms with me to help me get in the writing mood. They also get me out of my comfort zone by being extroverts and having me exchange numbers with countless moms on playgrounds. *insert nervous laughter here* All jokes aside, I love them so so much, and I'm thankful for their support on this journey.

I never imagined I'd have a "team" as an author, but life surprises us in the best possible way every now and then. Sally—thanks for being my best friend and gal Friday. You're the best partner and sounding board in this business. Christina—I'm so amazed by your talent and your analytical mind! Thanks for helping spread the word about these body positive romance books! Vivianna—I'm so thankful for your kind heart and how you take such good care of our readers. Corrie—Your heart for others shines through your work, and I'm amazed by the team of influencers and readers you've been able to pull together to share these stories! Tami & Sarah—thank you for running the crazy world of book shipping! I love that our readers get physical books with such care put in! Ziggy—thank you for filling in the gaps as needed! It is so fun to work with you! Hoss's Mods—thanks for keeping an eye on the reader's group and making it such a fun place to be!

My editors work wonder with the words I lay on the pages. Sometimes when I'm writing, I worry what reads will think or that my work is too messy. It's always a comfort knowing Trici Harden and Jordan Truex are there to make these stories reader-ready. The fact that they're two of the kindest humans ever is the cherry on top. I appreciate you both more than you know!

This project needed an extra eye from those who know the life of a mechanic! Thank you to Alissa, Amy, and Brian who read this story for accuracy surrounding Hayes's profession!

I love writing these stories knowing that Luke and Allyson are going to narrate them. They are such talented people and I feel so grateful that they're using their talents with these stories! Extra bonus? My brother Dakota edits the author notes for these stories in audio. It's fun working with family and being able to add that special touch!

To all the Hussies in my online readers group, Hoss's Hussies, THANK YOU. Seeing your excitement for Hayes's story made me so excited to get the words on the page. I hope I did it justice for you.

Finally, to the person reading this right now, thank you for letting me do the best job in the world. I am so honored that you would use your time and resources to read these words. I appreciate you more than you know.

The Hello Series

Hello Single Dad

Hello Fake Boyfriend

Hello Temptation

Hello Billionaire

Hello Doctor

Hello Heartbreaker

Hello Tease

Hello Quarterback

Hello Trouble

Hello Handsome

JOIN THE PARTY

Want to talk books with Kelsie and other readers? Join Hoss's Hussies today!

Join here: https://www.facebook.com/groups/hossshussies

Kelsie writes steamy rom coms that will make you laugh, cry, and dream of happily ever after! Her heroines are real, curvy women and her heroes are the kinds of men we deserve!

In all of Kelsie's books, you'll find heartwarming moments and plenty of laughter.

She currently lives in Colorado where she watches way too many rom coms, chases her three boys up the mountains (huffing and puffing), and writes books for lovely readers like you.

Connect with Kelsie (and even grab some special merch) at kelsiehoss.com.

facebook.com/authorkelsiehoss

instagram.com/kelsiehoss